THE WINTERMEN III:

At the End of the World

Brit Griffin

Markham Public Library
Thornhill Community
Centre Branch
7755 Bayview Avenue
Thornhill, ON L3T 4P1
Nov 2020

Copyright © 2020 by Brit Griffin

All rights reserved. No part of this book may be used or reproduced in any manner whatsoever without the prior written permission of the publisher, except in the case of brief quotation embodied in reviews.

Publisher's note: This book is a work of fiction. Names, characters, places and incidents are either the product of the author's imagination or are used fictitiously, and any resemblance to actual persons living or dead is entirely coincidental.

Library and Archives Canada Cataloguing in Publication

Title: The wintermen. III, at the end of the world / Brit Griffin.
Names: Griffin, Brit, 1959- author.
Identifiers: Canadiana (print) 20200330683 | Canadiana (ebook) 20200331302 | ISBN 9781988989242
 (softcover) | ISBN 9781988989327 (EPUB)
Classification: LCC PS8613.R535 W57 2020 | DDC C813/.6—dc23

Printed and bound in Canada on 100% recycled paper.

Book design: Heather Campbell
Cover Concept: Leah Lalande and Brit Griffin
Author photo: Alex Bird

Published by:
Latitude 46 Publishing
info@latitude46publishing.com
Latitude46publishing.com

We acknowledge the support of the Ontario Arts Council

THE WINTERMEN III:

At the End of the World

Brit Griffin

To John Patrick Griffin

and to Mary Griffin, my greatest champion

The territory no longer precedes the map, nor survives it. Henceforth, it is the map that precedes the territory.

—Jean Baudrillard, *Simulacra and Simulation*

Chapter One

"Think that's the place?"

Jeff brought up a pair of binoculars, said, "Hard to tell from the descriptions we've been getting. All the way down, every source saying something different. I don't know, they haven't been too helpful."

Susun nodded but thought otherwise. They'd been hearing: small shack by a fast-moving creek, cliffs on three sides, row of big conifers blocking the trail in. No way to get in without being seen. It sounded about right. She would have been careful, very careful, needing a place where she could lie low, stage a decent defense if need be. And the place Susun was looking at right now fit that description.

Susun and Jeff had been riding hard all morning. Now, as their horses were struggling to get through the deep snow, they felt like they were getting close. In the early morning, their horses' breath had hung in the air, the saddles creaking in the cold as they mounted up. But now it was warming, the snow sticky, slowing their progress. They were trying to stay close to forest cover, not wanting to leave themselves out in the open.

"Feels like we're so far from home," Susun said, "so far from Johnny."

"We'll find him," Jeff said. "Don't worry."

"I know."

Jeff glanced over. "Talos, as big and bad as they are? No

match for us."

Then Susun smiled and said, "Let's keep telling ourselves that."

It had been years since the mega-corporation Talos had taken over governing, starting out as a small security firm that had seen the evolving climate chaos as an opportunity. The fires, floods, crumbling roads and bridges, and finally the endless winter. Civil unrest. The whole ugly shebang. Governments of the day bailed, passing the buck over to the private sector. The business guys, they explained, could get things done. Could be more efficient, flexible. Forward thinking. What the government really meant was that the private sector was just more ruthless. Now, Talos ran everything. Except the Territories. And that was thanks to Johnny Slaught.

When Talos had blown through the north, they meant business. They wanted everyone out of the Territories, it was just too expensive, no good for the bottom line. So they rounded folks up, closed towns and highways, shipped everyone down to the sprawling mega-city near the Great Lakes. Contained populations, according to Talos, decreased risk, made for a more rational use of resources.

But Johnny Slaught decided to stay put, hunker down in an old hotel in the abandoned silver mining town of Cobalt. Talos had tried to budge him, throwing everything from starvation to outright assassination at him, but he was still there. Along with a group of people who also wanted to stay in the place that they were from and that they loved. Talos branded him a terrorist, called him the Winterman. The name stuck and the community stayed. Most of them wouldn't be there if it hadn't been for Johnny. He was the heart of it all.

So when Talos took Johnny, the community knew they were going to go get him back. But it wasn't going to be easy. And they were going to need to find help. Serious help. Jeff said they needed to go find themselves some help of the badassery kind. And so here they were.

"I hope this works," Susun said, thinking it was probably a miracle they'd gotten as far as they had. "We've been lucky, but from the looks of it, we're almost there."

"I am so ready to be over with this," Jeff said. "Seriously. Can't take another day of this weather. Like, I get the whole perpetual winter thing, but really, does it have to snow every day? Is it ever going to stop?"

"I hope so. And I think the weather's changing. I mean, you can almost see the ground in spots."

"I wouldn't be breaking out the lawn chairs yet. We're just farther south—that's going to make a difference."

"Yeah, but I think the air was different on the way down. Fresher, don't you think?" Susun said. The snow, thick and soft, was gathering on her dark hair. "Maybe even like spring. That's what I've been thinking. It smells sweeter."

Jeff said, "Official group optimist."

"Maybe. But this is just a snow shower. It'll be over soon."

"Well, snow or no snow, I am done with this horse-riding thing. I'm dying here, I ache everywhere. I'm never, ever going to be a cowboy."

"Yeah, don't think any of us pictured you as cowboy material."

Susun hadn't been expecting to come down here with Jeff. Chumboy Commando had seemed liked the best choice. Johnny's best friend. Best tracker, too, and with a string of solid contacts from big Lake Timiskaming right down through to Mexico. The community was on edge, though, wanted Chumboy to stay, just in case. They'd tangled with Talos often enough to know they could never let their guard down. So they did what they always did when making tough decisions: they drew straws. Jeff, he drew the short one.

Jeff, smiling, kept his eyes on the cabin below. "No, not a cowboy, not a tracker, not even a winter camping guy. And definitely short on patience. I thought we'd never get here. I mean, the guy's map, I couldn't tell a creek from a highway on it."

Susun had asked for a good map when they'd stopped to swap their snow machines for horses. Their contact was a cousin of a cousin of Chumboy's, went by the name of Hector. Chumboy had told Susun she couldn't miss him—he'd set up camp right on the shore to meet the needs of well-heeled travellers trying to cross the border into the U.S. and get as far south as they could. And for a price he'd let travellers know where roads were blocked and where they might run into Talos security crews.

Hector was stocky, round-faced, his chin covered in stubble and his hair down over his collar. He talked fast, told Susun no, he couldn't give her a good map. Couldn't give them any kind of map at all because there weren't any.

Talos had come through, maybe a few months back, taken every single map they could lay their hands on. Turned every abandoned gas station, convenience store, or tourist kiosk inside out. Went through abandoned cars, too. Serious about it. Killed a few people over it. He said word travelled fast, but not fast enough for him. They took his 1982 Ontario Road Map. They even took his 1973 *National Geographic* map of the Great Lakes. So no, he had no map to give. He could draw one, but it would cost them.

According to Hector's map, the trail they were on had taken them very close to where they wanted to be. From the top of the hill, they were able to see a narrow path leading down through a mixture of hardwoods, the bare stands of maple and birch not giving much shelter. They would be easily spotted. If they could get down the hill without being seen, they could get in behind the row of pine and cedar, could get a better look then at the wide yard and the small cabin at its centre. Should they just ride down? Hope they didn't get shot?

"I'm feeling like maybe I'm not ready for this. You?"

No, I'm alright. Think I'm losing my youthful good looks, though," Jeff said.

Susun glanced over at him. He did look tired. Older than thirty, that's for sure. But they probably all looked older than they should. She said, "No, you still look pretty good."

"Jordan still love me when I get back?"

"Absolutely. He'll find you even more ruggedly handsome."

"Thanks for that," he said. Then took a deep breath. "Well, we should probably do this before I chicken out."

"That a possibility?"

"It's always a possibility."

Susun glanced at him, remembering the look on his face when he showed the rest of them his straw. She could tell he was scared. She was, too. Going to look for Johnny meant going into Talos country. And there was nothing easy about that. The scraps of information trickling in told them that Johnny had ended up in the notorious Greenhouse zone, a sprawling complex of work camps on the outskirts of the City. Wasn't surprising he ended up there. Talos was always rounding up folks, forcing them to work. Telling people there was simply nowhere else to go to get food and shelter. Unless you were stinking rich.

Then the news got worse. He'd been moved to some sort of prison facility right inside the City. By then, though, Susun had committed in her mind to going, so she was going. The weather, she felt, was sending her a message. Even though it wasn't like the winter was giving up, there'd been melting, even several days of rain here and there. After months and months of nothing but hard, cold winter, it seemed like a good sign.

But they'd need help if they were going to mess with Talos, so she decided to take a chance, head south, see if they could get the help they needed. She told Jeff he could back out if he wanted, but she was going. He said he figured a road trip was in the cards.

It felt strange now, the possibility that they had finally found the help they were looking for. She was hoping it would work out. It had taken them a week just to make their way out of the north, reaching the City's northernmost border. They skirted along the edge of the City, then crossed the lake, taking the narrow snow road kept open by a thin but steady stream of travellers. They met up with their contact on the far shore.

Hector had told them not to take their snow machines any farther south, not unless they wanted to attract attention. Susun had asked him if there was more to worry about south of the border, and Hector had said he was a Mohawk, didn't believe in no borders, but could tell her straight up they wouldn't be getting gas once they got down there. Not without trouble, anyway. He also told them the snow was slushy as shit, would just slow them down, folks now talking about nothing but the thaw. That, he'd said, was all fine and good, but it was making people restless, already some reports of gangs forming up, running the roads looking for travellers. So, he said, only trade with folks you trust. Then he told them not to trust anyone.

They were using a bit of their gold stash, knew it might stir up interest, but it was the only way. It had got them the horses, supplies, and, more importantly, information. And that information had told them that their person of interest wasn't too far from the old border, holed up deep in a forest preserve.

Susun and Jeff had taken their time, sheltering in abandoned homes along the way, being cautious, making sure they weren't followed. In one house they hit the mother-lode, Jeff telling Susun that the folks in the area must know jackshit about scavenging. He was right. Back home, everything for miles and miles around had been picked to the bone. So when they opened the pantry door in the house and saw rows and rows of canned food, it was hard to believe. The homeowners had even left coffee behind, Jeff saying after his first cup that he could hardly take it, it was going to his head right away. "Better get me to a detox," he'd said. "Getting more of a buzz off this than the weed I used to grow."

Jeff was now surveying the clearing down below through the binoculars. Passing them to Susun, he said, "Someone's working up quite a sweat down there. Check it out, right along the backside of the cabin there, chopping wood."

Susun took the glasses. The cabin was tidy. Very tidy. A couple of large metal buckets on the porch, hung by the door, then along the side, four neat rows of stacked firewood, another row of chopped kindling, nothing out of place. Another small building set back and behind the cabin, then a lean-to. Then she heard the cracking sound of the wood splitting, remembering being a kid, watching her dad chop and stack wood through the summers, gearing up for winter. Never imagined things could change so much. Not back then when the seasons seemed carved in stone.

She studied the figure. Sweat running down the back of the white undershirt as the axe went up and then down again. Short hair, almost a buzz cut. But blonde. Had to be her.

Susun said, "Let's head down."

"Yeah? You're sure that's a good idea? Just ride in there?"

Susun didn't answer. Not too long ago she'd thought she

never wanted to see the woman again. She'd brought nothing but a trail of violence to their small community. Twice. But times change, and Susun was hoping to God they had found Mitch Black.

"We've come all this way, Jeff, might as well. Not like we have anything to lose."

"Guess you're right," he said, "but it feels like there still might be something."

"To lose?"

"Yeah, like a limb. Or my head. Man, this woman scares me."

She turned her horse, said, "Yeah, she scares me, too, but I think, maybe deep down, she's okay. Or maybe wants to be okay."

"Seriously, you've got to stop with the heavy-duty optimism."

"What are we doing here if we're not optimistic?" She sat for a minute, staring down at the cabin, tipped her face upwards and said to Jeff, "The sun feels strange."

"Everything feels strange. Like, surreal. Can you believe it? I'm some cowboy now, some Wyatt Earp guy riding down into a gunfight. I mean, I can hardly believe it, and like, I'm in the story, know what I mean?"

Susun just nodded, looked back to the cabin.

Jeff kept going, "Like it's pretend. Or a dream, yeah, more like a dream, like I'm going to wake up back at the old Fraser Hotel instead of riding down into some outlaw camp. I'm tripping out on some major Clint Eastwood here, big time."

Susun thought about that. The Fraser Hotel, with its candlelight and big kitchen and roaring wood stove. Johnny had said that when he'd thought about where to hunker down for the end times, the hotel seemed like a perfect fit. Big, old, and built back in the day to stand its ground against any fire. Didn't take long for it to fill up with folks, either.

Christ, she missed it. And missed, too, the way things used to be. Before the winter. She and Jeff had been playing 'what do you miss most' all the way down to the border, starting with the small things: a cold beer on a summer day, a long hot bath. Jeff said what he was really missing was a long hot bath with Jordan, then said, "Hey, sorry, at least I know Jordan's at home waiting for me. I know you must be worried about Johnny." Susun said, Yeah, she was worried, left it at that. She missed lots of things, but she was also a different person than she used to be. She could live without most of the things she missed. She could even live without Johnny. But she sure didn't want to.

Chapter Two

"In the speech, you wrote *a new kind of strongman*. I'd like to talk about that."

Eton Love moved behind his desk, straightened the small ledger, paused, then moved it to the far side, leaving his view of the large map spread out on the desk unobstructed. His attention now shifted to the map, taking in the blocks of grey and brown, the black and blue lines crisscrossing the surface.

"You didn't like the phrase?" Bob Scott asked, moving into the centre of the room to see Love better.

"No, no, I didn't." Love wasn't looking up, and Scott figured Love was letting him know he was pissed, could ignore him when he wanted. Letting him know there were other things that were more important. What Scott couldn't understand was Love's obsession with the fucking map, the man's latest obsession, all he did was gawk at it, then explode over some small detail, call for changes. Once he even tore the whole thing up. What a shitshow.

Scott asked, "Anything in particular offend you about those five words?"

Eton Love nodded, as if deep in thought, but Scott knew it was just a performance, so he waited. Love finally said, "I think it was the word *kind*."

Jesus Christ, this clown was a piece of work.

Bob Scott had been called into Love's office to discuss the opening event in what Love had dubbed "Project Domain: The beginning of the consolidation of the periphery." Love told Scott long titles were important, that people thought more words made something sound more important. Scott thought, but didn't say, that was pretty rich coming from a guy who once bragged nothing worth saying couldn't be said in a twelve-word tweet. But that was back in the day, before Talos was everything and everywhere. Hard to imagine anything before Talos. It had been Scott's life. He'd been there from the beginning, building it from the ground up. And now this—hands tied, sitting on the sidelines while this man-boy ran the outfit.

Love had asked Scott to join him at the Project Domain event because, he'd explained, he wanted a shared sense of purpose. A good working relationship. Love reminded Scott, as if he'd forgotten, that maybe Scott had run what was now the largest corporation in the world, but now Love was running the show. Time for Scott to get on board. He told Scott, "C'mon, Bob, we've got to show the people that everything is fine up here at the top, no power struggles, just one clear vision of a luminous future. So, on the big night, you're going to introduce me, say a few words, know what I mean?"

"I doubt we really have the same vision, Eton," Scott said.

Love replied, "Get your game face on Bob, you know how we do things around here now."

So Scott had delivered the brief introduction to the large crowd gathered under the roof of the People's Arena, saying in a tone that he hoped was both sincere and enthusiastic, "And tonight, the man with a sweeping vision of the future, a new kind of strongman, Eton Love. Come and witness the birth of the Domain." People cheered, the whole fucking farce dragging on for over an hour until they gave out bags of Old Dutch ketchup chips to the first lucky hundred through the door. That'd been Scott's idea. One of the Recon-Repo teams had come across a huge stash in some warehouse two hours outside the City. Looked like it had been some emergency supply depot that had been readied for processing but then abandoned. It had happened a fair number of times in the early days of the perpetual winter. Some town thinking it could tough things out with boxes of soup and a semi truck of disposable diapers but quickly giving up, loading its good citizens onto buses and sending them down into the City. Half those buses ended up like the emergency depots: abandoned. Some were left along snow-packed highways, drivers giving up on trying to push through a storm or navigate in the dark. Some went nose first into the ditch, others ran out of gas with no one to call for help.

It'd been tough in the early days, tough decisions in the face of daily chaos, plucking priorities out of thin air, trying to decide who to rescue, what to save. Lots of people and lots of goods fell between the cracks. Now, everything was accounted for, but back then, not so much. So when the Recon-Repo told him about the two truckloads of chips and candy, Scott was quick to pull the whole lot of it out of the general circulation and into Love's reserve. Fucking pathetic, that stale chips and boxes of four-year-old chocolate bars could be such a score, but there it was.

All in all, Scott had thought he'd done a good job. Afterwards though, Love was quick to ask him to meet ASAP, come up to his office to "deconstruct the event." Then he'd added, "It isn't a post-mortem, no no, it isn't like that, just a constructive review, a constructive deconstruction, as it were."

Scott, feeling that there wasn't anything too constructive about the meeting so far, asked, "The word *kind*?"

"Yes, at first I thought it was *strongman*. Thought that

sounded, well, I don't know, too brutal. Threatening."

"You were pretty clear, Eton, you wanted the message sent that you were in control. The big boss."

"Bob, seriously, just dial it back a bit with the defensiveness okay? You just need to think, and think hard, about what we want to incentivize, what kind of behaviours are we looking for, what outcomes."

"It seems to me it's all we talk about, instead of maybe more practical matters like how we feed everyone …"

"Bob, Bob, please, listen to yourself. For God's sake, aim higher."

Scott was about to say, *You know you are an annoying fuck, right*? but decided to say, "Ok, you're right, Eton, so let's go back to the speech. What's on your mind?"

"Great, great, Bob, good for you for changing the channel. Good. Ok, so the speech. The strongman, must confess, sort of warming to it, but then that whole 'new kind of' puts me in a tradition, right? But I'm not."

"Not what?"

"Part of the tradition. This. Me. I'm not just a new version of the old. I'm completely different. I've never been tried before, I'm …" he waved his hand as if dragging the right word from thin air, "a rupture. That's it, I'm a complete rupture with the old. Fuck the Anthropocene, right? This is a new fucking era, Bob, we need to get excited."

"Right, okay, Eton, so maybe simply 'strongman' would work better. Let's try that next time."

"No, see Bob, that's your problem."

"What?"

"You know, I wonder if you understand the things I try to convey to you. Important things. And because of that, your first move is always retreat."

"Eton, I'm trying here, but sometimes I wonder about where you're going with things. I mean, we're in a bad place right now, we have ..."

"Bob, you just retreat and wait, instead of coming back with something better."

"I thought I was giving you something better. We're talking about a few words, here."

"That what you think?"

Scott was having a hard time keeping his temper in check. This fucking little upstart was cramping his ass—standing there in his too tight t-shirt, small guy but muscled, working out at least two hours a day, buff enough but fucking useless. Too bad the last remnants of the City's corporate elite loved him, loved his big visions, his use of spectacle, his promise to restore civil society so everyone could get back to making money. Loved his quack therapies and ideas. Scott realized he had only understood part of the equation, that everyone wanted things to be predictable and safe again. What he hadn't realized is that some people, the people Love told him mattered the most, thought things could be better, that this breakdown was in fact, in Love's words, a radical reset that could be optimized.

Scott said, "Yeah. It's what I think."

Love smiled, "It's not what Ion Bakalov thought."

"Bakalov?" Scott surprised, "Since when does he have an opinion about anything besides the best way to hurt things? Chrissakes, Eton."

"There you go again, Bob, disappointing me. I wouldn't be underestimating him if I were you. And be warned, Bakalov is a man of many, many talents, and he's making quite a name for himself. He's on the move."

"Bakalov? Seriously?"

"Yes, he's impressing people, I think he could be our new

Renaissance man, military leader, hunter..."

"He's an animal exterminator, Eton."

"Well, Bob, he's actually a multi-purpose exterminator and some very important people, the people we need on our side, they're calling him our Winter Warrior."

"Who's calling him that?" Scott asked, then said, "No, never mind. That's just ridiculous. You're telling people that's who he is. You're calling him that and they're repeating it to one another. Jesus Christ, Eton, why him?"

"He's cleaning up the streets. It's a very visible role he has, people appreciate it when there aren't scores of horrifying dregs scouring through their garbage bins, breaking into their homes. When all the aggressive vermin, human and animal, are rousted and dispatched, people feel better. Safer. He just happens to have a very timely skill set. And I'm also impressed with him, because unlike you, Bob, Bakalov is ready to step out of his comfort zone..."

"His comfort zone? Listen to yourself, Eton. The first time I saw Bakalov he had just smothered his father at the Home for Dependents, with the man's own pillow. Said he didn't want to visit anymore, made him depressed. That, in a nutshell, is Bakalov's comfort zone."

At the time, it had made quite an impression on Scott. He'd been searching for someone to run the Facility, a jail for prisoners who were too dangerous or unpredictable to be working in the Greenhouse zone. Love had left the project to Scott, telling him it had to be bare bones, couldn't waste resources. But it also had to be the right kind of person to run the place. He might have important plans for some of the convicts. So no fuck-ups allowed. No one would give a shit what happened inside, but you couldn't have any security breaches, it being right in the heart of the City. Scott had asked Love why on earth he'd put a jail in the middle of the City. Love said it was a symbol. Of what? Scott wanted to know, and Love had said, "My strength."

Scott was racking his brain trying to come up with a jailer when an employee at WorkNow said he should try the Dogman, that the man was always in looking for work. Told Scott that in fact the guy had just been in and had left a junior employment counsellor mopping the blood and the snot off his face after making the mistake of telling Bakalov there was no work for him. "So is the Dogman a nickname?' Scott had asked. No, the employee said, the guy used dogs to run down everything and everyone. He told Scott that Talos had used the guy quite a bit, employed him to kill rats down in the tunnels, stray pets and coyotes out on the streets, got paid for every batch of twenty he brought in. Small time muscle jobs like clearing out homeless people on a strictly cash per head basis. Scott thought he sounded perfect, tracked him down and offered him the job. He was regretting that now.

"We've all done things we're not proud of, Bob, I mean you must remember your little fiasco, managing to lose track of an entire shipment of gold, gold that could have been so useful in the City right now? But let's not dwell on the past. And after all, you chose to give Mr. Bakalov a fairly significant role, right?"

Mentioning the gold. Bob Scott wondered what that was about. The fucking gold. It had almost gotten him out of this shithole. If it wasn't for that double-crossing bitch. He should have known better than to trust Mitch Black. He'd had serious doubts about her loyalty, though he had no idea whether she had even found the gold or gotten out of the Territory alive, that huge expanse of absolute fucking nothingness to the north of the City. Who knew what shit had gone down up there. He didn't. He had some information about sightings of her here and there over the months since, but nothing concrete he could follow up on. And at the moment, Black wasn't his problem. Bakalov was.

Scott said, "From controlling animal vermin to controlling human vermin, not a big leap, Eton. And to be frank, no one wanted to run the place, a mall converted into some bizarre mishmash of jail and training camp? No one with any real capability would take on a shitshow like that. But Bakalov? He didn't hesitate. But you know he has no real skills, no administrative ability, nothing. I mean for Chrissakes, he used to kill rats and coyotes."

"We were all something else before. But this is a new era and now we are different. All of us. Don't forget that."

"That's the problem, Eton, I'm not forgetting. I'm not forgetting, for instance, that you were with some half-assed startup that failed in its first year and now you're running the entire City."

Eton Love's expression didn't change, but he said, "That's right, Bob. I am running things. Think about that before you say something you might regret."

Scott was already regretting it, kicking himself. He should learn to keep his big mouth shut. And, yeah, they'd all been something else before, but Love had always been a vindictive little prick.

Love, letting Scott know he was in control of himself, not threatened, just disappointed, said, "Listen to yourself. I mean for one minute, just listen. Here I am talking about a radical new version of society. And you're still sulking over your demotion."

"Okay, Eton, I see your vision of the future. Fine, whatever. But your coffers are empty. We are barely producing enough food to feed the workers in the greenhouses let alone the demand here in the City. Our blackouts and brownouts down here are up around 50%. In the periphery, they're lasting for days, even weeks. Are you even paying attention to this? The City is going to be bankrupt—then what?"

"The answer is progress, Bob. The answer is Domain. Your problem—and you made it Talos' problem—was your lack of vision. The people are drawn to *me* because I offer them a glorious future. You? Your idea of a solution is to turn Zeus into a pencil pusher. My advice to you? Get some perspective before you're out of the picture completely."

Scott said, "From my perspective, Eton, most people are as worried about the present as they are about the future. You're lucky there isn't rioting every day out there. And your rich friends don't like chaos. Interferes with business."

"If you're worried about potential food riots, Bob, I think you should be reassured by Mr. Bakalov. He has all the talents needed. He is currently getting our new security force and some special ops teams up and running. He's started training some of the prisoners for the work gangs. I think we are well on our way."

"I think you're giving Bakalov more power than is wise."

"Be careful, Bob. Sometimes I appreciate your candor, but other times it just reveals your weaknesses. Your lack of perception. Ion Bakalov is perceptive, he listens, he thinks before he speaks. So, I wasn't surprised that when I mentioned my dissatisfaction with some of your work on the speech and how it came across, he had a suggestion for a very nice refinement. He said, 'Why not try *your new strongman?*' See? '*Your.*' See what that one word does? Now, see, suddenly I'm not a menacing figure, I'm not a despot, I'm someone who is looking out for the ordinary guy. I belong to the people. Protect them. You see?"

Scott was uncertain about what he should say. He had fallen so far down the ladder at Talos he really had nowhere else to go but out. But Bakalov? There was no fucking way the guy they called the Dogman was going to be the one taking his place, so he said, "I do see. It's a small adjustment but it makes a difference."

"Yes, that's right, Bob, good, yes, it makes a difference." He gestured down to the large map that covered his desk, "And this, my map? It's going to be the cornerstone of our society. We are going to redraw the world, and if you want to be in that world? If you want to be on that map? You better start being a team player, don't you think?"

Love looked up from the map, irritation now crossing his face, causing Scott to wait before giving his reply. There might be more coming his way, no point wasting words, or having to backtrack. He watched as Love examined him, taking in the grey trousers, suit jacket over a white shirt.

Love said, "You look too uptight."

"What?"

"It's not our image. We're relaxed. Relaxed, not worried about the future, but not stuck in the past, know what I mean?"

Scott was about to say he had no fucking clue what Love was talking about but instead tried, "Maybe the contrast is helpful."

Love pulled his eyebrows together, mouth turned down. "How so?"

"It makes you seem approachable, like I'm the past, but you're the new guy, more basic, less remote."

"Yes, it's true. My look, it's stripped down, basic black, yeah, I get it. You're bureaucratic and out of date, and it makes me look less pretentious, like the future."

"You are the future. A man for the people."

"I like it, Bob, I like it," nodding. Thinking it over, he added, "But we have to be careful, can't let that go too far. I mean, it's one thing for people to feel like I'm approachable, I get that, but they still need to understand that I'm the only one with the vision."

"Of course, Eton, you're their leader, not their friend."

"Their leader, not their friend. I like it." Love came around the desk, smiling now, slapped Scott on the shoulder, said, "See, Bob? I'm not hard to get along with."

Chapter Three

"Let's go," she said, patting her horse on the neck and nudging him a bit with her heels. The big roan preferred to take things slow and careful and there was no changing his mind. Susun liked that. Jeff wasn't as keen on his horse. When they had driven into the big shed to get their horses, and the roan and a small bay were led out for them, Jeff had said he was really hoping for something showier, didn't they have a nice black mustang or something? Hector had rolled his eyes, said, "If you want a mustang try heading to Detroit." Then he winked at Susun, said he'd see her soon. She asked how long it would take for them to get there and back and he said, "There's lots of trouble ahead on this road. If you're not back within a few weeks, I'm going to consider these snow machines mine. You be careful, and keep an eye on your hombre there."

The roan began moving down the trail towards the tidy cabin in the clearing, its big hooves punching through the soggy snow. The cabin disappeared briefly from sight as they got near the bottom of the trail. Susun reined in the horse, hesitating before emerging from the shelter of the big cedars that fanned out around the clearing. No sound of the axe.

"Guess it's now or never. Sure she's already seen us."

Jeff nodded. "Yeah, doubt there's any sneaking up on her."

When Jeff cleared the cedars he saw Mitch right away,

standing in the front yard, pulling on a sweater. Levi was coming out of the cabin behind her. That surprised Jeff. He heard Susun say something behind him like, "Well, I wasn't expecting that," and watched as Levi passed Mitch a shotgun. Pretty much like the last time Jeff had seen them together.

They'd been facing down Bodie Dejohn, one of the scariest dudes Jeff had ever run across. Looked like Dejohn had gotten the best of Mitch but then Levi turned the tables at the last minute, giving her exactly what she needed, a big old shotgun to blast a hole straight through Dejohn's heart. As Chumboy had said, Levi was a spooky little bastard. When he'd left town with Mitch, they all gave it about four hours before she dumped him off in some snowbank along the way. But here he was, still with her, hanging back but watchful.

Jeff kept moving until Mitch raised the shotgun, said, "You two can stop right there."

Susun stopped beside Jeff and they both just sat. Waiting.

Mitch was squinting a bit, the sun bright. She said, "You two are a long way from home."

"Thought you would have gone farther south," Jeff said.

"Don't give a fuck what you think. What are you doing here?"

"Maybe we could talk inside," Jeff said. Then he nodded at Susun and added, "She could use some water."

"I'm sure Susie can speak for herself." Mitch looked up at Susun. "This your new Gentlemen Jim?"

Susun ignored the question, said, "Hey Mitch, it's been a while."

Mitch said nothing, so Susun said, "It was hard finding you, if that's what you are worried about."

"Yeah, you could say I'm fucking worried about that. Think I'm living out here because I want visitors?"

Susun looked around the place. It was a nice spot, a few big pines around the house, limestone cliffs rising up behind it. Just the narrow trail in or out.

"Never would have found you without Chumboy's connections. He's got eyes and ears everywhere."

"That's fucking amazing, but I don't give a shit. I should just shoot you both right now."

"No one trailed us," Susun said, "and there weren't very many signs of life once we got past the City, anyway. No vehicles, just horse trails, a few small camps. You're out here on your own pretty much."

Levi had been standing quiet beside Mitch, mostly looking down at the ground. He turned now and headed towards the cabin. Mitch glanced at him, but said to Jeff and Susun, "Get down off those horses."

"We were careful."

"I bet you were. Coming down here with your B team, that's very fucking reassuring."

"We have as much at stake in no one knowing you're here as you do."

"I doubt that. Get down off those fucking horses."

They dismounted, Susun saying, "We're not here to cause trouble, Mitch."

"But you are causing trouble," Mitch said, glancing over as Levi returned, walking past her to Susun, giving her a jar filled with water. "You're having a baby," he said, nodding at her belly, slightly round beneath the loose white shirt, her coat hanging open.

Susun said, "Yeah, about five months along."

"Oh for shit's sake," Mitch said, rolling her eyes. "I can't believe you'd show up here like that. What the fuck were you thinking?"

"I was thinking we needed help."

"I'm not in the helping business."

Susun said nothing, just looked at her.

"Slaught the dad?" Mitch asked.

Susun nodded.

"Ah, well then this is an interesting situation," she said, looking at Jeff then back to Susun. "So where's Papa Bear?"

"Papa Bear's in jail."

It was quiet for a second, Mitch now frowning, thinking that it wasn't a possibility she considered when she saw them watching from the top of the hill. She said, "I see, so I guess that's why you've come? You need the huntsman's help."

Jeff sighed, said, "Like at least get your nursery rhymes straight. The huntsman is from Little Red Riding Hood. Not The Three Bears."

Mitch, already heading towards the cabin, her back to him, said, "Stick with Goldilocks if you want, dickhead, see how far that gets you."

ক

Chumboy left Harvey Larose and his son, Shaun, in the shed working on the wood splitter and headed up to the hotel with a sled full of firewood. There was a dim light shining out through the kitchen, but the rest of the old Fraser Hotel was in blackness, folks trying to conserve candles for when they would really need them, when the dark season returned. The longer daylight hours made things easier, but Chumboy found it made things harder, too.

It made slogging through the snow tougher, everything inside you feeling like it should be spring. Should be hearing the spring peepers singing, the geese coming in overhead. Chumboy took in the sky above. Today it was streaked with steely, thin clouds. No geese. Not in a long time. Not in a long time, too, those early mornings, hunkered down behind a blind of dogwood and willow scrub, the stubble of last year's corn showing though the snow. His Uncle calling the geese in. Loved it. Loved every minute of it. Maybe if there ever was a spring again, and if there were geese forgiving enough to come back, he'd take Johnny out hunting. Johnny would love it.

Pulling open the side door to drag in the sled, Chumboy saw Johnny Slaught's rifle in the rack, an old beat-up pump action. Chumboy had asked him a while back, "When you going to upgrade? That thing looks like it belonged to old John Browning himself." Slaught had said he didn't know who Browning was, and Chumboy told him that he was one of those bullet barons, big Mormon dude who was into guns, invented the pump action and later keeled over dead when working on the 9mm Browning. Slaught said he never did like the Browning. And that he was keeping his shotgun at least until the spring came back.

Chumboy was missing Johnny. He kept going over the chain of events that ended up with Slaught getting loaded into the back of an army truck and not being seen since. He just couldn't get his head around it, it all happened so fast, it was like he had missed something, that he should have seen it coming. Been more careful.

It had started out like any other morning, heading out early with Johnny, Max, and Jeff, going to see what they could find. That morning there was a pale purple haze across the sky, coming with the bitter cold. They'd almost bailed because of the cold. The week before had been balmy, one day almost pushing past the magic line of zero. Then it snapped back down, cold and blowing. None of them were looking forward to stepping outside, seeing the wind carving away at the snowdrifts.

As they stood around debating the trip, Tiny, the community's cook, started throwing open one cupboard after another in his kitchen, saying, "See? What do you see in here? And in this one? This one? What's in here? You know what you see? Jack shit, that's what you see. So if you want that served up for the rest of the month, by all means stand around whining about the weather. Otherwise, get the fuck out of my kitchen and get going."

It had become necessary to go farther and farther afield with each passing week, the areas closer to them were picked clean, six times over. This time they'd figured on trying the outpost, the last stronghold that marked the end of Talos' control and the beginning of the Territories. There were rumours that Talos was seriously restocking the security centre, a few travellers passing through Cobalt said they'd seen activity around the area, trucks in and out, all kind of security personnel. So the plan was a quick burn and turn down to the bottom of Thibeault Hill, then out to the outpost. Tiny had told them it was getting to be do or die time, he needed food—and lots of it. He said, "Bring me some goddam food for my kitchen. You bastards came here and set up a goddam hippie commune. Look around, we got over fifty people now and we're eating more goddam lentils than Jane Fonda, what the fuck?"

It was a good question. What the fuck indeed, thought Chumboy. But that day, the day they had headed down to the outpost, they were asking more practical questions, like if the trip would be worth it. It was a calculated risk, using fuel to go all the way there, hoping there'd be things they needed. They were banking on the rumours that Talos was having too much trouble maintaining order down in the City to worry about regular trips up to the outpost. So far, they'd been keeping a bare bones operation running just in case things ever did warm up. That way they could get in quick to lay hold of the timber and mines, get things up and running again. But now they were cutting back their presence even more, so they'd load the outpost up with a shit ton of supplies in one go, leaving just two or three guys to hold down the fort. If that was the case, there might be a fair stash of new supplies. There might be gasoline and food. And they desperately needed both of those.

So they'd gone. Four guys on two machines with sleds. Optimistic.

Chumboy could see it clearly in his mind, had gone over it so many times. They were crouching down in the woods behind the airport. Chumboy had a bad feeling about the place, wanting to wait and have a good long look before they went in. Max giving him grief for being too cautious. Even when they'd moved up, Max was chomping at the bit, Chumboy ignoring the kid, trying to focus on why there were so many tire tracks and footprints around the usually sleepy outpost. Restocking or not, it seemed to have recently been hella busy for a place that was a low priority for the City.

Just before they'd headed down to the outpost, Chumboy had told Slaught that as far as he was concerned, the winter was protecting everything, making everyone step back from taking and taking from the land, but Slaught said he wasn't feeling very protected. Chumboy said that might be true but sometimes folks didn't know what was good for them, and maybe Mother Winter knew best. Max got impatient, said talking fairy tales wouldn't get them gasoline and could they get a move on. Slaught had called him a restless young pup but Max just said they should get going and get it over with, never was anything exciting there except a couple of dumbass rent-a-cops.

After that, things happened too fast. Before he knew it, he and Jeff were running low through the bush back towards their snow machines, Chumboy yelling over to Jeff asking where Max was, Jeff looking back, panicked, said he was right behind them. They could hear men yelling, the harsh pop-pop of gunfire, Chumboy and Jeff scanning the field between them and the buildings. No sign of Johnny. Chumboy made the decision, telling Jeff they had to go, couldn't risk all of them getting snagged and losing the two snow machines, that they'd come back to get Johnny, but they had to get going.

That was three months ago.

They'd headed back down the next day, Chumboy going with Susun, saying to her if Johnny was still around they might be needing her medical attention and she had said, "That man pisses me off, always being the big hero." Chumboy told her the fella had an instinct for that stuff, wasn't much you could do about it, and that she sort of had the same instinct going on. She'd said she was still pissed off, joking a bit, both of them thinking, hoping, he was going to be there, hiding out, waiting for them.

But he wasn't.

The outpost was quiet when they'd gone back. No signs of life, though there were still supplies and trucks left behind. Like Talos would be coming back. Maybe soon. They searched the place, checking every closet and possible hiding place twice. No Johnny. They went through the three trucks that were there and siphoned out the gas. Then decided it was time to get the hell out of there. They rode home in silence, dragging a sled full of food and gas, but thinking about Johnny.

And he was still thinking about Johnny.

☞

Mitch stood leaning against the counter, Levi busying himself with the wood stove. Susun and Jeff were sitting on a pair of wooden chairs on either side of a table. The cabin felt close. Levi had left a small window open but it still felt hard to breathe. Or maybe Susun was just holding her breath, wanting this to work out so badly.

She'd arrived on Mitch's doorstep without much of a plan. Susun knew she needed Mitch. She was tough, resourceful, and she knew the City. And they needed that. Getting someone out of the Greenhouse zone would have been tough enough. In the middle of the City? Probably next to impossible without someone like Mitch. What she wasn't sure about was how to convince her to help.

Susun said, "So what we're asking isn't going to be easy."

"No fucking kidding," Mitch said, "but I'm not looking for easy, I'm looking for a reason why I should help you in the first place."

It was a hard sell. Mitch had spent time on Talos' most wanted list. Stealing gold will get you that kind of attention. And what Susun was asking her wasn't exactly consistent with keeping a low profile. So right now, odds were Mitch was trying to decide whether to send them packing or shoot them. No point rushing her, in that case.

Levi moved away from the stove. He looked better than when Susun had last seen him, heading out on the back of Mitch's snow machine, pale, clothes raggedy and the wrong size, making him look even smaller than he was. He was still pale, though, his black hair longer than before, tied back. Strange presence, content to just sit, staring at the wall, not seeming to mind the strained quiet of the room. But Mitch did, turning on Jeff and saying, "Stop fucking staring at me. It isn't helping."

"Sorry," Jeff said, "just stressed."

"You should be," Mitch said, "waltzing in here to ask for my help. And telling me you want me to break your Winterman out of a Talos prison? You got nerve, I'll give you that."

Susun said, "I know, it's a lot to ask. And the prison, it's right in the City core."

"The weirdest thing about it," Jeff said, "is that it's in one of those shopping malls. The ones with all the tunnels and stuff? I mean a mall? Must be some fucked up place. You know, like doing solitary in the food court, stuck in Tasty Taco's kitchen or something. Fucked up or what? And then there's the dogs, I mean, you can't make this stuff up."

Levi's voice startled everyone. "Dogs? What about dogs?"

Jeff said, "Yeah, well rumours are that they use dogs to guard the prisoners. Guess they have some real psycho running the jail."

"Bakalov," Levi said.

Mitch, surprised, asked, "Bakalov? How do you know him?"

"What? You know this guy?" Susun asked. "The guy who runs the jail?"

"I've dealt with him a few times," Mitch said. "He's a thug. Sells guns, black market shit. I think he did some muscle jobs for Talos. Best to stay clear of him." She turned to Levi, "So how do you know him?"

"From when I lived down in the tunnels, under the City. He used to come through with his gang, killing rats. He was scary, we'd just hide."

"Smart, to hide from a guy like him" said Mitch, "he's a real sicko."

Jeff said, "Christ almighty, must be a super bad dude if *you're* calling him a sicko?"

"Fuck you buddy," Mitch said, "you're the one that came knocking on my door."

"Okay, hold on, sorry about that, Jeff didn't mean that the way it sounded," Susun said.

"He sure as shit did."

Jeff could feel both Susun and Mitch glaring at him, could see, too, the worry in Susun's eyes, telling him to fix it, telling him to get things back on the rails. He said, "Susun's right, that was out of line. Sorry, okay?"

"Whatever, shithead. Anyway, it's a no-go, I'm not tangling with him."

Susun said, "We came a long way..."

"Go back."

"You might want to hear about Scott, first?" Susun said, playing her last card. It got Mitch's attention.

"Bob Scott? What about him? He still out looking for me?"

Scott had been Mitch's boss at Talos, had cleaned up after her when he'd sent her and an elite team up to the Territories to do some depopulating of the Wintermen's settlement. She came back with her team in body bags and no Winterman. Then he'd recruited her to steal some gold for him, promised her a cut.

"Think he was pretty pissed off after he sent you for the gold and then you left him high and dry."

"Heading back to the City wasn't in my best interest. But he doesn't know I have the gold. Anything could've happened."

"Maybe, but from what we heard, rumours started about the gold and he panicked, went public and pinned it on you. Launched a massive manhunt for you, had bounty hunters falling all over themselves. But then when Scott came up empty, Talos took a closer look at him. Too many rogue operations made him look like he was losing control. Rich folks got nervous, worried about a military coup so they took him out. Now I guess some baby-faced IT genius is running Talos. They say Scott was lucky to come out of it alive—working hard for corporate redemption, now."

"So what?"

"Well, it comes back to the missing gold. The City is broke. Running on empty. They need money. I mean if we hadn't had the gold that Levi gave us from your stash, we never would have made it down here. Gold is magic to Talos and everyone else out there. So if Scott wants to redeem himself, the best way is to come up with that gold. That means finding you again. You need to deal with Scott once and for all to save your own skin. The last thing you want is for that manhunt to get kick-started again."

Mitch was over at the table pretty quick, her hands clamped around Susun's throat, saying, "Aren't you a little Miss Smarty Pants..." Jeff jumping up, mostly to just get out of the way, saying, "Whoa there, Jesus, calm down." Susun just stared back, and Mitch said to her, "Might as well have sprinkled that fucking gold dust right to my doorstep."

Susun could feel the wall, hard and cold behind her head, the pressure on her neck not letting up. Mitch so close, eyes hard. Susun was having trouble swallowing but managed, "You brought it on yourself." But then Levi was there, hand on Mitch's arm, saying, "Maybe let go of her, I think we need to hear about Scott. Just to be careful."

And then Susun could breathe again, feeling all the tension in her neck subsiding. Mitch stepped back, getting right back to business, saying, "Okay, so what about him? He's back, so what?"

Susun rubbed her neck, still sore and feeling the hard edge of Mitch's anger. Everyone was on edge, had something to be mad about. But this wasn't going the way Susun had hoped. She'd been warned, Chumboy saying, "You're not going to find Florence Nightingale down there, you know, you're going to find Cruella de Vil." She'd said, "C'mon, she's not that bad," and

Jeff had said, "No, that woman is bad. Chum's right, she skins puppies."

She said to Mitch, "I thought we might have mutual interests."

Mitch, impatient, "That's your pitch? Some guy I fucked over wants to be a player in a place that's hundreds of kilometers away, and so now I should go there and risk everything to help some other guy I don't even like?"

"Look, this new head of Talos is squeezing every last drop out of everyone and everything. With things warming up, Talos has to start ramping things up, investing, getting ready. So nobody is staying in Talos without bringing money to the table. Scott can't be the guy who lost the gold. He's got to be the guy who finds it."

Susan was holding her breath, had nothing else to offer, knew her offer amounted to nothing. She had really believed Mitch would, for some reason just agree to help out. For old time's sake? Christ, what had she been thinking? The past two weeks, pushing on through washed out roads and frozen towns, the nerve-wracking process of trying to make safe camp for the night—it all seemed like a waste of time. Delusional.

Mitch, frowning, asked, "Did you just say it was getting warmer?"

"Yeah, haven't you noticed? It's warming, slowly, but getting warmer. It's all anyone is talking about."

"How much warmer?" Mitch wanting to know. "It still seems like shit to me."

"No, it's getting warmer. Everyone wants to believe it, too. They just want to think things will go back to the way they were. And this new guy at Talos is telling them that it will. I mean..."

Jeff interrupted, "Oh, what was it he said? Oh, right, one of Talos' big slogans, *We don't give in to Nature.*"

Silence, Mitch still thinking. Susun holding her breath.

Then Mitch said, "This is the deal then. I want gasoline, all the supplies we'll need—enough of both to get us there and back. Two snow machines. And all your contacts along the route, for safe passage back."

Susun, coming to life, said, "So you'll do it?"

"Can you deliver?"

"Yes, our contact at the border, he can help."

"Okay, then, we leave in the morning."

"Whoa, what's with the serious mind flip?" Jeff said, "A happy forecast is all it took?"

"Again, fuck you, buddy. It's my business. There's reason for me to be in the Territories. Just makes sense to travel there together. You have everything set up already, that just makes it easier for me. In exchange, can't hurt to swing by and help out with your Winterman."

"In the Territories?" Susun asked.

"Yeah, getting the rest of the gold."

"Your gold isn't here?"

"Most of it? No, it's safe and sound, tucked away until the great thaw. And if the great thaw is on its way, and there's power plays to be made, I'll be playing."

Chapter Four

"So, Ion, how is that project of ours coming along?"

"We are hard at work. Things are good, Mr. Love, very good."

Ion Bakalov liked Mr. Love's use of the word 'ours.' That was promising. And yes, it was *their* project, maybe even *their* vision. If Bakalov was careful. He ran his hand over his bald head, self-conscious, feeling big compared to this man, a very trim man in his black t-shirt and jeans, always in the black. He made Bakalov anxious, this man with his large desk, a glass of clean water beside him. Mr. Love was obsessed with his health, always drinking his purified water. Taking his herbal tonics. He was now perched on the desk, at ease. But he moved around a lot. Always moving. This man with his short attention span.

"I hope we have lots of promising candidates. We'll need lots. Hard workers. Or at least manageable."

Bakalov said, "They are all hard working when the dogs are on their tail."

"Good to hear—time to get them ready, start making your final selections. Will we have enough?"

"I believe so, Mr. Love. I already have some in training on the first length of the railway, part of our work clearing the Valley. They are working hard."

"Excellent. We are getting close to the final stage of our great plan, and we need these men ready. Are they ready, Ion?"

Bakalov shifted uncomfortably, did not like it when he was asked such questions because he never knew the right answers. "Some of them, yes, they are ready to be soldiers. The rest, they will be ready whether they know it or not."

"Perfect answer! Everyone comes to self-awareness at different times, no? For example, I have fully embraced myself. My vision. My discipline. I've gone through my fever dreams, come out the other side. I'm ready. I just need to know that you are ready, too."

"Yes, Mr. Love. I'm ready."

Love smiled. He was relaxed today. Some days he was jittery, pacing. Today was better. Love asked, "Do you know why these men are so important to me?"

Most of the men? They were worse than dogs. Dirty. Undisciplined. Maybe a handful would be worthy to be called soldier. But they could be brought to heel. "No, Mr. Love, I do not."

"Of course not, Ion, of course not, not to worry. I, however, have given this matter a lot of thought. You see, there are many ways of looking at the criminal element. Many ways. We can see them as evil. We can see them as, well, you know, as victims. But how I see them? I see that their presence prevents us from rebuilding our society. They take resources, space, our attention. They undermine order and control. And they have no allegiance, only to themselves. In short, Ion, they are vermin."

Bakalov could remember the speech Mr. Love gave, seeing him up on the platform, a single light on him, Mr. Love saying, "Let's clean the vermin out of the drains, out of the tunnels, out of the shadows and into the light of day, where they can see, clearly, their place in our City of Light." And the people that lived in the core of the City clapped, but with a hesitation. Bakalov could hear it, knew it was an applause mixed with fear. Bring the vermin into their world?

"Yes, sir, I remember you said that in your speech."

Love smiled, "And I meant it. We need to tackle these questions on many levels, Ion, many levels. Physical and symbolic. So, how do we stop the vermin from preventing the rebuilding of a great society?"

"Eliminate them?" Bakalov knew it was the wrong answer, but it was the only answer he knew.

"No, Ion, not eliminate them. Use them! Make them the very instrument of rebuilding society. There, we can all see them, there in the heart of the City, these vermin can be transformed into an instrument, a machine, a means of our renewal. They can build, *serve* our vision. That way, their lives will not be wasted. Will not be meaningless."

"Yes, sir." Bakalov did not understand what Mr. Love was talking about. How could those debased men be transformed? They turned into animals as soon as they were put into the Facility. Bakalov had been wondering about this since Mr. Scott had told him he would be running the Facility, taking care of prisoners, preparing some of them to be soldiers. Said it was part of Project Domain.

Love continued, very animated now, "It was Asimov, of course, who set me to thinking on this, did you know that? Have you read Isaac Asimov?" Not waiting for the answer, he said, "A genius. He saw the seeds of our destruction, way back in the 1980s. Saw that earth was doomed, that we could only save ourselves by moving into space. What a visionary! Sad that vision never had a chance." He paused for a minute, letting Bakalov know he was distracted by the sadness, by the failure of it all. Bakalov knew a lot about failure. "But," Love continued, "what really inspired me in Asimov was what he said about growth. That when we stop growing, when we have exhausted every frontier on earth, we will be in a prison of our own making."

Bakalov waited quietly. He was often unsure of where Mr. Love's mind might go, what idea it might land on.

"So, I thought to myself," Love continued, "what I am looking at here is not a failure but an opportunity. See what I am doing there? I am taking something that looks like a negative and, Bam! Making it a positive. And the positive? I could have spent my life behind a desk, I could have been trapped in mediocrity, but now? Now I have a frontier. A frontier to conquer."

He moved quickly behind his desk, running his hands over the large map that almost covered the entire desktop. "I struggled with this, Ion, struggled with being trapped in a prison of my own making, but it is ironic, is it not Bakalov, that here I am, stuck on this, this..." he searched for a word, delivering it with a tinge of disgust, "...earth. It was a prison, before this catastrophe. But then, is it really a catastrophe? No, because it has given me the opportunity to make my mark. I do have frontiers to open up, a society to build. I will take these prisoners, and use them to conquer my frontier, so I will not be a prisoner like them."

"I understand sir," Bakalov said, having missed much of what the man was saying because he was preoccupied by the map. The map that this man cherished looked like some cheap, tourist road map.

"Good, so let's get moving."

Bakalov said, "Yes, we make progress every day on your plan."

Mr. Love's plan. Bakalov thought about it daily. Open the railway that ran up into the Territory. Use it to reclaim the land, the resources, spread the Domain. It was hard work, clearing the tracks of snow, ice and debris after years of winter and many years of neglect. Bakalov's part in the great plan was small: make it possible for the train to leave the City. Clear and secure the tracks. That meant protecting the workers from the feral groups of men who lived down in the Valley. There were communities springing up all the time. Small groups of people with their insubordinate insistence that they could build lives down there. Their meagre efforts were doomed to failure. Nothing but tarps and twigs. But they could be dangerous. Telling each other they did not need Talos, that Talos was the enemy. That could not be tolerated.

He also had to keep the wildlife under control. The workers were afraid of the wild animals that lived in the Valley, the creatures hiding by day and then coming up into the neighborhoods to scavenge by night. The men were afraid of everything, thought Bakalov. He wished he had been offered better men to choose from. These men at the Facility were mostly lazy and fearful. And he wished he had a bigger part in Project Domain.

"Good, Ion, good. Now listen. The train is finished, ready to go. Make certain that you have the best of the best ready to go. Men with some motivation, with a strong will to survive. That's what we need."

"I have a system in place, Mr. Love, to help weed out the weak ones."

"Good, we can't afford dead weight at this point. We're on the clock, Ion. Make it simple, efficient and, to be blunt, cheap. Just get me my railway workers, my soldiers, my machine. Now why don't you get to it right now. Time for my meditation."

"Yes, Mr. Love, thank you." He started to go, then turned back, thinking of asking Mr. Love where he got the map, but the man already had his back to him, staring out the massive window that looked south over the City's core. Bakalov wondered what he saw when he looked out over the grey streets. What was his vision? Bakalov doubted there were vermin in the vision. It must be something clean and efficient. He could do his part for this vision. Today and every day. Him and his dogs.

Chapter Five

"I'm going to miss winter."

Johnny Slaught wasn't talking to anyone in particular. Just as well—no one was listening. Sounded like half the guys were asleep, their thick, rough breathing filling the room. And some tossing and turning on the two metal cots that had been snagged by the first guys in; no mattresses on them, but it just felt better being up off the floor and not curled up in some closet or along a urine-stained wall. The bed frames were a rare item, though, missed when the authorities had come through and salvaged most of the metal in the place, beds, railings, the whole nine yards.

Slaught hadn't been able to sleep, feeling unsettled with this bunch of guys, didn't know any of them and didn't want to. He sat with his back to the wall, staring out the window but seeing nothing, just darkness. Slaught figured at one time these must have been luxury apartments, all window, great view of the city. Now, at night, it was like a black curtain fell, the city below going into lockdown.

Slaught said, "There was something about the snow falling. The trees coated in snow. The skies in the evening. That blue, it's almost a green. Up north, anyway. Not here."

Somebody said, "Shut the fuck-up. Fucking colours. What's that bullshit?"

Another, "Poor puss missing his winter."

First guy said, "Asshole can't tell the difference between warm and cold. Jesus. It's never fucking going back to normal."

Slaught, frowning, thinking he shouldn't be talking to these guys but also wanting to, wanting to talk to someone, asked, "You don't think so? "

A new voice, aggressive. "Shut the fuck up, buddy, trying to sleep here."

Slaught glanced over but could barely make out the forms of the men in the room, the darkness too thick. He thought there were maybe a half-dozen, maybe a few more in the other room of the apartment, but each night it was different, and it was hard to keep track of the new guys coming in. They were all starting to look the same, himself included, the daily grime staining everything a dull beige.

It was the same every day. It started in the morning, the first brave soul opening the door, checking up and down the halls to make sure the packs of dogs that prowled the hallways at night had gone back to the kennels.

When the dogs were out, you weren't. It was as simple as that. If you were out there, the dogs would find you. So the days were okay, but you didn't hang around after curfew. As the sun went down, everyone headed up to the apartments, jockeying for the best spots before the last man in closed the door.

Guys still took chances though. Every now and again a straggler would burst into the apartment, pulling the door shut behind him in a panic as the dogs came tearing up the hallway. There were no locks on the door; a guy could come in at any point in the night, but there wasn't much incentive to hang around outside the apartments once curfew came, bringing the dogs with it. Slaught had heard of one room that was torn apart when a guy came in late, dogs on his heels. It'd been bad, some of the guys mauled and bitten before they'd beaten the dogs back and out. It was something you just didn't do—upset the order of routine. Put guys at risk. A few nights later, it was dealt with. The guy was found lying in the middle of the food court. What his fellow prisoners had started, the dogs had finished during the night.

During the day you could pretty well go where you pleased inside the Facility. Getting outside, though, that wasn't an option. Slaught, and every other guy, had tried. A guy could get lost looking for a way out, confused by the series of tunnels and hallways and stairwells. And in the end, every exit was either closed off or there were security guards keeping an eye on things. Try to put a boot through the glass? They'd just shoot you.

Wasn't much to do, either. Days were boring, that was the hardest part. Spend the days walking the endless hallways of apartments where the guys took shelter from the dogs at night. Walking the aisles where people used to shop, imagining buying a new pair of shoes, clothes maybe, electronics. Hard to believe he'd lived in a world where you just went and got whatever you wanted.

Slaught liked to get in early, snag one of the apartments near the stairs and settle down in the small L-shaped kitchens of the apartments, taking the far corner so his back was covered and he could see anyone coming. Slaught figured it had been a pantry area, where folks kept their pasta and their pots and pans, maybe. But that life was a long time ago.

Today though he had gotten in late, lost track of time while staring into the torn-up guts of what had been a shoe store, shelves and displays and any other scrap of valuables hauled away long ago by the salvagers, only one orphaned shoe flung down the hallway. By the time Slaught had made it to his regular apartment, his favourite spot was taken, a guy stretched out on his bedroll on the kitchen floor. Slaught gingerly picked his way across the room, placing his back against the wall near the big window. Cold, but safer than lying in the middle of the room.

He didn't know why he wanted to talk with the other prisoners. Maybe just wanted to have a conversation. Most days he kept to himself, even tried to eat alone. Not as though they had much time to chat. The meals were nasty and served just once a day. Gruel might be a good description. Guys would hang around, waiting for the smell of the food to spread throughout what used to be the mall's food court.

It was strictly first come, first served. Chef Big Donny would stand behind a metal grate with a small opening to shove out the next bowl. He was a good guy but he didn't take any bullshit. Tall, black crew cut, great smile you hardly ever saw—never when he was serving. He was all about keeping the line moving, trying to get everyone fed in the allotted time. If you were late, you missed out. You could either slink off and suffer, or try to take someone else's bowl. Slaught had already seen an easy dozen guys go down that way, their bodies just left in the food court for the day and then dragged off during the night. Some guys said they fed the dogs with them.

A voice in the darkness said, "Come on, you saying you like this better? Hot then cold, hot then cold. It sucks. Nothing but muck and cold and wet."

True enough, Slaught thinking of his time out in the greenhouses before he was moved to the Facility, out in the rain or sleet half the time, hauling dirt and salvage.

"Fuck winter." It was another voice, louder, and it angered the first guy who said, "Quit your pissin' and moaning."

The loud guy said, "Fuck you."

Slaught kept his eyes on the window, trying to concentrate

on what was out there, beyond the City, trying to picture Susun, trying to picture his home, up there in the snow with the wood stove and the cold clear nights and stars. What had seemed so goddam hard before now seemed like paradise. He'd do anything to be back up there at the old Fraser, doing his shift pushing snow or hauling wood. Sure never saw this fuckturnofevents coming. One minute he was on a salvage run with a few of the guys back home, next minute he's in jail.

 He could still see it, his last memory of being home, all of them crowded in the entrance way with the boots and parkas. Chumboy had been braiding back his long hair and then pulling on his bright red and black toque, saying, "Get ready to pucker up boys, we got some siphoning to do."

 The ride down had been fine but damn cold. Nothing out of the ordinary. But when they got to the outpost, coming up behind the building, Chumboy was uneasy, said all the tracks and the noise coming from the front of the building had him worried. Max said he'd go check it out, but Chumboy said he didn't like the idea of the young'un sneaking out there on his own, and that pissed Max off and he just bolted, slipping around the front. Chumboy told Slaught, "Gotta watch that kid, can't count on him these days." But then he was back, flushed, said, "It's fucking Grand Central Station out there." Chumboy grabbed the kid and pulled him in against the wall, asking, "Did they see you?" Max hesitated, said no, then said maybe, then flushed some more. Slaught said, "Jesus Christ, Max." Trying to think fast, but thinking they were fucked, he asked Chumboy, "Ideas?" Chumboy said, "None," which surprised Johnny because Chumboy usually had a way of seeing a way out. And then they were hearing some shouting and Slaught said, "Chum, they only saw one guy, right? I'm going out there. Get these guys back home, I'll figure something out." And with that he stepped out and walked around the front of the building, just as a couple of guys were running towards him. Hoping Chum could hear him, he said, "Well, well boys, that's a fine fleet of army jeeps you got there, but careful now, you might hurt yourselves with those tidy little Kalashnikovs."

And then there it was. Soon enough he was indeed truly fucked, down in the City, doing time with hundreds of other guys.

In the darkness of the apartment, Slaught heard the faint scraping of the metal leg of a cot along the floor, just a slice of sound, seeing the shadow moving like maybe it wasn't even there, a quick gasp of protest, then the spasm of a body taking the knife, the huffing of exertion as the first guy dug it in deeper and deeper until the rustling of the blankets stopped.

Slaught looked back out the window, thinking of the night back home, the white expanse of snow turned navy blue in the dark, the outline of the pale birch and then overhead, Orion taking his place high up in the night sky.

The sound of the body pushed off the cot and thumping to the floor. The creak of the metal cot as the guy with the knife took his place. Fuck almighty, Slaught thought, he had to get out of here.

ॐ

Susun could hear herself yelling as she was pulling herself from a deep sleep. She could hear the scrambling of bodies and by the time she sat up and leaned over to switch on the lantern beside her, Levi was up with his back against the wall looking more like a cornered coyote than anything human. Mitch was still on the bed but with knees planted firmly, SIG Sauer focused on the door.

Jeff rolled over, mumbled, "What, what's going on, what'd you say?"

Susun said, "Sorry, guys."

Mitch, still with the gun on the door but glancing over at Susun, "What the fuck was that about?"

Susun just shook her head, shrugged, "Didn't mean to wake everyone."

"Did you hear yourself, what was that?"

Susun sighed, "Sorry. False alarm."

Mitch said, "Not helpful. We're heading out in the morning, need our sleep. Jesus."

Jeff, now sitting up, said, "Whoa there, everyone relax. The energy is off the charts in here. "

Mitch, ignoring him, got up to check the windows and then carefully opened the door to take a look outside, leading with her gun, her heart still pounding. The night was cold, dark, the waxing moon looking like it was tumbling across the sky behind the fast moving clouds. Mitch wondered if they were in for bad weather. That's all they fucking needed.

Mitch said, "So get some fucking sleep and try to keep it down to a dull roar over there."

Susun turned out the lantern and the cabin was freed of shadows. The small window was edged with ice, the moon keeping the sky a deep blue-grey. It must be around two or so. Susun wondered what Johnny was doing, was he sleeping? She tried to picture him, tried to drag up some image of where he might be, felt the baby within her moving, stirring, upset too by the disrupted sleep.

Mitch, wide awake now, said through the dark, "So, what, you getting night terrors now?"

"Just a nightmare, I've been having it now for the past few weeks, maybe longer."

"About?"

"A map."

Mitch said, "A map?"

"Yeah, there's this map, it's so beautiful. And then it isn't."

Silence, then Mitch said, "Lady, you have no fucking idea what a nightmare is."

Chapter Six

When she woke up the sky was still dark, and it was pitch black inside the cabin. Must be around four. Mitch couldn't be bothered to try and go back to sleep.

She lay still for a minute in the darkness, going over things in her head. She was feeling okay about what was ahead, realizing too that she was maybe even looking forward to it. As soon as Susun had laid things out, Mitch knew she would probably go. Despite what she was saying at the time, and despite some very serious worries about tangling with Bakalov, she'd been excited, right from the get-go. Restless, maybe. As much as she liked waking up every morning in the cabin, getting to the routine of the wood and water and animals, there was something missing. And there was something, too, about these Wintermen. Like something unfinished. Well, maybe now she had a chance to finish it. And get the rest of the gold.

They'd be heading out soon. Mitch decided their best bet was to move fast. Susun and Jeff had taken their time coming down, cautious, worried about running into trouble. Mitch wasn't worried about any trouble. They could make the border in good time, see Hector and get their snow machines and the supplies they needed. Then head up, working their way into the City on a series of abandoned roads. There was security around the City, but it wasn't seamless and there were ways to get in along what Susun had called the "people's paths."

So that part of things was straightforward. It was Bakalov that was worrying her. Last time she'd seen him, she was buying some guns from him. The guy gave her the creeps. There were all kinds of rumours about him, all ending up in the serial killer basket as far as she could tell. But in a place where guns were almost impossible to get, he had them and she had needed them. It turned out to be her last gig for Talos—well, not quite Talos. That sonofabitch Scott. She couldn't get her gear from Talos since the job wasn't sanctioned, just a private little agreement between her and Scott about a shit-ton of gold that had been overlooked in the evacuations and was just waiting to be repo'd up in Winterman country. It was crazy—with food shortages basically leaving half the population malnourished or starving, it was still gold folks wanted.

When it was all said and done she'd scored the gold, joined up with Levi and headed south. But the load was heavy, slowing them down, so they had stashed most of it in a building near the outpost. They'd used the rest to trade their way right past the City and over the border, only having trouble a few times before they found this spot, deep in what once was a forest preserve. Too bad so sad about Scott not getting his share.

She got up, stepping over Jeff, then Susun, both curled up on the floor, and moved into the small kitchen area, where she dressed and then filled the kettle, set it on the wood stove. She added some wood to get the fire going, then sat back, staring into the flames.

Levi was whispering when he asked through the darkness, "When we're done, we can come back home, right?"

The word sounded strange to her. She'd never thought of anywhere as home. When you had a home, you had something to lose. "Home? Here?"

There was silence, she waited.

He said, "Yes, here."

She watched the flames catch, closing the door of the stove. Seemed odd that Levi would crave the picket fence and front porch. Nostalgia? Not likely, sounded like his childhood was a nightmare. From what she could tell he'd been on his own most of his life. Never mentioned parents. So home sweet home must be something in his imagination. Wasn't in hers; the idea of home bugged her. Meant obligation. Setting down roots. Boredom. She'd never been about anything like that. She doubted she'd ever see this place again, but said, "Yeah okay, we'll come home."

Chumboy found Tiny already up and heating the water for tea. "Up early," he commented.

"What's it to you?"

"Ever cranky, you, just making conversation."

"Well don't. Can't you see I'm working?"

Chumboy pulled out a chair from the big wooden table, wanted to have a few words with Tiny before the place was humming with folks.

Chumboy said, "Kitchen nice and quiet in the morning."

"Why are you yakking away then?"

"Just thinking you've made it a nice place. Homey, you know?"

Tiny pointed behind Chumboy to where the pale green paint was peeling along the metal railing, the industrial strength kitchen having seen better days. "Yeah, right out of *House* fucking *Beautiful* magazine isn't it?"

Smiling, Chumboy asked, "So how's our pantry holding up?"

"In the shitter."

"How are you holding up?"

Chumboy was just making his way towards what he really

wanted to talk about, though he was worried about Tiny, too. Tiny was a solid guy, always had a white apron strapped on and a backwards ball cap. Today it was a green and white ball cap, and Tiny wore a jacket underneath the apron. But every morning, Tiny was first into the kitchen, loading wood into the big fire box, getting things going before the day and the pressure started, every day having to feed over fifty people. Sometimes the numbers were up over sixty with travellers stopping in or folks farther up the line looking for comfort or safety in numbers if the weather was taking a turn for the worse.

These days a few folks were fleeing the City every month, heading back north towards what had been their farmsteads or towns before the winter had taken hold, thinking with the warming weather they might be able to make a go of it. But in some ways, it was even harder—the weather was unpredictable, warm then cold, snow then rain, then hard ice. And the ground was still well under the snow. Before Johnny had disappeared, they'd taken to going out and checking on folks. They'd already buried two families.

"I'm fucking a-one, Chum," Tiny said.

"Now you know I don't believe that."

"Of course you don't fucking believe it," Tiny was suddenly animated, mad. "You'd have to be a blind and moronic motherfucker to think I was a-one when I got half the fucking population trailing in here every day looking for Gordon fucking Ramsay."

Chumboy shook his head, "Nope, don't know the guy."

Tiny stopped working to stare at Chumboy. "You are one ignorant bastard, aren't you? Know all of this history bullshit about Rome and some fucking Mexican bandit looking primed for a gas station drive-by, and you don't know sweet fuck all about the things that really matter."

"Hey, Tiny, no dissing Subcommander Marcos, you know he's my hero."

"Some fucking hero."

"How could a guy who paid for a revolution by writing books not be your hero?"

"You know who my hero would be? A guy who could get me some bacon. That would be monumental fucking heroism."

"You might have me there, Tiny. As always, a hard man to argue with."

"So, no offence, Chum, but are you wasting my time for any particular reason?"

"Just enjoying your company, Tiny."

"Fuck you. Now what do you really want?"

Chumboy sighed, serious now. "Just wanted to let you know that word is Susun and Jeff made it to the border."

"When?"

"A few days ago, I'd guess. A guy showed up last night, stopped in before heading across the lake."

Weren't too many folks who took a chance heading farther up north without stopping in at Cobalt. Wasn't just that word had spread about the Wintermen, about their taking a stand against Talos. It was that once past the outpost, it was the first place that had any sign of order to it, where someone could maybe get a meal. Take shelter. Once through Cobalt, most either headed across big Lake Timiskaming to the Algonquin community there or pushed on farther north to the old farm belt. Sometimes folks would say they were headed over the lake to Quebec, but Chumboy would say, actually, no, that's Algonquin territory, reminding the travellers that in fact they were standing on Algonquin land as they spoke. That it had been that way since time immemorial.

Tiny asked, "Guy that told you reliable?"

Chumboy nodded.

Tiny said, "That it, though? Just that they were at the border?"

"Word travels, but slowly, right?"

Tiny was quiet for a minute, then said, "I told her she shouldn't go. Always was pig-headed, that cousin of mine. All the Latour woman are. Always have been."

"She's smart. They'll be ok."

"That what you wanted to tell me? Some slop about her being fine? It's bullshit, you don't know they'll be okay. You have no fucking idea. She could get hurt, running around down there pregnant. You'd think being a baby doctor, or midwife or whatever the Christ she is would give her some common sense. Jesus."

"Melinda says she'll be fine. Nothing to worry about. Susun's strong."

"Melinda? Our resident midwife-in-training? Now she's an expert?"

"Thought you got on with Melinda."

"I do. Bright girl. A saint to be putting up with my son. Just not convinced she's an expert on cross-fucking-border travel while pregnant."

"She's done a pretty good job with baby Gracie so I think she knows something about babies."

"So she's a great mom. What's that got to do with anything? Something bad could happen down there, Chum. And Susie's family."

"Tiny, I swear, half the people here are related to you one way or another."

"Yeah, well, the same could be said for you. Anyway, Susun's my favourite cousin, okay?"

"Fair enough. But she's going to be fine."

"I think we should have stopped her."

It had been a hard decision, everyone had a different opinion on what they should do, but in the end Susun had told them it was her decision to make. And that she was going.

Chumboy said, "She knows what she's doing. She's getting help. She's going to get Johnny out."

"You hear yourself? She's going down there to get Mitch Black, not Laura fucking Secord. Christ Almighty."

"Be honest. Black's a better choice than Laura Secord."

"Better choice for what? Violence and chaos? I've about had my fill of that bullshit, Chum. I'm looking for some peace and quiet. And chocolate. Christ, I'd kill for chocolate."

"You know, Tiny, it was sentiments like that that caused all the problems in the first place."

"What the fuck are you talking about?"

"Things people would kill for. Chocolate. Cinnamon. Beaver pelts. Oil. You name it, buddy, someone says those words and then it's mayhem."

"Laura Secord wasn't in a war over fucking chocolate, Chum. Jesus, where did you go to school? And I don't want to be distracted by your crazy bullshit. I want to talk about Susie, and how's she's running around down there, pregnant, with just Jeff. I mean, c'mon, Jeff? He's not exactly tough guy material if you know what I mean, and then Susie, with her headaches…"

"Headaches? What headaches? She didn't say anything to me about headaches."

Tiny shrugged, "I don't know, started a month or so ago, she'd be up before me, in here drinking tea, said her dreams were giving her headaches. I mean, Susie is special right? Kinda trippy, always has been."

"Her dreams…" Chumboy now sounded worried, but Tiny said, "Don't start with that stuff. I think her being out in the fucking winter apocalypse is more to worry about than a few weird dreams."

"What kind of dreams?"

"Dreams don't mean nothing, Chum. They're dreams, okay? I have dreams about a monkey drinking coffee, means nothing. It's crazy."

"Carl Jung might disagree with you."

"Fuck him, whoever he is, he probably dreams about coffee and monkeys, too."

"Well, he's dead and gone, Tiny, but he had some interesting thoughts about dreams. Thought a lot about the relationship between consciousness and unconsciousness, the role of myth and archetypes."

"Sounds like a world of bullshit to me."

"If you're not buying Jung, you might be interested in knowing that James Cameron came up with the idea for the *Terminator* movie in a dream."

Tiny, interested, "No shit? *Terminator One?*"

"Honest to god."

"Well, Susie's dreams sure as shit aren't as interesting as *Terminator One*, or *Two*. Well, maybe the third one, it was a fucking stinker, but she's dreaming about maps, Chum. Maps. Of all the boring shit to waste your time dreaming about."

"Maps? What kind of maps?"

Tiny shook his head. "She said they were like old maps, said the dreams sometimes felt bad and sometimes good. I mean, c'mon."

Chumboy was frowning, "Anything else?"

"You're worried about the maps? I don't believe it. She had a dream about a fucking map. Here, let me be this dream reader guy, okay? How about Susie was worried about getting down south, how to get there? And there you have it, a map dream."

"Humour me, Tiny, okay? Did she say anything else about the maps?"

Tiny sighed, "Yeah, she said sometimes the colours were pretty on them. I said, well that's really fascinating, Susie. She said sometimes she was unrolling the maps and other times she was looking for maps and couldn't find them. I said, Susie, you have me on the edge of my chair. She said sometimes the maps had monsters on them and she also said she was having the dreams every fucking night. Love her dearly, but she hasn't always been right in the head."

"Monsters? What kind of monsters?"

"Jesus, I don't know, Chum, I guess the kind you find on maps."

Chapter Seven

"What's on your mind, Ion? I know I've asked you for regular updates, but two visits in two days? I have explained to you about my need for focus right now."

Eton Love was drinking a thick green liquid out of a tall, slender glass. Bakalov could smell it as soon as he came in. Smelt of grass maybe, or like the earth. Repugnant.

What Bakalov missed was the smell of coffee. He had started drinking it as a child, his mother adding honey and lots of milk. Honey. Milk. Coffee. He wanted those things again. He wondered who got coffee now? Maybe Mr. Love's friends. He knew every now and again the young women who came to see Mr. Love would have coffee. Bakalov would like to drink coffee with one of those young women. Or vodka, that would be good, too.

"Yes, of course, sorry, Mr. Love. But it is about the expedition. I know it is leaving soon..."

"Yes, Ion," sounding impatient, "all the pieces are in place, we are just waiting on your railway men to clear the tracks. Is that why you are here? An update?"

"No, that is not why I came, but yes, there is good news. We had review of the train, everything looks, how do you say it? Ship shape."

"That is good news. So, then, if not that, what? What is so important for you today? Let's get to that."

Bakalov gestured towards the desk. "And this map, it is part of it, no?"

He could see Mr. Love suddenly suspicious now, Bakalov wishing his English was better, did not mean to alarm the man, ask him the wrong question. Mr. Love came around to the front of the desk, as if to block the map from Bakalov's view. "Why are you asking about the map?"

Bakalov backtracked. "No, well, I wanted to offer…" stammering, seeing the look on Mr. Love's face darken, panicking, he blurted out, "I know of maps."

"Yes, well, good for you. But how is that of interest to me?"

"I understand cartography."

"That so, Ion?"

Bakalov said, "Never mind, Mr. Love, I am sorry I have bothered you. I'll be going now, sorry to have wasted your time."

"No, Ion, stay, tell me, please, what do you know about maps?"

He was trapped. He should not have come. Asking for an appointment with Mr. Love was a serious thing. Bakalov was surprised when Mr. Love agreed to see him, he thought it must mean that Mr. Love respected him. But now Bakalov realized it was because Mr. Love was eager to know about the men at the Facility and the railway, not about Bakalov the man, just about Bakalov the rat killer and jailer.

"Sorry Mr. Love …"

"Maps, Ion. What do you know about maps?"

Bakalov had been working for Talos for over four years, at first just under the table, animal control, supplying guns, muscle, whatever Talos needed. Then he was hired for security, what Talos called "flushing." Keeping the tunnels and abandoned buildings free of vermin and the homeless. Worked his way up to head of vermin control. And now he ran the jail. And he was part of this Project Domain. Training workers, even soldiers. That was something, a good accomplishment. But that was not who he was.

He had repeatedly told the people in the WorkNow office that he was a cartographer. Each time Bakalov asked for another appointment to change his placement, the young man wanted to know instead about his kill-rate with the rats, telling him he showed real talent for vermin control. Then, a year ago, the young man asked him if he wanted to move onto the canine eradication project, keeping the feral dog problem in hand.

Six months ago, he'd heard rumours that Talos was ramping up their cartography department, all kinds of people were being hired. He went to the WorkNow counsellor, said, just tell someone that I am a mapmaker, that I want to make maps. The young man had leaned forward on his tiny desk, his hands clasped together, "Talos isn't interested in what you want," and Bakalov had reached across the desk and grabbed him by the back of the head and slammed his face down onto the tiny desk twice until the desk tipped over. Then Bakalov dragged the young man, who was now both yelling and sobbing, out into the hallway and dropped him in a heap onto the linoleum floor because he had run out of ideas of what to do with him, this young man whose face was now a mess of mucous and tears. Bakalov stepped over him, saying, "Tell them, understand, tell them I fucking make maps."

"I was trained as a cartographer when I was much younger, way before the Winter," he said to Mr. Love. "My father and grandfather were cartographers in Russia. Famous men, famous for their maps. They travelled everywhere. All over the world. Made maps."

Love now seemed surprised. "You've never mentioned that."

"I told WorkNow people."

"And what did they say?"

Bakalov pulled himself up to his full height, yes, he knew he was a big man, and he was proud, proud of his name, his lineage, his mapmaking. "They were not interested. They did not know what a cartographer was. One time, I said, 'Show me map, show me any map, I will tell how it could be better'."

Love was interested now, Bakalov could tell, the man moving back behind his desk, glancing down at his own map. "And what happened?"

"They told me there were no more maps. Not even subway maps."

"That's true, there are no more maps. Just this one."

Bakalov frowned, "How can that be?"

Love studied Bakalov, as if trying to decide what to say. Although the scrutiny was hard to take, Bakalov stood, waiting. He felt, at this moment, he was going to learn something important if he did not ruin things by speaking.

Finally Love said, "You see, Ion, people thought they didn't need maps. Google led us around and we got where we needed to go. We didn't need to know where we were, what was..." waving his arm, gesturing to his big window, "what was out there. Google did that for us. Brilliant. Maps? Irrelevant. Useless. But then this shitstorm happened and erased everything. Borders, highways, Google. Everything. Erased. So now, again, maps will be powerful tools. But there can only be one map. And it will be my map. So you understand?"

Bakalov did understand. He said, "One map, one truth, yes, I see."

"Yes! That's right, you understand." Mr. Love was now excited to talk about the maps. "You see, once I decided on my project, once I knew what I had to do, I realized the past and the future are incompatible. I don't want my vision for a glorious new future shackled to the past. We need a clean slate."

Bakalov, excited too, then, understanding the man, understanding what it could all mean, said, "Tabula rasa."

"Exactly. My, my, Ion. I *told* Scott he underestimated you! You can appreciate how—in a burst of excitement, in my zeal—I wanted all of the maps disappeared. The past disappeared. Especially maps of the City, the Territories. Our nation. No trace, no hint of the past to... *infect* the imagination. I got them all, from tourist centres, libraries, everywhere."

"Where are they?"

"Burnt. I had them all destroyed."

Bakalov did not know what to think of this.

Love said, "And now, you can also understand why I keep this map so close to me. It is possible that other maps out there, maps of Niagara Falls, maps of Bueno Aires, maps of the London underground system. But you see, these places, they don't exist anymore as far as we know. They are under snow, swept clean by this transformative event. History doesn't matter. Now, for us, there is only the City. What lies beyond our borders does not exist until we create it, understand?"

"Yes. And that will be the purpose of the expedition? Of Project Domain?"

"Exactly."

"Then, Mr. Love, I tell you, I came today to request permission to be part of the expedition."

Bakalov watched as Love stepped away from his desk and gestured for Ion to sit down. "Sit, Ion."

The chair was small, he sat uneasily at the edge, felt suddenly too big, awkward. Love came around and perched on the edge of the desk, Bakalov noticing again what a small man he was, slender, almost delicate, like a woman. He had muscles, yes, but from the gym, not work. Bakalov wondered how he had become so powerful.

"Tell me, Ion, why should you come on the expedition? Every mouth we bring along will cost us."

"Many of the men from the Facility will be on train. I could control them, keep them working. I know them."

"Yes, that's true, Ion. That is a valid point. So perhaps we can consider this a job interview then? How about that? It's unconventional, maybe, to take the rat collector and make him a foreman, but that's why they love me, right? So tell me, Ion, what do you bring to Project Domain?"

Bakalov could see the man encouraging him, but maybe doubting him, too. Mocking him? Bakalov held up one of his thick fingers and said, "One. The expedition. It will make maps, yes? I will make good maps. The best maps. In Soviet Union, my father, his maps could tell you how far away you can be from a bridge and safely smoke cigarette to go unseen. Can tell you how far voices will carry. Tell you what kind of trees there are in area, how old the trees are, where old mines are, how many bridges and how long the bridges are. I can make you those kinds of maps."

"Interesting. But I have a team of cartographers already."

In the moment, getting on the expedition mattered most. He held up another finger. "Two. The vermin. It will need controlling, the men and the wildlife. The wolves especially. You will have problems, I think, bringing food and men up to where the animals are wild. You will need a hunter."

"I can see you have given this some thought."

"Yes. I think about it."

"But why, Ion, why all the thinking?"

Bakalov said, "I show you something. Please."

"Show me what, Bakalov?"

Bakalov was trying to find the right balance that demonstrated both his importance and his willingness to serve. "I show you destiny. That I was meant to serve your vision."

Bakalov stood, reached into his pocket and brought out his wallet. He gently pried apart the billfold and drew out a piece of paper. He looked for a place to set it down, moved towards a low-lying coffee table and squatted down, gingerly unfolding the paper and smoothing it out. Love leaned over the chair to get a better view. A map.

"My grandfather made this map. 1980. It is a map of the City. See? It must be destiny. I am here to help fulfill your vision. My father, here in this map, has shown me the way."

It was a very simple map, vivid turquoise against a buff background, the two lakes, Ontario and Erie, and a small circle to mark the city that had been called Toronto. "Your grandfather was in Toronto?"

"Soviet mapmakers were all over world."

"Why haven't you shown me this before?"

"I worry for my map. Every time I open it, unfold it, fold it back, it wears more."

"So what good is it if it is too fragile to use, Ion?"

Bakalov folded the map back up carefully but also as quickly as he could, tucking it into his pocket before Love asked for it. He would never give it up. He'd taken a big chance showing it to Love.

"I do use this map, Mr. Love. I use it to remember. To inspire me."

"I see." Love paused, then said, "You know I could take the map."

Bakalov had decided, when he thought to show Mr. Love the map, what he would do if the man tried to take it from him. He said, "Yes, I understand that. Of course I do. But I hope you will see fit to allow me to help with your project. And keep my father's map."

"Very eloquent, Ion. I have to say I'm impressed." He paused for a moment, then said, "You keep your grandfather's map. For now."

"I understand, sir, of course."

"And I will consider this wolf business. Our wildlife management strategy, I guess."

"Wolves are cowards. Cunning. Will kill anything they can."

"I've only seen them on calendars, Ion, so I will take your word for it. But for now, it's time for my meditation. I will contact you once I think over your proposal."

"Thank you, sir. Thank you."

Bakalov closed the door gently behind him. He was glad Mr. Love had not demanded that he hand over the map. It would have forced him to act, he might have even had to kill Mr. Love. He didn't like to think about that. He was happier thinking about killing wolves. Perhaps his luck was changing.

༄

It was hard to know for sure, but Slaught figured there must be close to three hundred prisoners in the building. Was that what they were, prisoners? Something like that. But why take a bunch of healthy men out of the greenhouse system? It was a mess, understaffed, crops not being tended, large die-offs. Didn't make any sense to him. And there was no one to ask. Except the dogs.

There seemed to be a few different packs, usually three or four dogs in each one. Big, short-haired things. Only saw them at night when they acted as some sort of fucked up, feral security system. Effective as shit.

He'd never really recovered from his first night at the Facility, probably nobody did. The day started off bad enough. One minute he was getting ready for his shift in the greenhouse, next thing he knew, he and a dozen other guys were loaded into a truck, told to sit down and shut up. Which he did.

A few hours later they pulled up at the front of some luxury apartment building right in the centre of the City, were pushed through a lobby littered with broken glass and trash, shoved into a mall and then just left there. No explanation, no nothing. Door closed and that was it.

Slaught had looked at the two guys closest to him and said, "What the fuck?"

They'd all felt scared. Bunch of them headed deeper into the building, but Slaught hung back with a few other guys trying to get his bearings. One of them tried going back the way they'd come, but the doors were boarded up and chained from the outside. The guy started to push and kick at them. Slaught said, "Hey man, you're going to wear yourself out that way," but the guy was losing his mind. Slaught tried talking to him some more but he was just yelling and pounding on the door and the other guys were saying to leave him, everything was fucked up and they should figure out what was going on.

They moved carefully towards the escalators, hearing a murmur of voices. Slaught said, "This is surreal," and the guy beside him said, "Just plain fucked up, like out of *Omega Man*, you know, the movie about the undead, and the main guy, it was Charlton Heston, could only come out during the day. Saw some chick with an afro. Well, it was the 70s, right?" But he stopped telling them about the movie when the food court came into view. There were at least two hundred men, some crammed into the cheap plastic chairs, most standing. But all of them eating out of an assortment of containers, a few guys over by a serving counter that was covered with a metal grille. Getting their food pushed out to them.

No one really even looked at them as they stood at the top of the escalator debating whether to go down or not. Slaught said he thought it was best to stay up where they were, watch for a while, but the other guy said that it must be some sort of restaurant, and he was hungry. But still they stood, watching the mass of men dressed in mostly grey and beige, spooning up their food at a frantic pace. The *Omega Man* guy said he couldn't take it, he didn't care if they were eating sewage, he was starving, so he started cautiously down the escalator. He was halfway down when a group of men in uniforms came out from behind a big set of double doors. They were wearing some sort of coveralls with the fucked up Talos happy face logo on them, and hauling big garbage pails. The men who were eating got up pretty quick, dumping their plates into the bins and then moving, all of them, straight for the escalator, taking the stairs two at a time. Hustling. *Omega Man* guy backtracked up the escalator to get out of the way. "I'm outta here," he said to Slaught as he ran past. Slaught said, "No, wait, we gotta figure out what's going on, why everyone's leaving," but he just took off. Slaught laid a hand on a guy as he pushed past, asked, "Hey man, what's going on?" The guy didn't stop, just said, "The dogs. Get moving." And so Slaught did.

And that—asking or not asking—usually determined whether a guy would make it past the first night in the Facility. If they thought they could figure it out on their own, thought they'd be smart and keep to themselves down in the mall areas, stretch out for the night on the torn up remains of the benches, they made a bad choice. The dogs would find them. The packs of dogs were unleashed just as it was getting dark, bounding and braying and hungry for blood. If you weren't safe inside one of the apartments on the upper levels, you were in big trouble.

First morning in the Facility, Slaught was walking through the food court and saw two bodies. One crumpled up in a fetal position. The other was being dragged by the feet towards the exit by men in the same uniforms as the day before. A second man in coveralls grabbed the crumpled-up body by the scruff of the neck and started to drag it, too, towards the exit.

Slaught went over, saw it was the door-kicker and the *Omega Man* guy, and asked, "Hey, what happened?"

The man in the coveralls didn't answer, just kept making his way towards the doors.

"So who was he?" Slaught asked, feeling like the man's name should at least be spoken, acknowledged.

"Doesn't matter." The man was big, bald, hauling the guy behind him and not even glancing at Slaught.

"Do you even check for ID? You'll need to notify next of kin, right?"

The man snorted a laugh, "In here, you have no kin."

Slaught watched as the body was hauled across the scuffed floor, leaving smears of blood, then called after them, "Come on, you could pick the guy up at least, show some respect!"

The bald man looked back at Slaught and said, "I like to leave it for pups to lick up, let them get every last drop of the bastard."

Chapter Eight

"Bob, your face, if you could only see yourself. All pinched, the tension. You need some strategies."

"Strategies?" Scott asked. "For what, Eton?"

"Uh, okay, first off, right now, I want to clear up a small thing. To be honest, I'm not feeling the 'Eton' thing. Would prefer you tried out Mr. Love—it feels more comfortable for me, I'm positive it will feel more comfortable for you, right? And the strategies, Bob, they're for your stress. It is out of control."

Scott was definitely feeling stress after receiving a message from Love calling him over to the Talos head office. One word on the message: money.

But money was something Scott was having a hard time getting his hands on. On the way over to Love's office he was racking his brain, trying to think of any possible tax, levy, toll, or untapped source of revenue, but was drawing a blank. And Love was pushing ahead with this fucked up Project Domain bullshit. How was Talos going to pay for it?

He'd hustled up to Love's office, noting the two security guards posted outside his door and another two at the end of the hallway. That was new.

Love, not really giving Scott a chance to respond, asked, "So, Bob? Anything to say?"

"You're asking for money... Mr. Love. And I just need to be honest, it isn't easy. All our big donors are getting tapped out, we've gone through all possible repossessions and take-overs, the opportunities are getting thin on the ground..."

Love interrupted. "This conversation isn't what I was hoping for. I'm not interested in what we don't have. I am interested in what we could have if you put your mind to it, put your heart into it. See, it's a shift in thinking I'm asking for here, I need you to change, become, you know, a better version of yourself."

"Look, Eton..."

"You need to get past that, Bob. It's Mr. Love. Try again."

Prick. "Yeah, alright, Mr. Love. I know we need the money, and I know you think it's out there somewhere, but I am telling you, we have repurposed, stolen and scrounged every scrap of wealth out there and there just isn't enough, not to send you and what you're asking for, teams of soldiers, geologists, miners, cartographers, up into the hinterland."

"Bob, again, the disappointment. Because you are thinking about the wrong things."

"Okay, I'll bite. What should I be thinking about?"

"You should be thinking about the weather."

"The weather? That's all anybody thinks about. What is to be gained by thinking about it any more than we already do?"

"You know that the past several months have shown a steady increase in temperature."

Scott frowned, "Still pretty shitty out. Cold. Sleet..."

"It's warmer, Bob."

"Not much."

But Love was slowly shaking his head. "You haven't really been paying attention, have you?"

"What? Are you saying the weather is actually changing?"

"Yes, the weather is changing, Bob. You think I leave these things to chance? I have teams," Love was animated now, waving his hands around for emphasis, "so many teams, all kinds of teams, doing all kinds of research, reporting back to me, so I know, I know what is going on. I need to know, because I am in charge. Understand? I know what's going on. It's getting warmer."

Scott said, "Well, that's good news." Scott wondered how long Love had known about it. He had a hard time processing the information; on one level he'd just given up thinking things could ever be normal again. He added, "That's actually amazing news. So what are you thinking? Do we need to start with some sort of transition team?"

"Bob, Bob, Bob. You really are yesterday's man, aren't you? Playing catch up now? Not to worry, this is what I have been waiting for. I'm ready."

"Right. Okay. So what now?"

"Implementing my vision, that's what we need to be doing. No time to be playing Overlord of some low rent dystopia. You need to get on board with me, right now, if you want a role in our future."

"Well, I am thinking we need to start working our way through all of the neighbourhoods, maybe have some sort of risk assessments, see which ones are fit to repopulate and if we can start expanding the grid . . ."

Love sighed, stood and went behind his desk. "I'm an optimist."

"Okay?"

"So I am going to try one more time with you. Once more."

Scott put his hands up. "Fine. Go for it."

"See this? This map?"

"Yeah. It's not that road map you had before."

"That's right, good, paying attention a bit now. So we used the old map to get started. But this is new. Unsullied."

"It doesn't have much on it as far as maps go."

"You say that, but I don't think you really even know what you are saying. This map is the first step in recreating society."

Scott, trying to sound calm, "I understand you have a big vision. Good. We need that. But we also need to be thinking about what the return to normalcy will look like. You have big ideas but we need practical ideas on how to make our City more liveable."

"Don't tell me what I need to think about. You need to think about this, Bob: when spring comes, who is going to come out on top? Who? I am. Not fucking China, not fucking New York, not fucking Germany. Me. And the City. Understand? It is THE City. And we are going to have lights again. And heat. Everyone will have heat. And we can drive our cars. And buy things. All the things. All the fucking stuff we should be able to fucking buy. Why? Because I am the man. So you listen to me when I tell you to go find me my money."

Scott said he'd get right on it, closed the door quietly behind him. Jesus, the guy was really losing it. Scott nodded to the man standing at the top of the stairwell, but the guy just looked past him. None of the four guards were dressed in the camo uniforms that Talos security used, instead they wore all-black uniforms. Didn't even have the Talos logo. Scott said, trying for casual, "Pulling guard duty for Mr. Love are you? You with Talos security?" The man didn't look at him, just said, "New Army."

Scott said, "Must have missed this one. What's New Army?"

"You'll have to speak with Mr. Love, sir."

What the fuck? Love must be getting worried, creating his own little army to look out for him. Well, Scott was more than happy to give him something to worry about.

Chumboy's Auntie Verla was telling Tiny that he made a good cup of tea. The woman was small, grey hair pulled back into a braid. Wearing multiple sweaters. Pink cardigan over a faded blue tunic, mustard-coloured turtleneck underneath it all. She said, "Now all we need is some of that sweet milk and we'd be good."

Tiny asked, "Like that Carnation stuff?"

"Yes."

"You like that canned milk?"

"It's sweet."

Chumboy said they'd keep their eyes out for some next time out, but doubted any would still be around. "Cupboard is bare out there, Auntie."

"Cupboards are never bare, just have to know where to look. Be patient."

"Well, I don't know, Auntie," Chumboy said, "on our last trip, we went pretty far north, all the way up to Larder, only came back with two small sacks of flour, a dozen tins of those godawful pea and carrot mixes, and a few pounds of dog biscuits."

"Your pup must have been happy," she said.

"Well, I managed to grab a couple for her before Tiny here repo'd them from me."

Tiny said, "Protein is protein. You soak those suckers long enough you'd think it was spam."

"Didn't taste much different."

"Anytime you want to be the underappreciated cook of the fucking new age I'll give you my apron. Until then, you eat what I serve." Then Tiny said to Auntie Verla, "Sorry about the cussing."

She just shrugged and smiled.

Tiny asked, "So what brings you over here?"

The small woman said, "Just a friendly visit. Good cup of tea."

Tiny wiped his hands down the front of his apron and said, "No offence, but you have a way of showing up just before all hell breaks loose, so I thought I'd see if I should be getting on my Kevlar or not."

"You think I bring the trouble, Tiny?"

He shrugged. "Doesn't really matter how it all goes down, I'm just trying to learn from the past."

Chumboy said, "I wanted you to tell her about Susie's dream."

Tiny looked at Chumboy, then to his Auntie, asked, "The dream about the monsters?"

"Yeah, the map."

"You guys cooking up some sort of hocus pocus shit? I won't have it in my kitchen."

Auntie Verla said, "I like those words: hocus pocus."

"No offence, again, Verla, but I just don't share your perspective on that. "

Auntie Verla had a long, slow sip of her tea, and looked down into her mug. Tiny said, "What? You reading some hoodoo in there? Getting some messages in your tea now? Jesus."

Auntie Verla looked up. "Tiny, what are you talking about? People don't get messages in their mug of tea."

Tiny, confused, thinking that Auntie Verla was always talking about stories, and visions, and all of that mystic stuff, asked, "People read tea leaves, though. That's a thing, right?"

"I'm not some old lady chasing tea leaves around my cup."

"Alright, sorry about that," Tiny said, "just trying to figure out why you'd come all the way over here to ask me about some crazy dreams my cousin was having?"

"How many times did she dream this map?" Auntie Verla asked.

Tiny said, "You didn't answer my question."

Auntie Verla just sat and waited. Tiny said, "Okay, well, I don't know, maybe half a dozen times. Maybe more."

"Same dream?"

"No. She said something about sometimes it was a good map and sometimes a bad one. Deep stuff, right?"

But Auntie Verla said yes it was deep, something to be taken seriously. "When a dream changes, grows, it is telling a story maybe."

"Is that what that Jung guy thinks? That the dream itself is telling the story? What does that even mean?"

Auntie Verla shrugged. "I don't know who you are talking about. Why don't you talk to me about Susie's dream instead of these other guys?"

"Okay, fine. What else?"

"Did Susie say if she was in the dream?"

Tiny looked at Chumboy now, asked, "What's going on? You think Susie's sick or something?"

"Well, was she in the dream?" Chumboy asked.

Tiny said, "There were monsters, or beasts, I don't know what she was saying half the time. She maybe said something about touching the map, or picking it up, but I gotta be honest, I just stop listening to her after a while, she doesn't make any sense half the time. But you know what? Right now, right here and now, I'm going on strike, no more slop for anyone until one of youse explains to me what's going on."

Chumboy said, "Look at it this way, Tiny. Dreams can be important ways of sensing the future, or processing what is happening right now in a person's life. So a reoccurring dream about a map, especially one that seems to change, that's interesting. This dream must be strong, I mean it's giving Susie headaches, right?"

Tiny, shaking his head, said, "Seems to me like you guys are making a big deal out of Susie's anxiety. Big trip into the unknown, has a few bad dreams about unchartered territory, there it is. That Jung guy would probably say the same thing."

Auntie Verla said, "You see it just as it is."

Tiny wondered if Auntie Verla was being sarcastic. "Yeah?"

"Susun is going into the unknown. We all are. We just need to think about why she is being shown the map. Why she is having this dream for us."

"For us? No, that's not how it works. It's just her dream. When I have dreams that I'm back in high school, and then I realize I'm not, fucking jubilation, it's my dream. It's for me. C'mon, you know what Susie is like."

Auntie Verla nodded. "She's hearing or seeing things we can't hear or see yet. Maybe because of the baby."

"Do pregnant women get weird dreams?"

"Important dreams, Tiny. Dreams to bring babies into the world."

"I don't know about all of this dream stuff."

Auntie Verla was looking into her tea again. She took a sip and said, "You make a good mug of tea, Tiny."

"Thanks, Verla. But I gotta say, I think you guys are overreacting."

Auntie Verla shook her head. "Tiny, when women start dreaming, we need to start listening."

Chapter Nine

"Take whatever resources you need, but do one final cleanse. I want that valley empty, cleared and cleaned up."

Love had shown up unexpectedly. Bakalov was honoured to have Mr. Love come see him in his warehouse, where he lived and worked, trained his men. Trained his dogs there, too. But he was also worried. Was the man checking up on him? Mr. Love had complained that Bakalov was wasting his time when he requested meetings, but now Mr. Love was coming to see him?

Bakalov said, "It is good to be clearing the Valley out, this wild place so close to the City. Acting as a highway for pests and vermin. I am proud to be doing it."

The Valley was one of the few places in the City where regular Talos security forces rarely went. Neglected, it attracted all kinds of folks with their plastic tents and rummaged lives. Bakalov thought the self-proclaimed 'back to the land' communities were communitarian, socialist bullshit. Most couldn't last anyway, it was a tough go. The ones who did, Talos had Bakalov take care of them.

"Clearly we can't move ahead unless the Valley is under control," Love said.

Love looked different today, wearing a black parka with fur around the collar, black boots, a black watch cap. Bakalov was surprised—he looked comfortable in this outdoor gear. Made him think Mr. Love was more adaptable than he had believed.

"It will be the last area of the City that Project Domain will pass through," said Love, "and I need to use that opportunity to show I have things under control. I control the City, I control the Valley, I control the periphery. And so I control the entire Domain. Understand, Ion?"

Bakalov said, "Of course."

"So then the priority is clearing the railway tracks, making the journey out of the City seamless. Beautiful."

"Yes, of course. The clearing of the track is complete to the three hundred-kilometer mark. We are making good progress. I have backtracked now, left three crews to keep the tracks maintained. And I am working on a final sweep through the Valley itself."

"There is a lot at stake here, Ion. We have to eliminate the chaos, make the wild tame, you do know what I mean, don't you, Ion? The Valley is the most visible place of resistance. There are men and women out there living like animals. And animals living out there with no fear of humans. No limits. Just the other day, a pack of those wild dogs or wolves or whatever they are, they took a child. Two years old. What could the family do?"

Bakalov said, "That is unacceptable. How could that happen? Where were their parents, the security?"

"Oh, Ion, I don't know, maybe it didn't happen. You know what I mean? Whether it happened or not isn't what matters. What matters is that it could happen. We cannot tolerate areas beyond our control. That is what is unacceptable."

"Yes, of course," Bakalov said. Feeling the need to explain what he knew about such things, he said, "And it is possible, probable even, when these beasts are left to themselves. They get bold. So when they are hungry, they will take chances, these animals. Come into villages, or on the edges of towns, take children, even adults sometimes."

"Well, we can't have that. There are some important people, generous contributors, who live along the Valley, because they feel safer out there than in the City's core. And they don't want their personal security forces wasting time chasing down coyotes and raccoons. So get out there and trap them or shoot them or whatever it is that you do. I need you to double your efforts. I want all the vermin gone. I'm trusting you with this important work."

Bakalov didn't think that hunting down vermin in the Valley was important work but he was pleased that Love had come himself, showing up out of the blue with three big trucks loaded with personal security guards.

"Of course," Bakalov said, "I will accomplish this."

Love looked at Bakalov, feet planted apart like a soldier, hands behind his back. He tried to imagine this man murdering his own father. Took in his massive build, sloping shoulders, the huge bald head, mouth tight-lipped and the goatee trimmed and exact. Big arms. He had no trouble seeing it. Just looking at the man you could tell brutality was his second nature. But to trust him? That was the question. Could such a monster be subservient? He looked right into Bakalov's washed out blue eyes and there was nothing there but a willingness to serve. The eyes of a perfect butler.

"I know you will, Ion, I know you will. That is why I came in person. To show my confidence in you, yes, but also to let you know how important this task is. The train, the machine that will bring renewal to the City, it starts out through the Valley. Once it is cleared, then we push north, make the land useful again. Because you know what is happening? Nature is giving up its resistance. Winter is done, exhausted. I know it. I can feel it. It is our right to have spring again and spring will come."

༂

"I don't think my horse likes me," Jeff said. He glanced back at Susun. "You, however, look like a regular Calamity Jane."

"Maybe less talking, okay?" Mitch said.

Jeff sighed, rolled his eyes, but Susun, too, preferred silence. The crunch of the snow under her horse's hoofs, the occasional bird singing. That was fine. Nice even. But she wanted to think.

She was glad to be leaving behind the dense woods, the mid-afternoon sun now warm on her back. They'd spent the morning slogging through overgrown trails, brittle tree branches slapping back, the horses winded from the deep and uneven snow. They'd be on firm footing and then plunge through a foot of snow, Jeff almost tipping off his horse as it went down on a knee. Levi jumped down and helped the horse steady itself, stroking the horse's neck and talking to it, its breathing coming in puffs, nostrils flaring. It was a hard go. Jeff said he was never, ever going to ride a horse again.

It was easier going now that they were moving along the edge of an open field. When they had been struggling through the bush and snow Mitch had gotten impatient, telling Susun to pass over the map, surely there was a better trail to follow. Susun had brought out the small, hand drawn map Hector had given them. Mitch said, "You call this a fucking map, Jesus."

Susun explained it was all they could get. Told her that Hector, the man who'd given them the horses, said there were no more maps, and told them his little map was like homemade hooch. Contraband.

Mitch said that was pretty fucked up. What the fuck would Talos want with all the maps? She then told Susun she could put away her Dora the Explorer map, adding, "Well, that solves one mystery."

Susun asked, "What's that?"

"Your nightmare. Worried about no map, no guides. Pretty obvious."

"The dreams started before I left. I've been having them for a couple of months now."

Mitch stared at her for a second, taking her measure, and said, "Guess you're a fucking psychic, then."

ৎ

Bakalov climbed onto a table in the food court. Most of the guys were already drifting in. It was early, but they never knew exactly when the meal would be served and it was better to be safe than sorry. Slaught was up near the top of the escalator, had descended a few steps when the big man with the grey teeth shouted, "Vermin."

He didn't need to shout. All of the men were quiet, watching the Dogman and the three guys with him. This was new. Probably bad. Some of the guys starting to edge their way out of the food court, prompting the Dogman standing on the table to yell, "Stay put."

Everyone did.

"I need twenty men. Volunteers. Strong men."

The men started glancing at their neighbours, not clear what was coming next. Bakalov was pleased with the confusion and fear in the room, realizing now they were afraid of him. Afraid of Ion Bakalov. He had power over these men. He said, "Twenty of you can walk out of here today with me."

From the back, "To do what?"

"Go hunting," he said.

Bakalov was surprised at the group of men, so passive, just

gaping at him. He had already selected the strongest men, had them out working on the railway. Now he would need to turn some of these men into proper soldiers. It might be tough at first but he could do it. He said, "It makes no difference to me if you volunteer or I choose you. None at all. But if you volunteer, you don't have to come back here."

A young man, hunched down in his parka, right up at the front, asked, "Hunting what?"

"Doesn't matter," Ion answered. And it was true. You hunt a rat, you hunt a man, doesn't matter. Maybe you need a different approach, but in the end, they either run or fight, and then you see how you do, what kind of hunter you are.

Bakalov watched as the men were glancing at each other, waiting for someone else to say something, for the other guy to act, wondering if he was on the level. Questioning it. Would they really get to go free? No one wanting to speak up.

Bakalov said, "So none of you have the courage to be the first one?"

The young guy in the parka stepped forward, asking, "What happens after the hunting?"

Bakalov liked the question—showed the young man was thinking. "If you're a good hunter, you can stay with me. We form special force. What's your name?

"Jimmy. My name's Jimmy. So, what kind of 'special force'?"

Bakalov shook his head. "You make decision now." He wanted to push the young man, see if he could take the risk.

"Okay, I'm in," he said, scuffling his feet a bit, trying to look bold but coming off maybe a bit awkward, not used to being the centre of attention. Bakalov said to him, "Pick nineteen men to go with you. Pick young, strong men."

Jimmy hesitated, and Bakalov watched as the men around him collectively started to move away, nothing sudden, but a shifting away from him nonetheless. Jimmy looked a bit panicked, turning to the first guy beside him and saying, "Okay, well, you." Then he turned around and pointed to a guy with a beard and glasses, one of the lenses broken, and said, "And you." Like he was picking kids for a ball team. The guy with the broken glasses said, "Fuck you, I ain't going anywhere with you."

From the table-top Bakalov could see the man clearly, just past Jimmy, and so he shot him. It was loud, guys pulling away from the sound. Jimmy was bent over, hands over ears as if he could block out being shot himself.

Yelling now, because Jimmy was still covering his ears, Bakalov ordered, "Jimmy! Pick your men, finish the job." And Jimmy slowly looked up, looked down at the bearded guy, his glasses lying on the ground. He had fallen straight backwards when the shot hit him just above his heart, and now blood was pooling on his chest. Jimmy then took in the scene around him, the men backing away, the fear in their eyes, and turned to a big guy wearing a black hoodie under a ski jacket. "You," he said.

Jimmy had no more trouble picking his nineteen men.

༒

They were bored. Slaught figured that's the reason they talked. Well, sometimes they talked so they could pick a fight. But they fought because they were bored, too.

Slaught found the days long, the nights unbearable. During the days you could at least walk around the mall, climb the escalators, wander through the trashed hallways thinking about how things used to be. The evenings, though, they were another story. There was no upside to hanging around downstairs once supper was over. So everyone went up, looking for their spot for the night. And then, well, sometimes it was fighting, sometimes talking, but always the itch of boredom and anger and fear.

But tonight, the guys were both bored and amped up. The shooting earlier, the whole scene with the Dogman, even the idea of hunting, of being outside, was fucking with their heads. They talked about the guys who had gone with Bakalov, some saying they were fucking suck-ups, a few guys saying they were just losers and probably wouldn't be coming back. But Slaught could tell they were all suddenly thinking about being outside. What things would be like if they ever got out of here. They had been playing 'what if' for the past hour. What if you got outside and everyone was dead? What if you got outside and there were only dogs out there? What if you got outside and it was summer?

One guy, head shaved and a tattoo on his neck, had started, "Okay, okay, I got one for you. What if you've got yourself outside, almost free, and those fucking Dogmen track you down, tell you to surrender because there's this beautiful girl they're going to kill—what do you do?"

Two of the guys didn't even seem to hear, one gnawing on his thumbnail, trying to get purchase on it between his teeth, the nail bitten almost halfway down to the cuticle from what Slaught could see. The other guy seemed catatonic, Slaught wondering if he was stoned, wondered if you could get stuff in here. Maybe there was a whole subculture of trade he was missing out on. Maybe just as well.

A third guy, early thirties, beard matted and dirty brown, took the bait. "That's the problem right there, though, you're dealing with a bunch of motherfuckers, right? So they say, 'You die, the girl will live,' right? But you can't take that to the bank, know what I mean? They're probably going to kill the girl anyway. So what's the point?"

"But if you say fuck it, then what? Watch them kill her?"

"Where's the girl from?" asked the bearded guy. "How do you know they even have her?"

"Don't be fucking stupid," tattoo guy said. "This isn't real, dumbass. They have her, okay?"

"Okay, man, okay, just thinking through the different possibilities."

Getting back to his story, tattoo guy said, "Brutal, right? I mean, you gotta wonder, could I really watch her die? That's going to break me up, man. I might rather, you know, make the big gesture, go out shooting..."

The guy took the thumb out of his mouth, and said, "What? That's fucked up—die just so you don't see her get whacked and stacked?"

"Yeah, man, that's the thing, right? It fucks with you, you got no way to win." A skinny kid, getting into it, "And what, you give up just because you're a coward? Not tough enough to watch her die? She's nothing to you, man."

"I mean it'd be one thing to say, yeah, I don't want to see that," said the bearded guy, maybe trying to redeem himself. "So I make the big gesture, give up, save the girl, looks good, but then is it really just because you can't take the heat..."

The thumb guy finishing it, "Then get out of the kitchen, right?

"Fuck yeah, man."

The skinny kid said, "No way, you take it like a man, watch her die, say to the man, fuck you. Fuck you and your rules."

"Awesome. Best response ever, bro," the guy with the beard said.

Slaught thought the conversation was taking a weird turn, asked, "So, what about the girl?"

The men stared at him.

The bearded guy said, "What about her?"

"Well, the woman is at the centre of the whole thing, right? Try to see it from her point of view."

The skinny guy, sounding angry, "I ain't pretending I'm a chick."

"You're missing the point," Slaught said.

"Yeah, that right, wiseass?' said the skinny kid. "And just who the fuck are you to tell me that?"

Slaught felt himself getting angry; he was bored and afraid, too. He said, "I'm the fucking Winterman, dipshit, that's who I am."

Chapter Ten

They weren't used to being outside. The twenty guys had been loaded into a big truck and driven across the City. The truck bumped along for over an hour until it came to a stop. Bakalov came around the back to pull open the tailgate, told them to jump down. Hurry up, they had work to do.

It was cold and dark. Jimmy went first, trying to take command, telling the other guys to get a move on. Most of the guys wouldn't look at him; Jimmy figured they were pissed about being picked, about being out here. They'd all heard the rumours about the Dogman's private killing fields and now Jesus fucking Christ here they were, all of them scared, but also blaming Jimmy. Like it was his fault they were out there. How was he supposed to know that things were going to go south so fast? All he'd done was ask a few questions. It was fucking insane.

Jimmy could hear the guys starting to grumble. The traps and bait were heavy and carrying them in the snow was hard. They weren't used to work, spending most of their days loafing and walking and loafing some more—not much else to do. Jimmy was struggling, too, trying not to show it, tossing the bag of bait up over his shoulder, following along single file behind Bakalov and two of the other Dogmen. Three of Bakalov's dogs were on leashes, bringing up the rear with the fourth Dogman.

Bakalov stopped, turned, holding up his hand as a signal to stop. "Alright, some instructions. Jimmy here is going to divide you into groups of four. Two scouts. Watch for a good spot for the traps, keep an eye out for wolves. The dogs should let you know if they're around. One guy sets trap, other guy baits it. Simple." Then he turned and passed a gun to Jimmy. "Here. For being the first to volunteer. Make sure everyone is working."

Jimmy stared at it, uncertain about whether he should hold on to it or put it away but then seemed to notice all the other guys looking at him and shoved it into his pocket.

"That's not where it goes," one of the guys said. "Put it in your pants."

Jimmy said, "Don't worry about it and get moving." Taking charge.

The dogs came pushing past them on the trail, nearly knocking over a tall, thin guy wearing a hoodie and hunched up with the cold. "I don't like the dogs," he said.

"The dogs mark their trail," Bakalov said, "and the wild dogs and coyotes will come later, see what has been on their territory. So we set traps along this trail."

The hoodie guy didn't say anything. Jimmy told him to grab the bait and get going. He was warming up to his role, liked bossing the guys around, it felt good. The hoodie kid was struggling to get a firm grip on the garbage bag wrapped with tarp that held the bait. He said, "This fucking stinks."

Jimmy said, "Don't worry about it, you already stank," and Bakalov laughed. The hoodie kid gave Jimmy a look that said, 'Yeah, little fucker, you're going to be sorry soon enough.'

"What are we doing?" It was the first guy Jimmy had chosen.

Bakalov said, "We are getting rid of the wild dogs. The coyotes and wolves, too. They have been getting bold. Mr. Love says that is not how the City will be. There will be order, no chaos."

"Who's this Mr. Love guy? Dumbass name, anyway."

Bakalov looked at Jimmy. "Is this man your friend? You picked him first. What is his name?"

Jimmy shrugged and answered, "Yeah, I know him. His name's Boyd. He's alright." Saying it but not sounding like he really meant it, Jimmy thinking maybe the guy was going to be a fuck-up. Then he'd get blamed. Jesus.

"Boyd," Bakalov said, "you show respect. You be quiet, do your job. We don't have a problem."

Boyd set down the bag of bait and said, "It's heavy. I don't like it out here." He looked cold, moving from foot to foot, agitated. Jimmy moved closer to him. "Boyd, come on."

"What's your problem? I just said what everyone is thinking."

Jimmy glanced quickly at Bakalov, then said under his breath to Boyd, "Trying to get yourself killed, asshole?"

Boyd shrugged, looked at Bakalov, sniffed a bit and asked, "So what's with the killing of the dogs? I thought you liked dogs."

Bakalov said, "Boyd, you need to learn that there are many kinds of dogs, just like there are many kinds of men."

"I'm not much interested in dogs, 'cept bitches," Boyd said, sniggering.

Bakalov stared at the young man for a few seconds and Boyd stopped. Boyd looked at Jimmy. "My feet are freezing. It's too cold out here," he said.

Jimmy said, "Once we're moving, you'll warm up. Let's listen to Mr. Bakalov so we can get to work and get this job done."

Boyd said, "Fuck this, I'm going back."

"You can't just go back, asshole," Jimmy said. "You were lucky to get out."

"Dude," Boyd said, "this guy is whacked, I'm going back."

"Hey, we signed up for this, let's just keep going."

"*You* fucking signed me up."

All the guys were paying attention now.

Bakalov moved closer to Jimmy and Boyd, "You think this is a discussion you can have?"

Jimmy turned to Bakalov, panicked, and said, "Sorry, Mr. Bakalov, he'll change his mind." Then to Boyd he hissed, "Just pull yourself the fuck together, okay?"

Boyd said, "This is bullshit. Knock yourself out killing puppies, but I'm outta here. Going to go wait in the truck."

The other guys didn't move, watching as Boyd pushed his way past Jimmy. Bakalov waited until Boyd had moved about ten feet down the trail, walked after him a few paces until he had cleared the group, then shot him in the back, turning away before the young guy had even crumpled down into the snow. "Jesus Christ!" Jimmy said, then asking, peering into the darkness, "Is he dead? Did you kill him?"

"Doesn't matter. The wolves will find him soon enough. Let's be quick with our work. We don't want to meet them on the way out."

Jimmy looked at the lump in the darkness on the trail, his friend now just a shadow. He thought he heard Boyd moaning, but he was cold and he wanted to be moving, to get this night over with. And he was scared now, but sort of excited, too.

Bakalov started walking. Jimmy, following behind, not looking back now, asked, "Is this like a regular thing? Will we be coming out here again?"

"Let's see how we do tonight, what kind of bounty we can get. It is hard work."

"I can work hard. I've worked hard before. Back in the day."

"You, you can come for training. The rest of them were forced to come, so they will need to prove themselves."

Jimmy asked, "Do I get to keep the gun?"

"Only if you use it properly."

"Oh, I'll use it properly," he said.

Bakalov said, "I will tell you a story. I had a friend with dairy farm. His cows, they were bothered by the wolves. They had attacked his cows, scared the farmer's family. So he calls me for help. I go, bringing my AR15 and my 9mm pistol. We wait four hours and nothing, no wolves, it is getting dark. He wants to leave, go have his supper. He doesn't know how to wait. To hunt. But then he says, look, there, must be a wolf, a small black movement against the snow. And I say no, that is no wolf, look how it is moving, it is a porcupine maybe. I shoot it, turned it to red mist, splattered there against the snow. The wolves, I tell the farmer, will smell the red mist now. And we wait another hour. He complains; his feet, they're cold. Said he was leaving, but I told him, No, just wait. And then they came, five of them, mangy dirty wolves, heading towards the stain of the porcupine on the snow, hungry, not really paying attention to anything but the smell. I said to the farmer, I like to unleash carnage, and then? I aim, snick, snick, first puppy, then second, third one through the air, tangled up in his own guts. Sent them all back to hell where they belong."

Bakalov paused, relishing the memory, then said, "You see, firepower? It wins. Wanting to kill, it wins. The farmer, he had neither. He needed me. You pay attention, people will need you. That is how you use your gun properly."

ঝ

Aimless wandering. That's how Slaught spent his days. At the greenhouses, they worked. Hard. Here, the boredom made him feel more tired, so he kept moving, tracing his same path every day.

He headed down to the food court where most of the guys

congregated off and on during the day. Things felt more animated than usual. The guys who'd gone out hunting the night before were holding court, bragging, talking about the bait and the dark and the guy getting shot. And about how Bakalov had promised that guy Mumford that he could leave but then sent him back in. That was a raw deal. That was the big bald guy. Ion Bakalov. The Dogman.

Slaught usually kept to the edges, along the walls, didn't like to leave himself exposed. The energy in the food court was disruptive, edgy, and something was telling him to get out of there. If he'd learned anything from Chumboy, it was to listen to his gut. He decided to cut across the food court area and go back down into the hallways.

But then up ahead, four of the Dogmen appeared, including that Bakalov guy. Where the fuck had they come from? Standing near the bottom of the escalators, arms crossed, surveying the crowd of men. They were right in his path.

He stopped as three of the Dogmen started fanning out along the perimeter of the food court, one of them barking, "Sit down, everyone down!"

Guys who weren't at tables looked confused—where did they sit down? Some started towards the few empty chairs when another Dogman yelled, "On the ground, get the fuck down on the ground!"

Slaught could see the bald man moving away from the escalator towards the centre of the food court, dressed in a big camo parka that made him look even bigger. The man went a few yards then stopped at the edge of the food court and glanced back, noticing Slaught. Probably because he was the only one still standing.

The man shouted at him in a thick accent. "You were told to sit!"

Slaught thought it would just be easier to sit down as he was told, but he guessed today wasn't going to be the day he picked easy. He said, "Don't see why I should."

And there it was. If it hadn't been about him before, it was now.

The Dogman stared at Slaught, and then began to backtrack towards him. Now every guy, even those who usually tried their best to mind their own business, was watching. Slaught watched, too, as the Dogman walked slowly towards him, the other three staying put, guns trained on the rest of the population. There must be almost three hundred of them sitting there. Christ almighty, three hundred to four. They were wasting great odds.

Then the Dogman was a few feet from him saying, "You should sit because you were told to." Saying it like it was just the truth. He was taller than Slaught, barrel-chested.

"So who are you?" Slaught asked.

The Dogman showed a slit of a smile. "I am Bakalov. Now sit down."

"Yeah, I heard you but just wasn't clear on what the reason for it was."

"Reason? Because I told you."

"Listening to someone for no good reason can get you in trouble."

Bakalov said, "I remember you, you were the one wringing his hands about the dead man. Worrying about his mother."

Slaught could smell him now, diesel maybe, not something you caught a whiff of much anymore. Something else, too, a little sour maybe? Reminded him of something; he wasn't quite able to put his finger on it.

Bakalov gestured to the men sitting in the food court. "These men, they are smart. They want to eat. They sit down when they are told. They get to eat. I think you will wait until I finish what I came here for, and then I am going to help you be smarter."

"So what did you come for this time? Don't see any dead guys laying around for you to feed to your dogs."

Bakalov smiled again. Fuck, it was an ugly sight, the man's mouth just a mess of grey and menace. "I'm not here for the corpses. I'm here for the Winterman," he said.

Slaught realized now that in some way he had seen this coming. As soon as he'd gotten to the food court things felt off. Must have been him shooting his mouth off about being the Winterman. Someone grassed him up. But why would it matter?

Slaught said, "Well, let me save you some time. I'm the Winterman."

"You?"

"That's what I just said."

Bakalov frowning, "But why should I believe you?"

"Don't then."

Bakalov stared at him for a few seconds, scanned the crowd, and said to a group of men close to him, "This is the Winterman?" But the men shrugged, not meeting his gaze. Then Bakalov seemed to make up his mind. He jerked his head towards the doors and said, "Let's go."

"Where to?"

"You have trouble listening. I said, 'Let's go.'"

"You tell me where."

Slaught watched while the man pulled a small pistol out of the inside pocket of his parka and gestured towards the door with it. Bakalov said, "I could shoot you right now."

Slaught hesitated. He figured leaving with the guy would bring nothing but trouble. But he was also pretty sure none of the three hundred guys here would do anything if Bakalov beat him to a pulp right in front of them. Still, once in that tunnel, it could be game over.

"You could, I guess, but I figure you are wanting me for a reason. See, there's always a reason, and I just want to know what that reason is."

It seemed to take forever for the meaty fist to come up and slam into the side of Slaught's head. Slaught felt his neck jerk sidewise as he sailed down towards the floor. His first thought was that the guy packed a powerful wallop. Then, as his face met the floor, and he caught the smell of the dark stains that coated the front of the man's boots, he thought he recognized the sour smell from before. It was like the smell of a butcher shop, all blood and guts.

Chapter Eleven

"Christ, he's filthy," Scott said, and put his hand to his face. "He stinks, too."

Bakalov—dragging Slaught by the collar like a sack of potatoes—paused and asked, "Should I leave him out here, in the hallway?"

Bakalov had heard from one of the soldiers on security detail at the Facility that some guy called the Winterman had shown up in the population. The soldier had heard some of the prisoners talking about it and asked him if it might be important? Bakalov said maybe, then sat down to think it over.

He remembered that bitch—what was her name again? Black, that was it. Remembered her from when she bought some guns from him. He'd said he'd buy her a beer, but she just dropped the money in his pocket and took the guns. Too good to even hand it to him. The guy next to him said she was some stuck up Talos operative, and maybe those Wintermen she was hunting would take care of her, take her down a few notches. And now he had the Winterman. Life was funny.

It was information. And Mr. Love was always telling him that information was a form of currency. So Bakalov had thought about how he should spend this currency that he had just acquired. He thought of going straight to Mr. Love with it. But instead he decided to drag the piece of shit up to Scott's office. In case it wasn't that important.

It would look right. Scott was his immediate boss, but also the boss of the woman that was supposed to hunt this Winterman and put an end to him. It would be interesting to see what Scott made of it. That would give him an idea if this was important. Important enough to take to Mr. Love.

He had to half drag the man to get him loaded up into the truck. The man was heavy, but not so big that Bakalov couldn't take him down with one solid hit. So much for this Winterman.

And now he had him in front of Mr. Scott. And Mr. Scott seemed interested.

"No, no, bring him in," Scott said, stepping back as Bakalov hauled Slaught to his feet and pushed him into the office. Slaught staggered, stumbled forward, finally sinking down to his knees on the floor.

Scott looked down at the Winterman, the matted hair and beard made sticky by blood seeping along the man's left temple. His coat grimy, stained. The sole peeling away from the bottom of one of his boots.

Scott said, "Good Christ, Bakalov, the man looks like shit. What do you do to them over there?"

"Nothing. I do nothing to them. They do this to themselves."

"Is everyone in the Facility in this state?"

Bakalov shrugged, "Perhaps. We don't inspect them."

"What if some disease flares up and spreads?"

"Then they get sick, maybe die. It is one way of keeping down the population."

"You know, Bakalov," Scott said, "you aren't fit to run that place. I don't think you're fit for much. Except maybe shooting dogs."

Bakalov smiled. "But you promoted me yourself," he said.

"Which means, Bakalov, I can demote you, too."

"Mr. Love thinks I am, as you say, fit for the job."

"Well I think I'll have a talk with Eton." He used the man's first name, trying to show maybe that he was closer to Mr. Love. Bakalov wondered if that was true. He had a feeling that Mr. Love did not trust Scott.

Scott said, "You have to start thinking these things through. The Facility is overcrowded as it is, but worse yet, it is in the middle of the City. If this place was out in the hinterlands, quite frankly, I might not give a shit, either. But we can't handle any kind of rioting, break-outs, or pandemics. We don't have the resources. You need to have protocols in place."

"Protocols?"

"Yes, protocols, procedures, rules."

"Yes, we have rules. This man here, he broke the rules. That is why he is here."

Scott had almost forgotten about Slaught. "Right. Here, get him up on a chair." Scott brought a plastic chair over, asking, "Is he ok?"

Bakalov kicked Slaught, barking, "Get up, get up in the chair!" Slaught pulled himself up.

Bakalov said, "If he isn't okay, it's his own fault. He gave me trouble."

"I think that's what he does: gives trouble. Did you tell him anything?"

"Tell him what? I don't know why this man might be of interest to anyone."

"Did you tell anyone else you were bringing him here?"

"No. I remembered you have hunted for this man, so I brought him here."

Scott nodding, "Good."

"So why does this man matter?"

Scott said, "You don't have to worry about that, Bakalov,

you can head back to whatever it is that keeps you busy."

Bakalov hesitated. "I can wait. Take him back when you are finished."

"I'll call. Or better yet just leave it, I'll have a couple of my men escort him back."

Bakalov nodded. He was reluctant to go but saw no choice. As he was leaving, he said, "Watch this one."

He closed the door. Mr. Scott did not have any security outside like Mr. Love did. His office was small, cramped, not like Mr. Love's big room at the top of Talos Tower. Maybe Scott wasn't an important man after all. Maybe he should have taken this Winterman straight to Mr. Love. Maybe he still should.

༄

Scott waited until Bakalov shut the door behind him before crossing the room to get a glass of water. He eyed Slaught as he passed him the glass. "I have a few questions for you," he said.

Slaught drained the glass and held it out to Scott, but Scott just stared at him as if by touching the glass he could catch some prisoner-borne pandemic. Slaught's ribs ached as he bent forward to set the glass on the floor and he sat up slower than he expected. He was in bad shape.

"You paying attention?" Scott snapped his fingers. "Slaught, I'm talking to you."

Slaught was having a hard time focusing, the throbbing behind his eyes was distracting and made him want to just lie down, but here he was, sitting in this stupid plastic chair.

Scott said, "So this is what the famous Winterman has come to. You should see yourself. What a mess. Hardly the great liberator, eh?"

Slaught brought his hand up slowly to the side of his head,

the blood there sticky. Tried to clear his head. And the guy in front of him just wasn't shutting up.

"Slaught?"

Squinting up at the man, "Can you stop talking for a minute and let me think."

Scott laughed, "Are you kidding me? Do you know what is happening? Even where you are? I could send you back into that place—wouldn't even have to put a price on your head and you'd be dead within a day. All the young bucks over there trying to prove themselves."

"Listen, buddy," Slaught said slowly, must've taken a few good whacks across the mouth, too, jaw aching, lips puffy, "not sure if you've been in there, but most guys have more to worry about than trying to prove themselves."

"I can just call the Dogman back if you'd rather talk to him."

Not the Dogman. Not yet. Slaught said, "Like to know who I'm talking to."

"Bob Scott."

Slaught didn't say anything, trying to place the name, thinking maybe it meant something to him, but he couldn't search past the pain.

"Slaught? For Chrisssakes, snap out of it."

Slaught was wondering if he had dozed off, his head snapping back. Now he gripped the thin arms of the chairs, feeling them digging into his palms. He tried to focus. "Can you not talk so loud?"

"You better start listening, Slaught. Right now, you're drinking water and talking to the Vice President of Talos. Don't talk to me? You can go back to Bakalov. Understand? So why are you in the Facility?"

"Wrong place, wrong time, I guess."

"You were down here, in the City?"

Slaught shook his head. "The outpost." Figuring Scott could find out anyway, no point not answering, but the name, Scott, and Talos, there was something there, why couldn't he put it together? Fuck, his head hurt.

"Okay, Slaught, so I am going to ask you a few questions. You're going to answer me. Are we clear?"

Slaught nodded. "What's on your mind?"

"Gold. That's what's on my mind. Specifically, where is it?"

Right. There it was. The whole nine yards: Talos. Gold. Mitch Black. Hadn't thought about that jackpot in a while. Guess he'd had other things on his mind.

"How would I know?"

"What happened to it?"

"Never saw it."

"So you know about the gold?"

"People came looking for it, that's what I know."

"But she had it?"

Slaught hesitated, yeah, Black had it, sailed outta town with it, but he didn't think he owed Scott any kind of explanation. "By 'she,' do you mean Mitch Black?"

"Don't waste my time, we both know who and what we are talking about. Did she have the gold?"

"I thought you two cooked up the whole treasure hunt together. Regular Bonnie and her armchair Clyde."

Scott leaned in to Slaught, hissed, "Answer the fucking questions."

"I never saw the gold."

"But you know about it?"

"Yeah I knew about it. I already told you that. You and her were going to grab the gold and then do a splitsville. Then a bunch of fucking maniacs came riding into town, shot things up, shot each other, then it was all over. Glad to see everyone clear out."

"So Black left with it?"

"I guess. Never actually saw it, myself."

"Where is she now?"

"She's not exactly my pen pal."

Scott said, "I can get Bakalov to help you tell me what I need to know."

"I'm telling you everything I know. Never saw the gold. She left town. Didn't leave a forwarding address. And I've been stuck down here for months."

"You could help yourself by telling me. Give me something here, Slaught, I'm trying to work with you."

"Is that what this is, you trying to work with me?"

Scott stared down at Slaught for a minute. He walked to his desk, looked around the office and finally grabbed the large framed photo of fucking Eton Love. He went over to Slaught, and swung hard, smashing the picture across the side of his head. Slaught tipped off the chair and fell to the floor. Broken glass everywhere. Christ almighty.

Slaught couldn't do much but lie there. He could see Scott's shoes—they were polished. He thought how different they were from the Dogman's.

"Sit up, for Chrissakes."

"I was."

"Get the fuck up off the floor."

Scott was clearly better at kicking then hitting. Slaught was glad he was wearing his stupid down parka—it provided some padding as Scott kicked his ribs. He was coughing now, couldn't help it, his ribs feeling like they were in a vise. Slaught pulled himself to his knees and almost crawled back up onto the chair.

He took a deep breath, trying to focus. "So why is Black so important now?"

"You're not asking the questions, here. I am. Where was she headed?"

"South."

"Everything is south of your shithole town. You better give me something."

"Got nothing. Nothing for you, nothing for Talos. I don't know what she did or where she went. I don't even like her. You forget she tried to kill me?"

Slaught was tired. Dragging himself back to the jail and curling up in a corner looked pretty good right about now. Caring about what Talos wanted or needed wasn't high on his priority list. Slaught said, "Now can I go? Someone going to take me back?"

Scott leaned forward, and Slaught was suddenly struck by the man's anger and desperation, right there at the surface. Bad combination. Scott said, "I need to find her."

Slaught shook his head and said, "Can't help you Scott, but a piece of advice? Think twice about that itch to find her. Nothing good ever came from getting tangled up with Mitch Black."

Chapter Twelve

Bakalov was pressed for time. He had to get back down to the Valley while there was still daylight, check the traps and then return for a meeting of the railway work crews. He liked the meetings, they made him feel important. Telling men when and where to work. Telling them their progress was not good enough. Telling them to work harder. But he knew if he wanted to keep his job, and become more indispensable to Mr. Love, he needed to use his currency. So he made a detour to go see Mr. Love.

"All of these impromptu meetings, Ion, it's really getting out of hand," Mr. Love had said when the security guard showed Bakalov into the office. Snow was falling outside the big window.

"I felt this was important enough," Bakalov said.

"Then out with it."

"There is a man called the Winterman. A criminal. I just brought him to Mr. Scott. He met with him in private."

"Private?"

"He asked me to step outside."

"Interesting. So Scott asked to see him?"

"No, Mr. Love, I heard the Winterman was in the population. I remembered that Mr. Scott had dealt with this man when he was head of Talos so I brought him to Mr. Scott."

"And Bob was interested in him?"

Bakalov said, "Mr. Scott seemed very interested."

"The Winterman? Refresh my memory, Ion, wasn't there some manhunt for him? Some sort of rebellion up in the Territories."

"I only know that Talos sent a team up there, to clear out the people in the Territories."

"So, this Winterman, has he been in jail since then?"

"No, Mr. Love, the mission failed. Only one of the team survived. A woman."

"Oh, wait a minute, is that the same Talos operative that went off the charts? And there was a manhunt for her, too? This the whole gold fiasco thing?"

Bakalov said, "Yes, she was sent up there twice. And failed twice."

"And this Winterman, what is he in the Facility for?"

"Treason."

Love was distracted by this. "Really? Treason? How can we have treason if there is no country? Sounds so archaic."

Bakalov shrugged. "He was caught at the outpost, trying to take Talos property."

"I see. Yes, Talos is the state, the nation. Interesting. Alright, and this Winterman, did Scott say why he was interested in him?"

"No. And he did not want me to stay."

"But did you ask him?"

"Yes. He would not answer me."

"Well, isn't that interesting."

Bakalov also thought it was interesting. Maybe something worth finding out more about. Mr. Scott wanting to hide things.

"Listen, Ion, why don't you bring this Winterman over to me in the morning. I could have a chat with him."

"I will bring him, Mr. Love."

"Excellent. I'm dying to meet him. I think he's my first outlaw."

ও

Shit. It was later than he thought.

He'd been wandering away from the food court, pretending he was going shopping, playing a game in his head. What was he shopping for tonight? Maybe for sneakers. Soap, maybe. Chrissakes, though, it was fucking hard to stare into what used to be the liquor store. He'd stood there for a good half hour, daydreaming, taking in the gaping, grimy space that at one time held rows and rows of booze, whiskey from Scotland, wine from France. Imagine that world, so big but still small enough to ship wines and rums and whiskey. And that weird shit that his dad drank, the bottles of peach schnapps he'd pack when he was heading out for the week to the hunt camp. He'd tell Johnny he should come along this time, he was old enough; they were going to turn the woods around their cabin into their own mini Vietnam, shooting at the trees more than the deer. Did he want to come? Off they went, Johnny maybe thirteen or so. Later he asked his dad what the Christ were grown men doing drinking shit that tasted like syrup? But they'd gotten a deer and hung it up in the shed and had all gone out with their flashlights to look at it, the creature hanging upside down, brown eyes still staring. Johnny was drunk, sick on the thick, sweet liquor, asked his dad if the deer was crying and all the men laughed.

He'd stood there too long thinking about it. Must almost be curfew, and soon the dogs would be out. He'd better get moving.

Running up the stairs, he felt winded, and pulled himself up with the railing. Thought about trying the sixth floor. Glanced down the length of it. Things were already getting dark, the dim emergency lights at the top of each stairwell showing enough light that he could see all the doors shut on sixth. He kept moving. Checked the eighth—all the doors closed. That was strange. On the ninth floor he peered down the hallway; the apartment at the end was the only open door. Then he heard the snarling coming up behind him. Those things could sure sniff a man out. What'd Big Donny call 'em? Demon dogs.

He ran, his lungs aching. Man, he was out of shape, sitting all day, his legs rubber as he sprinted down the hallway. He could sense the dogs clearing the stairs, the sound of claws scrambling up the cement stairs and then silence as they hit the carpet, already shredded by their nightly prowling.

He reached the door and hesitated before going in. Always had to be careful. It was quiet, but something was off. Behind him, though, the dogs were snarling, and the sound of panting made him want to jump into the room. He could make out the big shapes of the dogs, half shadow now in the dim light. He thought maybe there were three or four of them. He stepped into the dark, listening to the space, trying to shut out the low growling of the dogs. Didn't want to be surprised by someone waiting inside, hiding in the dark with his own demons.

The dogs were quiet now and hesitating, too, seeing him stop, watching him in the darkened hallway. Slaught stood in the doorway, ready to go in, but then the sound of boots pounding up the stairs came from the opposite end of the hall. A guy plunging around the corner from the stairwell into the hall. Young, maybe eighteen or so, scared of what was coming behind him and not paying attention to what was ahead.

The dogs turned, snarling now, maybe feeling trapped. The guy came up short. He was trapped now, too. Frozen.

Slow motion now, the dogs crowded together, growling, the beasts clocking onto the smell of fear that had materialized at the far end of the hall.

Slaught made up his mind, launching himself back down the hall towards the kid. He was thinking of football, of the run down the field, as he came up behind the dogs, plowing through them. He couldn't see them but he felt them, the solidness of their bodies against his legs, the sharp tearing at his shins. He kept going, calculating that his size and momentum would get him there. He just wasn't sure about getting back.

Slaught yelled then, "C'mon, let's go, the place at the end!" He reached the kid and clamped his hand tight onto his shoulder. The kid was staring into the dark, trying to make out the bodies of the dogs that seemed just one thick lump of snarling shadow. Slaught had to drag him towards the door, glad the kid wasn't too big. The dogs could see better in the dark than they could, and Slaught had to let go of the kid to throw one off of his arm. The dog yelped and slipped back.

Slaught was almost at the door when he sensed it—movement in the apartment. He thought maybe someone was in there. And then a face leaning out from behind the door, barely visible in the shadows, weasel thin and smirking; eyes connected with his, head shaking. The door closed.

"Fuck!" Slaught yelled. What the fuck to do now? He flattened his back against the wall, grabbed the kid and said, "We're going back down, then up." He began dragging the kid back down the hallway towards the stairs. The kid yelled, "But the other dogs..."

"Let's worry about these ones, ok? We're going to get to that stairwell. Then go up."

The kid kept stumbling along with Slaught, the dogs, too, keeping pace. Every now and again Slaught could feel them taking quick lunges and snaps. He and the kid were both yelling, at each other and at the dogs.

Slaught said, "Get ready. You go first. I'll hold them off, but you get the fuck up those stairs and watch for me coming."

The kid said, "How long do I wait? The other dogs..."

Slaught tightened his grip on the kid's shoulders. "Close that door on me these puppies will be the least of your problems, understand?" The kid nodded.

Slaught moved into the middle of the hallway, shoved the kid towards the stairs and yelled, "Go man, now!"

Slaught turned, facing the pack now. They were close; he could smell them, see their shapes, moving sideways, creepy in the dark. What did they say, try to make yourself big? Fuck. He wasn't feeling very fucking big right now. He lunged at the dog beside him, trapping it against the wall with his body and landing a few heavy blows to its head, the dog clawing and squirming.

Yelling, Slaught hit the dog again, then released it, stepping back, thinking he just needed to move about six more feet and he'd clear the hallway. But now what? A slight change, the dogs stopping, quiet suddenly, like they were listening. He listened, too, in the dark, and heard the scramble of claws from the stairwell. Was it the pack the kid was worried about, getting close? Coming from where—up or down? Probably from below. Would the packs fight each other? Worth a try.

He listened until the sound of the claws on cement was even closer, then he bolted, ran smack into the pack of scrambling fur and claws that was just hitting the top of the stairs. As he busted through them, the pack on his tail slammed into them as well. A snarling tangle of rage erupted behind him as he bolted up the stairs. They were coming, but they weren't fast enough, slowed down by their own colliding aggression. He saw the open doors along the hallway, then the kid at the first door. Slaught wondered if many other guys would have waited. He lunged into the apartment and the door slammed shut behind him.

༄

Slaught, wheezing, heard the dogs clawing at the door, snarling and snapping at each other. He tried to catch his breath, slow his breathing. The kid was crying through a string of curses. Fuck, fuck, fuck.

Slaught asked him his name, and the kid managed, "Raymond, Ray."

"Okay, Ray, we're good now."

Raymond, almost yelling, said, "Did you see that bastard? Did you see that fucking bastard, he closed the fucking door on us? Saw us coming, the fuck." Funny, for Slaught it was also the look on the guy's face in the doorway, not the snarling dogs, that was burning him up.

"You know him?"

"Seen him before, I think."

Guys in here tended to keep to small groups, or to their own company, like Slaught. Chances are he might never run into the guy again unless he went looking for him. A face to remember. Couldn't see much in that hallway, but the smirk on the lips, Slaught would remember that.

"I can't fucking believe it—could you believe it? We were so fucking close. Fuck him, how the fuck could he do that?"

Slaught said, "Ray, guys in here, they do shit like that. How long you been here?"

"Four months, maybe."

Slaught was surprised, "That long?"

"Yeah, lots of us have been here that long. You?"

"A month."

"I've heard we're never getting out of here."

Slaught didn't say anything, didn't like hearing shit like that. Ray said, "Still can't believe that guy saw us coming and did that."

"That's why you don't take chances. You get in early, go up high."

"You were late."

"Got lazy. Can't afford to be lazy in here."

"I'm never going to forget that fucking asshole's face. Never."

Slaught said, "You get some sleep," but wondered how the kid could have spent four months here and still be surprised by shit like that, still surprised that they were no different than the dogs. No, maybe that wasn't right. The dogs, they were just being their dog selves—hunters, guards. But the guy in the doorway? What was he being?

Chapter Thirteen

Slaught couldn't fucking believe this.

He'd gotten Ray up, shaking him, saying, "Time to go, Sunshine." Walked him down to the food court. Ray told him that Big Donny was his uncle. "See ya later, gotta go help out in the kitchen," he said. Then Slaught was just heading out of the food court when that sonofabitch Bakalov showed up with his Dogmen squad and said he was due for another field trip. Slaught said, "Sorry to disappoint you by surviving your little ambush last night." He figured Bakalov probably had some stooge in the place doing his bidding. But Bakalov just shoved Slaught towards the exit, saying, "Move it."

And now he was in front of some clown called Mr. Love, the guy wearing, what? Leisure wear? Looked like he was getting ready to go for a jog. Love said to him, "So I am trying to remember, Winterman, what exactly is your story? Help me out here?"

And his place. Christ almighty, Slaught didn't think places like this still existed. Clean couches, a little glass stand in the corner with bottles of booze. A fucking ice bucket. The whole fucking planet was an ice bucket, and here was this guy playing James Bond. What the fuck?

"You like scotch, Winterman?" Love had seen him eyeing the liquor.

"Guessing you do."

Love, suddenly breezy, said, "I don't mind it now and again, a nice peaty one. Hard to find, though. Brandy is really my go-to drink. Bakalov here probably likes vodka. Would you like to join us in a drink?" Love asked, opening the decanter, pouring a bit of the brandy into a glass. Slaught caught the sweet sticky smell from across the room. Christ, it smelled great.

Love poured some clear liquid into a glass, passed it to Bakalov, who looked a little uncertain, Slaught figuring this wasn't business as usual. Love asked, "And your preference?"

"Nothing for now, thanks. Not enjoying the company."

Love crossed the room and flopped down on the couch, then leaned forward, glass in hand, animated. "I heard you had a rough night? You look dreadful." Love leaned back, frowning, "The Facility not working out for you?"

"Guess good news travels fast in that place."

"It's Bakalov's job to know what's happening inside," Love said, then stood abruptly, "and what's happening now is that you are a marked man. It is only a matter of time, I would imagine, before your luck runs out. And I'm the man who can help you."

"That right? Maybe I don't want your help."

"We could spar all morning, Winterman, but my time is exceptionally valuable so I would prefer to get to the point."

Slaught shrugged, "It's your party."

"Yes, it is, isn't it? So this is what I want. I want you to help me."

"I thought you were going to help me."

"Yes, that's right. Consider it a quid pro quo."

"Right. Well, don't worry about me. And I told the other guy, Scott, I don't know where the gold is."

Love's expression changed. Just a faint flicker of, what? Hard to say, but something. Love said, "You're not here because of any gold." He gestured to the large map mounted on the wall,

"You're here because you know the Territory and I need a local guide. Simple as that."

Slaught said, "Are you kidding me? Why would I want to be your fucking guide?"

"Your whole tough guy thing is mildly entertaining but I'm needing something else from you right now," Love said. "We are mounting an expedition into the Territory. You know the terrain, the settlements, the people. You could be helpful to have along. Smooth things over with the locals. Get the idea?"

"You're going up north?"

"Yes, I just explained that to you. Trouble processing?"

"What for?"

"What for? To bring progress. That should be obvious, even to someone like you."

This Love guy with his weekend muscles and smug attitude was making Slaught's head hurt. Things were bad enough down in the City, and Talos was going to haul its fucked-up brand of civilization north? Jesus fucking Christ.

"Maybe your idea of progress and mine are different."

"I have no doubt about that, Winterman. My vision of the future is, well, it is simply dazzling. Bold. Rare. Beyond the likes of you. That is why you're in the Facility and I am launching the most ambitious and compelling rupture in the history of humankind. But it's your lucky day. Your measly skills, interestingly enough, may land you a place in my epic venture. So you can either come along as my guide or I can throw you back in there to get eaten alive by the pack. Human or otherwise."

Being confronted with a choice was jarring. He hadn't had to make a decision in months, which suddenly struck him as weird. Wasn't like him to just go along with things. To not make up his mind, to not act. What the fuck was he still doing in the Facility, anyway? Wasn't like him to just be sitting around, waiting for something to happen. Maybe that was his problem. He thought the future was written so he'd been waiting for it to happen. Waiting to be let out. Waiting for spring to come. And maybe that was the reason he was still stuck in this grim fucking place. Maybe the future wasn't the problem. Maybe it wasn't what he'd do once the spring returned. Maybe it was what he was doing right here and now. In the winter.

"Take me back."

Love shook his head. "Disappointed. That is how I feel. But it's your decision. You can go back to the Facility for now, maybe spend some time thinking about any loved ones, friends, family you might have up there in the Territory. Yes, think about them."

"What does that mean?"

"So you do have loved ones up there? That's so touching, I just assumed you were one of those lone wolf types."

Slaught didn't answer, watching the man now, trying to understand. Some bad combination of boyishness and lethality.

"I understand that your commune, or whatever it is up there, had a rather negative experience with Talos. But I am bringing a new era to the Territories. A rebirth. You either get on board or get out of the way. I'm unstoppable. So I don't need to explain to you what is going to happen to all those individuals who try and resist."

"Resist what exactly?"

Loves smiled. "Me."

༊

"He's gone through the ice, Dad's with him but we can't get him out." Shaun yelled, as he barreled into the work bay where Chumboy and Melinda were splitting wood. "It's Old Man McLaren."

Chumboy, already moving towards the door, asked, "How far?"

"Not far, just at the edge of the lake."

Melinda was running for blankets, Chumboy yelling after her, "Let them know inside to get ready for him." He turned to Shaun and said, "Grab the ladder," then ran to get the toboggan and headed for the main path, Shaun catching up and dropping a rope and the ladder onto the toboggan. The snow was sticky and sinking under their weight, slowing them down.

They hit the edge of the lake and could see Larose kneeling, trying to slide a branch across the snow and ice towards McLaren. The old man's head and one arm were visible but the rest seemed to be under the water.

Larose looked up, worried, yelled, "Think I'm losing him."

Chumboy gauged the distance from the shore to McLaren. Their ladder might just make it. As soon as they were close enough he slid the ladder off the toboggan. "How long has he been in there?" he asked.

"I'm not dead, goddammit," McLaren said. "I can hear you. Ask me the questions."

"Can you get your other arm up on the ice?"

The water moved, steely under the grey sky, and McLaren slowly, with what seemed a good deal of effort, pulled his arm up to the surface. Chumboy figuring the arm was numb, heavy and wet, hard to maneuver. "Try just flinging it up there if you can," he suggested.

"Not a goddam Frisbee," McLaren said. "Can't feel a damn thing." But he finally dragged it up out of the water and onto the ice in front of him.

"Alright, great. We're going to slide this ladder out. Think it might come pretty close so let's see how this goes. Want you to get your legs out behind you, alright, flat as you can, stretch right out."

"These boots," the man said, "heavy. Might as well be wearing cement shoes."

"Can you get them off?"

McLaren said no, couldn't move them, couldn't feel them.

Melinda was looking worried as she joined them at the lake's edge. She said, "Slow down that breathing of yours. Try and relax as much as possible, it will make this a lot easier."

McLaren nodded his head. Getting tired. Chumboy said, "Here it comes," sliding the ladder out, the slow scratch of the metal across the ice, snagging here and there. Everyone watched as it came about two feet shy of McLaren's reach, his fingers outstretched and grasping, as if sheer will could keep it coming.

Chumboy scrambled back up, grabbing the toboggan and saying to Larose, "Okay, we're going to tie off the toboggan and I'll go out on it. You push me out but keep a hold onto the rope. Then I push the ladder out farther, and you pull us all back in."

"Don't think you're too heavy?"

Chumboy patted his stomach, "Nope, been cutting out those carbs lately. Now let's go before I chicken out and leave this crazy old man to freeze to death."

"I heard that," muttered McLaren.

"You were meant to."

Chumboy lowered himself onto the toboggan. Larose pushed and Chumboy used his arms to propel himself forward, shoving the ladder ahead of him, and then it was within McLaren's reach. "Goddammit, my hands, they're frozen," said McLaren.

Chumboy pushed it closer. "Try hooking your elbows over it."

It was awkward at first, the ladder jutting out over the water beside McLaren, but he was able to get one arm hooked inside the last rung. "Pull the goddam thing," he called, and Larose started pulling back slowly, both Shaun and Melinda helping, too. Then as the toboggan reached the edge of the lake and bumped over the lip of the shoreline, Chumboy said, "Slow and steady."

The ice gave way not too far from shore, but they had enough momentum to keep the ladder coming with McLaren holding on, Chumboy saying as the old man reached shore, "That's some ugly fish we got here." Then Melinda was there with Shaun, pulling off the man's gloves and coat, throwing on dry mitts and a hat, covering him with a blanket, saying, "Let's get a move on, don't want him losing any digits."

They hustled him around the lake, taking turns pulling the toboggan to keep the pace brisk and soon enough they were back inside. McLaren said, "That would've been a helluva way to go."

They got him bundled up in blankets. Seeing the expression on Chumboy's face, the old man said, "Stop looking at me like that."

"Well, gotta say, an old timer like you? Thought you'd know better than to head out there on your own."

McLaren shook his head, said, "Don't I know it. It was damn stupid of me. Got so used to the hard cold, stopped being careful out there on the water. Just went across that inlet there like I do every day and next thing I knew I was up over my arse in water. Wish things would quit changing up all the time, a feller can get damn confused."

Chapter Fourteen

Bakalov had taken a few more rounds out of Slaught before he dumped him back inside the doors, so Slaught wasn't surprised when he woke up to hear a few guys saying, "Leave this guy here and the dogs won't even bother climbing those stairs tonight."

When Slaught tried to roll over and push himself up, they backed up a bit, one of them saying, "Whoa, wasn't sure you were even alive."

Slaught managed, "Me neither."

The three guys were already walking away, one of them saying, "Man better get himself cleaned up, he's walking bait." Slaught thought that was good advice, but where? He sat up, did a quick check and figured he was just banged up, but nothing seemed broken.

He slowly heaved himself upwards, felt like gravity was giving him the gears, putting some extra force into keeping him on the ground. It wasn't easy getting on his feet. He could hear men slowly heading towards the food court, the mumble of their voices and shuffling of the feet. Zombie time. Pavlov's zombies. Fuck he hated supper.

He limped past the food court, felt a few pairs of eyes sliding towards him. He scanned the crowd, trying to find the face of the bastard who had locked him and Ray out last night. What would he do if he spotted him, anyway? So he kept moving, wondering if it might be best to skip dinner, hunker down early. Didn't think he could take another run in with the dogs. But these guys were smelling blood, too. Probably suspicious, wondering what kind of guy leaves the Facility but ends up back there. Two days in a row. Heading into a dark room with some unknown pack of them was probably something to worry about. Love was right, he was taking a big chance.

He saw Big Donny appear behind the grate, moving back and forth, getting the line set up, and then disappearing into the kitchen. He could already smell the food, and again that mixture of nausea and hunger washed over him. Fuck, if he ever got out of there, he was going to go and worship at Tiny's feet. It might have been touch and go some nights, but at least most of the time you could tell what you were eating. Big Donny's favourite kitchen appliance must be an industrial-scale blender. Mash it all up and you don't have to worry about what you're serving.

It seemed to be taking Big Donny longer than usual to reappear with the cauldron of gruel. Some of the men were starting to grumble. Slaught noticed that Ray and a few of his pals were hanging around at the edge of the food court. Didn't usually see Ray on this side of the grate; he was usually in there helping Big Donny slop out the gruel. Slaught wondered if something was up.

Sounds of shouting from the kitchen, the guys looking around to see what was going on. Then there was Big Donny, yelling, bursting through the metal doors and coming right out into the food court, tearing off his apron as he came, yelling, "Listen up you motherfuckers!"

And they did.

Big Donny kept going, "I've had it. I feed you every day, and every day it's the same shit and you don't want to even know what it is. I think I've served you bastards just about everything there is to serve. But there's no fucking way, no fucking way on this planet, that I'm serving you dog meat. No fucking way." He paused, then added, "I fucking loved my dog."

And with that Big Donny stalked back into the kitchen, walked around to the counter and slammed the grille shut.

Then all hell broke loose.

It started with yelling, then a surge of men towards the kitchen as the yelling grew even louder, Slaught getting caught up in the push of bodies, feeling a couple of hands on either side of him. Couldn't tell if he was being dragged or pushed but he was moving, the crowd and the chaos not giving him much choice. The momentum was taking him towards the kitchen where the swarm of guys started to pound on the metal grille, swearing, hollering for Big Donny.

Slaught was trying to get a handle on what was happening but the crush of bodies had landed him right at the front. Then there were strong hands on him, Ray holding onto his arm, that was strange, and then he was being pushed through a door he never noticed before, maybe six guys coming through with him. He was hauled down a short hall and then Christ almighty he was pushed into the kitchen. Big Donny was there and some guys he'd seen with Ray sometimes.

Big Donny grabbed him and shoved him back towards the kitchen door, saying, "Get a move on, Winterman, you got someone waiting for you."

Slaught, trying to get his bearings, process what was happening, asked, "Fucking Bakalov?"

Big Donny grinned, even as the wall was shaking under the barrage of rage and hunger on the other side of it. "No, looks like you got yourself a get out of jail card. Nick of time, too, there's a price on your head. So get moving before I change my mind. Take the hall until your first right."

"What'll I find there?"

Ray said, "We're just the messenger, man, just the messenger."

Slaught hesitated, and asked, "Why aren't you coming?"

Big Donny answered, "Didn't say we weren't, we'll be coming, but get the fuck outta here before Bakalov arrives. Deal was we buy you some time." He turned to Raymond, "Let's get this party started."

Slaught could hear the noise level escalate behind him, could hear Big Donny yelling from inside the kitchen. He moved carefully down the hallway, wishing the bastards clamouring for puppy chow weren't so loud, making it hard to hear. He couldn't tell where the narrow hallway led, saw washroom signs up ahead, should he slip in there, wait and see? Maybe it was Bakalov. Slaught reached up, felt the crusted-over blood along his temple. He wondered if he had boot marks up there, too.

He stopped in the hallway. Behind him the sound of mayhem, men's shouts, the screech of metal on metal, Slaught wondering if they were tearing the place apart. He hoped Big Donny and Raymond were okay, and felt funny about leaving. Why leave alone? Couldn't they all get out at the same time?

He just felt like sitting down. Sitting down and maybe curling up on the cement floor and going to sleep. Giving up? But he told himself to get his shit together. Keep moving.

He was getting close to where the hallway branched off, and he had no way of knowing which way to go. He'd almost reached the end, and then there was Levi, stepping out from the shadows of another hallway up ahead, saying, "Unless you are planning on staying, maybe you could hurry it up."

Earlier that morning, they'd headed across the City to the Facility. It had still been dark, and the group kept to the shadows until they found themselves close to the City core. Then Levi had taken them down into a disorienting series of underground pedestrian walkways and subway tunnels, each one more desolate and decrepit than the last. They finally stopped on what seemed to be an old subway platform, and Levi told them to wait there, keep a watch and stay quiet. He was going to sneak into the prison, to see if Slaught was still there. And to get some help getting him out.

At the last minute Mitch said she didn't want Levi going off on his own. Levi dug in, said it was the only way, the place was full of men. He wouldn't be noticed. She would. It was settled when Levi said, "If you don't trust me, you should just say so."

And that was that, except it didn't stop any of them from worrying, huddled at the far end of the subway platform. He slipped in and was back in just over two hours. He said that when he went back in for Slaught it wouldn't take as long; he'd been slowed down trying to find some of the boys he used to run with in the tunnels—unless all the boys were dead, they'd help. Susun wanted to know what made him think they would be in the Facility, and he gave her a look and asked, "Where else would they end up?"

Turns out there were a few of them there, and they helped him find Big Donny, who had confirmed that Slaught was still alive. Susun asked, "Are they friends?" and Levi said he didn't think you had friends in there, just people willing to leave you alone.

Levi said he was surprised that none of the boys he'd lived with in the tunnels had remembered the disused subway tunnel. They'd gotten pretty excited, realizing they could just walk right out of the prison, but Levi had asked them to wait at least fifteen minutes after he left with the Winterman before they used it themselves.

Mitch wanted to know how long it was going to take Levi to get out with Slaught, how long should they wait. Levi said they couldn't wait any longer than an hour. The truck would be leaving then, and it was their only chance to get out of the downtown core. Mitch said there was no way she was leaving him behind, and Levi answered, "If it takes me more than an hour, I'm already dead." As Jeff watched Levi leave, he'd said, "Man, that's one downer of a dude," and Mitch told him to shut the fuck up.

So they'd waited, quiet, in the dark tunnel, listening to the dripping of water and the scuffling sound of rats. With a half hour still to go they heard something from farther up the tunnel. The hollow, echoing sound of boots coming down the stairwell, then the door opening. Mitch pushed Susun behind her into the darkness, whispering to Jeff, "Get back, just in case." They all held their breath as the footsteps approached. Mitch poked her head around the corner and said, "Well, well, Papa Bear's back," and Slaught said, "Christ, I was just talking about you."

ॐ

Slaught, almost giddy, leaned in and whispered to Susun, "It was like being in another world, going through those secret tunnels. The kid knows his way around that shit-pit."

Then they were on their way, riding in the back of a Talos work truck, crammed in with about two dozen temporary workers, everyone hunched down and keeping their eyes to themselves. Only Slaught seemed relaxed, asking, "So where is this taking us again? I can't believe I'm sitting here next to you."

Susun said, "We can talk later, okay?"

Slaught could feel the tension. In fact, all of them were pretty quiet, none of them making eye contact with him. Guess they didn't want to say anything that might draw attention.

Fair enough.

Except. Except he felt like singing, shouting, standing up and twirling Susun around in the air. Things he had never really felt before. How to describe the feeling? Relieved? Oh yeah, fuck, unbelievably relieved. Relieved to not be curling up in some grotty corner of some trashed apartment. Relieved not to be running for the rooms, relieved not to be eating the slop. Relieved, yeah, but more than that. Happy? Nah, not enough. Exuberant? Maybe, wasn't quite sure, he'd have to ask Chumboy later, ask him for the word that could describe it so he could tell people later, tell them the story of his time in the big house.

They'd gone through a series of tunnels and finally ended up outside, the sidewalks packed with workers hoping to get on the trucks to take them up to the green zone for the midnight shift, waiting for work. No one was really talking to him, just telling him to keep moving. As if he needed reminding. Emerging into the daylight, feeling outside air on his skin, he was both disoriented and almost weak with relief, but also felt a steady lifting of weight from his shoulders. He took his place in the line-up, eyes on Susun, following her lead, unable to believe how solid she was. So beautiful. And seemed pretty calm.

But the math was worrying him. He could see the three trucks lined up along the curb up ahead. Between him and the trucks, there must've been a hundred folks.

Slaught had the impression he shouldn't talk, should make himself invisible, so keeping his voice quiet, he said, "Uh guys, we're not gonna make it." But Susun said, "Don't worry, okay? Just keep moving."

Slaught noticed that some folks were being waved away, told to get out of the line. There was some pushing and shoving up ahead and a few Talos security were walking the line, pulling out troublemakers. Folks were crowding up behind them, too, the crush of it all pushing Jeff out of the line a bit. Mitch grabbed hold of his coat and dragged him back into the line-up, Jeff letting her, looking scared and not saying anything as she shoved him into Slaught's back, saying, "Stay the fuck put, okay?" The closest Talos guard yelled, "Everyone settle down or you're out, got it?"

Slaught figured they didn't stand a chance of making it onto one of the trucks unless there were more coming. For all he knew they ran all night. If they didn't make it, he wondered what the plan was, then, trusting that they had a plan. But then the guard started walking up the line asking every dozen or so people for their red cards, show me your cards, red cards? Anyone got a red card? And Susun leaning out to the man, showing him five red cards and saying, "This group. Five of us." He gave them a quick look over and pointed, "That truck there, get moving."

Susun just nodded, Slaught thinking it was interesting, seeing her taking charge like that. Those steely nerves of hers.

She led the way, pushing past the crowd and heading over to the truck. A thin fellow, tattoos along the side of his face, held out his hand to help her up. And then they were all in, crowded into the back of the big covered truck, like a repurposed army truck, the trademark Talos happy face with petals around it marking it as a greenhouse vehicle. The lean guy then said, "You folks, slide down along that bench, make room for a few more, and then said to Susun, "Tell Chum that Moose says hi," and Susun nodded. Slaught tried to catch her eye, did she know this guy? Susun saw him and said quietly, "Everything's all set for us, okay?" Slaught noticed she wasn't smiling, and realized she hadn't smiled yet, not even when she'd first seen him. She'd only said, "Let's get moving, we're on a tight timeline."

    Slaught wanted to put his arm around her, kiss her, but knew it would be the wrong thing to do. He settled for sliding in next to her and sort of leaning into her but looking straight ahead, like everyone else. Then the truck started rumbling, and he looked at the faces along the benches, a few people actually sitting on the floor that was covered in mud and snow and wet, and Slaught said, "Chrissakes, folks, I know it's the end of the world, but could just one of youse smile?"

Chapter Fifteen

Jimmy Mumford knew he'd made an impression. About fucking time someone took notice of him. Bakalov said after it was all over that Jimmy was going to be his right-hand man.

Bakalov had sent Jimmy back inside the Facility to keep an eye on things for him. Told him, yes, he'd be a hunter and soldier, but for now he needed him to keep being a prisoner. Said to keep an eye on the guy called the Winterman. Important people were interested in him. Jimmy thought it sucked big time, still being inside. Thought maybe Bakalov was full of shit. But what could he do about it?

Then he was caught off guard by the riot. Big Donny shouting something he didn't really catch except it had something to do with dogs. And then guys were fucking losing their shit. When they couldn't budge the metal grille they started hurling chairs, trying to pull tables up off the floor, grabbing anything, sometimes each other, to throw at the metal barrier between them and food. It was fucking mental, Jimmy thinking he had to get the fuck out of there and then, out of the corner of his eye, he saw three guys slip through a door he'd never seen open before.

It swung closed before he could get a glimpse through it. He started to move towards the door, still a ways to go when a larger group surged towards the same door, just pulled it open and poured though, leaving the door open.

And Jimmy ran for it.

In the mayhem and the yelling and rancor filling the food court not everyone noticed this new exit. Jimmy reached the door and no one else seemed to be paying any attention so he went through and closed it, slipping the lock back into place behind him. Then he moved slowly, trying to get a sense of where the prisoners had been heading. He could hear noise down the hallway so he followed that, seeing a door open at the end but then voices behind him, flattening himself to the wall and hearing Big Donny saying, "Get your stuff together, Raymond, we should get moving, there'll be plenty others coming soon enough."

Time to move, before Big Donny saw him. Jimmy ran down the hallway, then another long hallway and onto a subway platform, hearing voices ahead of him. Following the sound, heart pounding, questioning himself each step, keep going? It could be his one chance. He came to a set of big metal doors. Slowly pushed them open and peered out. Fuck. It was the outside.

He could just fucking leave, get absorbed into the City. Never go back. But then what, living rough and going hungry, back on the streets? Or go back inside where it wasn't much different. Or spend his days with Bakalov dragging himself through the snow to shoot mangy dogs, cats curled up in the underbrush. That sucked, too. Then he had another idea. A gamble, maybe. But why the fuck not?

He slipped out through the door. Saw it would be easy to shut behind him, just slide the big bolt across the top. Should hold anyone coming out behind him for a bit, anyway. He pushed it closed and slipped the bolt over. He headed down the sidewalk, caught a glimpse of a few guys from inside hightailing it down an alleyway. The stench of sewage was hanging in the air, it was fucking cold and the streets were slushy. He didn't even have on a proper coat. He hoped this was going to fucking work for him. He circled around the building, keeping to the wall, eyes down on the pavement like everyone else he saw. He slowed down as he approached the security gate at the front of the Facility.

Two Dogmen were sleeping in chairs inside the lobby area. Jimmy banged on the glass until one of them woke up, grumpy, slouching over towards the door scowling, and Jimmy yelled, "You'd better call Bakalov. You got big problems."

"Who the fuck are you?"

"Just call him."

"I'm not fucking calling him, now beat it or you're going to end up inside this shithole." Jimmy felt very smart when he got to say, "That's what I'm talking about, asshole, that's your problem. I was inside that shithole all of five minutes ago."

They had to wait a bit until one of the guards tracked down Bakalov and he arrived on foot, two of his dogs pulling their leashes taut. Bakalov said to Jimmy, "Show me," then nodded his head to the other two Dogmen and said, "Let's go."

So Jimmy retraced his steps, the dogs agitated and making him nervous. He told Bakalov that about a dozen guys had gotten out before he'd put the place into lockdown. They reached the door and they could hear the men on the other side, banging against it, wondering why the fuck the door was shut, and Bakalov brought up his AK-47 and just started firing into the door and the shouting stopped.

Then Bakalov slid the bolt and they could hear running and yelling and Bakalov sent the Dogmen ahead, told Jimmy they'd stay back for a few minutes in case of ricochets, then they headed down the series of hallways, stepping around the bodies of a few guys who'd been caught in the tunnel. One Dogman was waiting outside the door to the kitchen, and asked, "What about these guys?" and Bakalov looked into the kitchen. Big Donny and Raymond were standing there, just looking back, saying nothing, and Bakalov asked Jimmy, "These men?"

Jimmy said no, they had stayed in the kitchen, seemed like they were trying to get things under control and so Bakalov kept moving and Jimmy hung back, made eye contact with Big Donny and mouthed, "You owe me now," and Big Donny said, "Yep, you betcha."

༚

"Uniforms?"

"Yes, Bob, uniforms. I want you to find uniforms. You are in charge of requisitions, aren't you?"

"Ok, Eton..."

Love held up his hand. "Wait, Bob, hold on a second. First, we've been over this and I was very clear that we are not on a first name basis. But I've given this some further thought. And I don't think Mister is working for me anymore. It's just not my vibe, know what I mean? So I'm thinking Commander. I went through a lot of possibilities—you know, the usual: President, Prime Minister, really don't like that one, even toyed with Chancellor for a while, Emperor..."

"Emperor?"

Love shrugged, "Too Roman, yeah, I know. But I like how it ties into our civic endeavours, right? But the problem, Bob— God I love saying your name, it's just so basic—anyway, the problem was Emperor *Who*, right? I mean 'Emperor Eton' or 'Emperor Love,' neither of them works. Not really. 'Commander Love,' not bad right?"

Scott wondered if Love realized how crazy he sounded. At first, Love's energy, his drive, it worked. Love had come out of nowhere when Scott and his entire administration had been demoted, the Talos Board taking to Love because he had this can-do energy, and ideas about the future. He was going to solve all the problems. He stayed up all night working. They liked that, the manic energy. But now, well, maybe that manic energy was getting out of hand. He wondered if the board was noticing?

Maybe it was time to go have a word with a few of those board members.

"What kind of uniforms?"

"Do I have to do all your thinking for you? I mean I'm trying to draw the big picture for you, right? Could you handle a few details for me? Could you do that? I mean, come on, you worked with the military, you should know what's out there in terms of resources. After all, they were disbanded by you, right?"

"Okay, so we're reinstating the military. Thanks for the heads up."

"Oh, are you feeling left out? Well, whose fault is that? You know, again, Ion was fast off the mark, he created his own special unit, got them uniforms, even some basic training. Ahead of the game. You could be learning, but you would rather live in the past."

Bakalov has his own unit? "What kind of a unit?"

"An elite unit for security and hunting for the expedition. I'll have my own security for my cartographers. For my map."

Scott glanced over at the large map now mounted behind Love's desk. "You think someone is going to go after your map?"

"You ask that only because you don't appreciate the gravity of what I'm creating. The map is the heart of everything. The foundation. And I want more security. Ion cannot do everything. He can watch my surveying teams while they are in the field, but we need some regular types, to keep the workers working and all of that. I mean it's bad enough our workers look like street people. And make a note that we'll have to keep them out of sight till we clear the City. We don't want our visuals ruined."

Scott saw no point in arguing. "Okay."

"And it would be nice if these uniforms could match the train. It's going to be black. I have a designer coming in, but we don't have time right now, I need the first batch ready to go yesterday."

"What's the rush?"

"I'm talking about the Domain, Bob. My Domain. It's almost ready to go and we need to be putting our backs into it. Do I have to do everything? Isn't it enough that I'm both big picture guy and methodical detail guy? All I want from you is some fucking uniforms."

"Right, sorry."

Love crossed his arms, staring at Scott. "I am not sensing that you mean it. In fact, you have been under-performing on every responsibility you have. You've brought in next to nothing in terms of financing. I mean it's a good thing I wasn't relying on you to deliver. And I just don't know if you are showing me the right motivation. And, somehow, you forgot to mention that valuable asset you came across. Keeping that to yourself?"

"What asset?"

"The Winterman."

Fucking Bakalov. He was becoming less and less useful to Scott. But clearly more and more useful to Love. Scott said, "Not sure why you'd be interested in him."

"Well, you were interested."

"Because of exactly what you were talking about. Money. This is about that gold shipment that went missing. This Winterman might have been one of the last people to see it. When I heard that he was in the population at the Facility, it would have been remiss of me not to question him."

"I see. Well, I found him somewhat underwhelming but I think he could be useful."

"How's that?"

"As a sort of local liaison. A guide, if you will."

"You might want to rethink your assessment. This Winterman could be a liability to your entire vision."

"Intriguing. What are you thinking?"

"Talos has a history with this guy. We nearly had a full-blown insurrection because of him. Then he somehow, maybe, got tangled up in this missing gold, plus stealing gas, guns, and food supplies on a regular basis. What that means is this guy could stir things up, even from inside. He knows his way around the Territory, has connections, knows the locations of dissident populations."

"When you put it that way, he suddenly seems much more useful than you."

"What are you talking about?"

"I'm talking about who gets on the train and who doesn't, Bob."

ᛯ

Jeff said, "Fucking déjà vu. And I mean that in the worst possible way."

They'd spent the last hour bushwhacking into the camp that belonged to the Uncle of a guy called Ricky. Ricky's Uncle Delbert had been burnt out and murdered by Talos some two years back, Ricky showing up in Cobalt sometime after that. He'd decided to stay, become part of the community. It'd been Jeff's idea to stop there on the way back up. They'd want to get clear of the City, get past the Greenhouse zone, but they couldn't make it all the way up north before dark. Jeff had said that Uncle Delbert had quite a stash of guns, that when he'd been there with Ricky there'd been a working wood stove, plenty of firewood, and a trail in. Not much of one, but a trail. And it wasn't too far from their drop off point.

They'd taken the truck almost to the Greenhouse zone and then the lean guy with the tattoos had pounded on the window and the driver had pulled over, the five of them getting up and jumping off the truck and into the snow and darkness.

Slaught was surprised, felt like they were in the middle of nowhere. Susun told him to wait while Jeff and Levi went with her to get the snow machines, that they should be hidden somewhere close to the drop off point. Mitch saying to Slaught, "Missy's gotten bossy while Papa Bear's been away." Slaught said nothing, but wondered why the fuck she kept calling him that.

They'd returned after fifteen long minutes, riding three snow machines and dragging sleds with supplies. Another hour riding in the dark and they hit the cabin, Jeff saying he hoped it wasn't as spooky as the first time he'd come there, when there were animal parts and car parts all jumbled up together in some sort of hillbilly nightmare. But it was just as bad as he remembered.

As he got off the snow machine, the headlights catching a length of a deer leg resting on top of a car hood, he said, "See, I told you guys. And you thought I was exaggerating."

They worked for a bit, clearing snow out from the doorway, getting the stove started. Levi heated up some stew and made some tea. Susun would look over at Slaught every now and again and smile, but she was distant, all about getting down to business. Slaught figured it was the adrenaline, maybe the stress; hard to disengage when you were in the middle of a shitstorm.

He could wait. It was tough because the cabin was small and he felt conspicuous. Everyone was getting to work and he was just trying to stay out of the way. He offered to go get some more firewood, but then Jeff said, "Okay, look, I wasn't going to say anything, dude, but you are rank. I need you to go do something about that." He rummaged through the closet, pulling out a plaid shirt and work pants, and said, "Here, try these, Dead Delbert was about the same size as you, put these on. And seriously, just get out of those rags, burn them or something. I mean, you know you're covered in blood, right? Could you go roll around in the snow or do whatever people used to do in the old days to get clean? And what happened to you in that jail?"

Slaught said he could try and answer those questions when he came in, but Jeff was right, he needed to clean up. Jeff said they could melt some snow, get some hot water happening if he wanted, but Slaught said snow would do just fine. Jeff said the exfoliation might do him some good anyway, take away some of the grime and blood, make him a brand new man. They could deal with the beard when they got home.

"Whatever you say, Jeff, I'm just happy to be able to go outside."

Jeff came up with a wool jacket and a down vest and Slaught said that was fine, it wasn't that cold out anyway.

He stepped out into the night, breathed deep and looked up, but the skies were cloudy and a light snow was falling. He couldn't see Orion but knew he was up there. He could smell the birch smoke as the wood stove got going. Christ almighty, it was amazing.

He knelt down, taking the soft snow into his hands and rubbing them together, thinking it was pretty warm out. He rubbed more snow over his face, through his beard. Weird, he'd never had a beard before. How long had he actually been in there?

He started to get cold as he changed, hurrying, taking a minute, though, to scrub his feet with the snow and then sorry he'd done it because then he was really cold, hustling to get the wool socks on and pull on his boots, changing into the classic work shirt and pants combo that Delbert must've put on every morning. Slaught could just imagine him, shirt buttoned up, going out to load in the wood before things went to shit and Talos decided they wanted him off the farm he'd had for sixty plus years.

He pulled on the jacket and vest, warmer now but his feet were stinging a bit. Stood for a few minutes taking in the cool air and dark grey sky and was ready to head in when the door opened behind him, the soft, yellow light across the blue snow, then disappearing as the door closed again.

Susun said, "Hey, you."

"Hey, yourself."

She was beside him, arms crossed and looking up into the night sky.

He said, "Thanks for coming to get me."

"Were you surprised?"

"Surprised to see Levi. And Black. Never thought I'd see the pair of them again." He felt like they were talking around things that mattered.

"Chumboy had to stay back, with the community. Otherwise he would have been here. He misses you. Badly."

Slaught turned to her, put his hands on her shoulders and said, "Yeah, I miss him, too. But I know it's always going to be you who's saving my ass."

She smiled. Not much of one, but a smile. He said, "It must have been something. How'd you and Jeff end up with those two?"

"We went and got them. Wasn't sure we could pull it off without someone like her. Turned out Levi was a big help, too, though."

He nodded. "Christ almighty, you really went to the wall for this. Hope you don't regret it."

"Don't make me," she said, sounding playful, but there was something there, underneath it.

So he asked, "What's on your mind, Latour?"

She waited for a few seconds, staring off past his shoulder. "Motherhood."

Slaught was still holding onto her shoulders. He felt maybe he should be holding on tighter, nervous now, excited maybe, trying not to get ahead of himself. He asked, "And why's that?"

But she just looked at him, her dark eyes drawing a line in the sand. He said, "Hope that means what I think it does. That why Black is calling me Papa Bear?"

Her look softened. "Yup. You've got about four months to get your shit together."

Slaught looked down at her belly but she didn't seem very big. Four months. That was soon. He said, "Could call him Orion."

Susun was shaking her head but smiling, too, now. Said maybe Pleiades would be more appropriate, and Slaught said, "A girl?"

"Think so."

He was thoughtful, not saying anything, and she said, "Not liking Pleiades?"

He shrugged. "It's okay, hard to pronounce though. What about Molly?"

"Christ, Winterman, you have no imagination at all."

"Latour, you have no idea what I'm imagining right now. I couldn't even put it into words."

Maybe he'd given up when he was inside, he thought, but he wouldn't be doing that again. Ever.

Chapter Sixteen

"She was spotted and no one did anything?" Scott yelled.

Bakalov shrugged. "Communication is slow. By the time we got reports the woman was no longer around. And I'm not City Security, do not have resources to look for her."

"It didn't occur to you that her presence in the City and the Winterman's escape from the Facility might be fucking related?"

"I have other things on my mind. More important things."

"More important? I'll tell you what's important…"

The man was red in the face, Bakalov wondering what would happen if he provoked Scott further, would he bring on a heart attack? "I don't think you will, Mr. Scott. The Expedition is leaving soon. You don't even seem ready. Mitch Black is not important. She is simply a mercenary. There are dozens of them in the City. Dozens. I don't think you know what is important."

"Listen Bakalov…" Scott began, and then stopped. "Wait, do you know her?"

"I have done business in the past with her, yes. In the early days."

"And you never thought to say anything. Does Love know?"

Bakalov shrugged, "It is my job to relay important information to Commander Love. This? It is not important."

"The gold, you fucking moron. She can take us to the gold. Let me spell this out for you, because clearly you can't think worth shit. She has gold. Lots of it. Your boss needs gold. Desperately. Therefore, he needs Black. He can't afford his absurd northern expedition without money. Lots of money. And where is that going to come from?"

"The Commander has money. Think about it. He has luxury there, all around him. He has money from somewhere. His train. It is a beautiful machine. Expensive. He has rich friends, maybe, I don't know."

"All his rich buddies are tapped out. You can only go back to the trough so many times and even his most loyal backers will get pissed off. The medical services, the power into our priority neighbourhoods, controlling those mobs of homeless. Those things cost and we're broke. So your Mr. Love needs money."

"He is Commander."

"Call him whatever the fuck you want, Bakalov, but if you want to impress him, find that woman."

"You don't know for certain she even has the gold. How do you know this?" Bakalov asked. He added, "You just know that you don't have it. That doesn't tell me anything. You don't even have proof this gold existed."

Bakalov watched the red in his face return; the man was easy to provoke. Bakalov thought there probably was gold. That this man had cooked up some deal with the woman. And she outfoxed him. That's what made Scott so angry. Humiliated. No bitch could outfox Bakalov, ever. He wondered about killing this man right now, getting it over with. It was inevitable that he would have to. But maybe wait? Wait until Scott was completely on the outside.

Maybe also wait until he found the gold. He could hear himself saying to Commander Love: "I have found your funding." Or maybe, "Commander, I have solved your problem." Or better, "I have found something that might help you." Make it seem not too important. Then he could do whatever he wanted.

Bakalov said, "I am preparing for departure—that is my priority. You will have to worry about this Mitch Black yourself."

Scott said, "Listen, the two events are linked, I'm telling you that. And I'm going to mention it to Eton."

"If I find her, I find her. I will bring the bitch to you. But I am not looking for her, you understand?"

"Yes, I fucking understand, Bakalov. But you understand me. We—you and me and your wonderful Commander—we need to find this woman."

"Send some men after her. Men you can trust."

Scott said, "I don't trust anyone."

"Then go yourself, Mr. Scott. My father always said if you want something done right, do it yourself."

Scott stared at him. Finally he said, "Fuck you, Bakalov."

Bakalov, glad now that their cards were on the table, said quietly, "No, Mr. Scott, I don't think so."

❦

They had figured they'd better take a look at the outpost before heading further north. It'd been busy as all hell the last time Slaught had been there—if it was still Grand Central it might mean Love was headed their way sooner than later. Best to have a handle on that.

They'd circled wide when coming in to the outpost, keeping to the cover of the bush that ran along the north edge of the property. They stopped their machines, parking and moving up on foot. Couldn't hear much. Susun said she thought maybe they should get in a little closer. "You okay with me and Jeff checking things out?" she asked Slaught.

Jeff said, "I mean, given what happened to you last time? I mean if you want to, your call, right?"

"He's a big boy," Mitch said, "sure he can handle it."

"Yeah, no, I'm good. Happy to hang out here, I'll keep a look out," Slaught said, thinking how strange it was to be back at it, up to their elbows in snow and trouble, and how damned good it felt.

"Me too," Levi said.

Slaught watched as they skirted around the building, easing their way along the side. He said to Levi, "So, you and Mitch?"

Levi didn't say anything, slate eyes travelling back and forth along the rim of snow banks that circled the parking lot of the outpost. Some serious concentration going on there.

Slaught said, "Nice weather today, eh? Bit overcast, but mild."

"Don't talk, I'm trying to listen."

"Yeah? What are you hearing?"

"Right now? You."

Slaught was quiet, taking in the tall spruce trees, black-green against the grey sky, the wind moving their branches around. Slaught liked the way it looked, like the trees were waving. Thought he might have never noticed that before. It was like he had a new way of seeing now, everything so vivid.

Slaught glanced at Levi. The kid had focus, that much was clear. Wasn't exactly the best company, but still, Slaught was enjoying standing with him, being able to make small talk, think about something other than dogs and feeding time. Asked, "What are you hearing now?"

"Nothing."

So they stood in silence.

By the time Susun and the others came back, the clouds overhead were bunched up and moving, maybe getting darker.

"Found nothing," said Susun.

Slaught said, "Empty?"

"The whole place, cleaned right out. Feels desolate," she said.

"Hard to believe it's the same place, it was so loud and busy when we were here," Jeff said to Slaught. "The trucks pulling up, men moving in and out, supplies. Now? Not a single vehicle. Nada."

"I was hoping there'd be something here," Slaught said. "Something to help us figure out what Love has up his sleeve."

"There was something," Mitch said. "Your girlfriend here was too busy checking out some wolf tracks to notice the mess of vehicle tracks leaving the outpost and leading out towards the old highway. Truck tracks, sleds, and lots of them. Not the freshest, but still visible. Looks like there was plenty of traffic."

Susun frowned. "Yeah, I missed that. Sorry. I was distracted." She'd noticed a sparse trail of blood, followed it as far as the bush with Jeff. There were tracks, too, a coyote, maybe a wolf. Hard to tell. When Susun bent down to get a closer look, placing her hand inside the paw print to get a sense of its size, it felt like she got a shock, like the track poured right up and into her. She'd snatched her hand back and said she had to sit for a minute and rest. Jeff told her to take her time, then helped her up, saying she looked a little pale, and walked back with her once they were done.

Jeff said, "Like, seriously, your brain must be wiped after all of this. You just need some sleep. And some of Tiny's home cooking."

"You okay?" Slaught asked.

Susun pushed her hair off her face and took a deep breath. "Sometimes, it's hard to explain, it's like I feel too permeable. That I can't keep things on the outside." She saw the blank but concerned look on Johnny's face and said, "Nothing to worry about. Must just be the baby."

"Well, tell her to settle down," Slaught said, "Jeff didn't mean to scare her with talk of Tiny's cooking."

Susun smiled. "So, back to the tracks, maybe Talos has just left? Too hard keeping the outpost open?"

"Why, though?" Mitch asked. "The outpost is about access, maintaining a connection to the Territories."

Slaught said, "Unless they're relocating it, maybe that's what Love meant, moving it farther north? Reopening the territory."

Mitch, skeptical, said, "Well then, where are they?"

"That's a good question," Slaught said. "Hope we don't run into them farther up the trail."

Already moving, Mitch said, "We should check, follow these tracks, see if they're abandoning ship and heading south or maybe relocating somewhere else around here. Can't see them giving up this outpost without a good reason."

Susun glanced up and said, "Let's get on with it, then. We can give it a half an hour or so but then I want to keep heading north, don't want to be riding in the dark, especially with snow coming."

অ

The tracks led south, and there were a lot of them. Maybe when he was grabbed they were pulling out? Slaught couldn't remember much about that day. Dragged across the snow, the guards knocking him around and throwing questions at him. Then they tossed him in the back of a truck with a bunch of guys who looked worse off than he did. Said they were employees of Talos, all of them dinged up and dirty. Didn't remember too much more after that; woke up at the greenhouse barracks. Pulled the early morning shift, saying to the guy next to him, "So what kind of a job is this, anyway?" and he'd answered, "Whatever kind they want it to be, buddy, you're in for it now."

After a while the tracks started converging, becoming so thick it was more like a road than a trail. Susun killed her engine and the five of them sat trying to figure it out, the tracks all running alongside a long, snowed-in mall.

Slaught remembered being younger and coming down to shop there, leaving early in the morning, then spending the day, eating lunch in the food court and heading back north in the mid-afternoon, his mom not wanting to drive at dusk when the moose might be up on the highway. He thought of the food court back at the Facility. Man, life could sure be fucked up. He said, "So this is weird."

Jeff said, "Maybe Talos needed some retail therapy?"

To their left was the sprawling remains of the shopping mall, at the far end a parkade. "From up there," Slaught said, "we'd have a good view."

They rode over, then decided they'd walk up since the snow had only drifted over the entrance of the first level. They pushed through that and made their way slowly up. The place was littered with crap, shopping carts, food wrappers and other debris. Nothing of value, though. By the fourth level Slaught figured they'd have a good enough view, walked the perimeter looking for any sign of activity. At the south-east corner they picked up the trail of the tracks.

"So they sort of bypass the mall," Jeff said. "Oh, okay, I see, they run into the bus depot over there." Then he added, "What kind of moron would downgrade from an airport to a bus station?"

And then it clicked. Slaught seeing the map spread out on the big desk in Love's office, the thick black line running from the City upwards through the white expanse to the north.

"The railway."

Mitch frowned. "What?"

"It was a bus and railway station. They're setting up shop at the old railway station. They're coming up on the train."

"The train? What would make you think that?"

"Saw it on a map."

Mitch said, "A map? Well, that's quite the coincidence."

"What does that mean?"

"Ask your girlfriend, she's been seeing them in her sleep."

୧

They hadn't stayed too much longer, the rest of them wanting to head north before the weather got bad. Mitch said she and Levi were going to circle back to the outpost, said it'd been swell hanging out with them but they'd be just as happy not to see them again.

Slaught said he wanted to thank Levi, and told him, "Hey man, thanks, must've been hard going back down into those tunnels. I owe you one."

Levi said, "No, you don't owe me, but I don't owe you, either."

"What the fuck?" Mitch said, "I was there, too."

But Slaught just said, "I know you Black, you got a real heart of gold."

She was thinking about that as she and Levi pulled up in front of the auto parts garage, swung around behind to the blue storage container. She was thinking, too, about the gold, what they could do with it. Have a hell of a time in the City. Doubted Levi would go for that. Did it matter to her, that he was so different? She'd gotten used to him, his silence. His calmness. An intense guy. Sometimes she'd catch him looking at her, pale grey eyes so sad and hard at the same time. Like he was waiting for something bad to happen. Other times he'd just be staring off, eyes not so wary. Maybe dreaming of something. She had no idea.

They cleared the snow away so they could get the door of the container open, working up a bit of a sweat. Mitch looking over at Levi, quiet, steady, focused on the task at hand. He was something else.

He turned, went to his sled to get the pry bar, jamming it in underneath the metal door, always surprising her with his strength, popping the door and pulling it open.

Empty.

She stared into the container. Levi, watching her expression, leaned around to look in himself. He said, "Didn't think anyone would look here."

"This was the container, right?"

"Yeah."

She looked around. "What the fuck."

Levi shook his head, asked, "What do you want to do now?"

"Find the sonofabitch who stole our gold."

"It wasn't our gold."

Mitch looked at him. "It will be when I get it back."

"So what are we going to do?"

Mitch surveyed the bleak trail leading to the container, the row of industrial buildings, doors mute and sealed with snow, roofs collapsing. "We're going to tear this fucking dump of a town apart until we find it."

Chapter Seventeen

The train left the City with a considerable amount of fanfare. It was painted brilliant black and on either side of the front engine, in large and ornate gold lettering, was the word 'DOMAIN.' It was a beast, powered not just by an engine at the front but also by an engine in the centre and one at the end. The first six cars were reserved for Love and his cartographers. Love's car was sparse but elegant, his large wooden desk hauled in there by four men from the Facility who were then somewhat less impressed with their own boxcars crowded with racks of bunks—those farthest from the wood stove almost unbearably cold.

The bulk of the boxcars housed the workers and equipment. Towards the back was the kitchen car, Big Donny getting the privilege of sleeping in there with his cooking crew. He picked his nephew, Raymond, and a couple of hard-working pals to make up his crew. When he saw the kitchen, crammed with cardboard boxes of canned soup, beans, and rat poison, he said, "Fuck me, it's right up there with the Ritz."

The very last car of the train was Scott's, Love telling him just before they left, "You're going to be like our quartermaster, but not quite as important. Just tracking supplies, no decision making on allocations, okay? We'll see how you handle that responsibility before we give you any more."

Scott wasn't surprised when he was told he'd be staying in the last boxcar, this insane expedition being all about symbols.

Ideals. Propaganda. And that's why, on either side of the central engine car, railcars were set aside for Bakalov and his army brats, then another few cars for regular security. Love saying as they'd boarded the train that the army was at the 'heart' of his expedition, his warriors for the Domain, and his cartographers and surveyors were its 'mind.' Jesus Christ, what a farce.

He had to admit though that he was impressed that Love had actually pulled it off, had gotten the train ready and organized. That he'd gotten all the Talos Board members to back the expedition, that he had enough resources. Scott thinking Love must have squeezed every last cent out of the City. Scott hadn't thought there'd been much left to squeeze.

And everyone had come out to watch them go by. Crews had cleaned up the route, taking away the rubbish, Bakalov and his boys going in ahead of time, kicking down and dragging away all the tent cities and their inhabitants along the tracks. The City almost looked normal. Normal except for the pageantry; long black and gold banners hung from the streetlights and from balconies as they chugged through the City, Love saying "Classic colours. Couldn't do better. They say 'empire' without saying 'Rome,' know what I mean?" But Scott said no, as it happened, they were the colours of his high school basketball team, and Love had said, "You really have a weak sense of self-preservation, don't you, Bob?"

Weak sense? Maybe. Maybe not. But at least he was beginning to get his exit strategy together, knowing now that the only reason he was on the train was because Love wasn't going to leave him behind in the City. Didn't trust him. With Scott alone and possibly able to re-establish some of his old networks, he just might be able to make inroads with the City's elite, those few dozen families still doing business. And Love wasn't having that. Scott was on the train so Love could keep an eye on him.

Bringing up the rear. Couldn't have been a clearer message to the power elite who'd watched the train roll out of the City to open up the hinterlands.

The plan was to push past the old outpost right up to Cobalt, use it as a regional base. There was at least a settlement there. A population at their disposal. Set up a barracks. Love was unleashing his surveyors and cartographers, making the most of the downtime while workers cleared the tracks.

But why? That was the question that no one seemed willing to ask Love. Love with his crackpot ideas about diet and meditation and his fucking Domain. Good Christ. It was like a madness. All the people that mattered, all the wealthy and connected families Scott had worked with, and socialized with, it was like they had absorbed it, too. You couldn't talk to them anymore about anything other than Love and the Domain and his grand vision. Scott had tried. In the days before the train had pulled out, he'd reached out to a few of the families he thought might see reason. But no luck. Everyone, it seemed, was on board.

But they weren't actually on the fucking train. He was. They couldn't see how crazy it was up close. Now that the train had stopped for the night, the dark and the cold had gotten a firm grip. The day had been freezing, too, though. Scott had spent his day huddled around the stove in his railcar, trying to record expenditures. Love had demanded an itemized list of every single thing, had said, "You know how you build an empire? By knowing every nail, every hammer, every man you use to build it. You keep track. That way, Bob? There's no corruption. Just purity. A new way of doing things. A new history."

Scott doubted it. This wasn't history in the making. It was a fucking shitshow. And it was brutal every fucking cold kilometre of the way. And that wasn't the worst of it. It was almost as if the farther from the City they got, Bakalov got worse. Bigger. Meaner. Bolder. He had his army now, a group of young guys, called them the Twenty. Had apparently put them through some basic training. And then armed them.

That's when Scott got worried enough to walk the length of the train to Love's car, having to ask the guard outside, one of Love's private security guys in his black parka, his balaclava rolled up into a toque, if he could see Love.

Once inside it was like he'd stepped back in time. The train car was outfitted with Love's antique wooden desk, the map on the wall behind it. Another unfinished map spread across the desk, a side table with white linens for Love's meals. Jesus.

Love, standing with his back to Scott, hands clasped behind his back, staring down at the map on his desk, said, "I hope this is worth interrupting me. I need to focus now—I just finished my training session with Bakalov and it pulls all the energy into my core."

"Okay, right, my apologies, Commander, but I do consider this very serious. Those guys your man Bakalov is arming? They're criminals. They're from the Facility for Godsake. Giving them guns is a recipe for disaster. They could easily turn those guns on us. On you. We have no idea how to control them."

"I think Bakalov has it well in hand."

Scott sighed, "But do you have him well in hand?"

"Questioning my authority?"

"No, it's not that. I just think maybe he didn't think it through well enough. Who knows what they are capable of."

"Anything different than you, Bob?"

"What does that mean?"

"Your capacity for self-reflection, well, I mean it's non-existent isn't it? Look at yourself. What has happened on your watch? Property confiscated. Stolen, really. People *killed*. All in the name of establishing some sense of order. Fair enough. I don't quibble with that. You made some hard decisions back in the early days of the winter. But then you put your own interests ahead of Talos, ahead of the greater good. You should reflect on that."

"What is this about? You want to go back over all of that again?"

"I want to remind you that being on this train gives you a chance to start over, to have a clean slate. Focus on that and let Ion handle the rest."

"What, so this is just some opportunity for self-improvement? Because of your benevolence?"

Love finally turned around. The youthful face dark and tight. Love seemed thinner, and Scott wondered if Love's "training regime," as he liked to call it, some crackpot combination of fasting, exercise, and his "deep-thought time," was taking its toll. Maybe he wasn't sleeping enough, either, his emotions more extreme. And right now, Love was looking very angry. He said, "If you don't get it together, we won't need you in the City."

"Meaning?"

"It means if you're lucky, you might make Territorial Administrator, and if not, you'll be up here with the rest of the so-called criminals, clearing roads and restoring infrastructure. It means, Bob, you're probably not coming back."

ༀ

What Slaught wanted was time alone with Susun, but what he got was a welcome home party, Tiny saying he'd voted against it because Slaught wasn't worth the fuss and he looked like shit. Said, too, that he'd hardly missed him, but then he cracked open a bottle of liquor, causing an uproar, Jeff and Jordan accusing him of hoarding.

Slaught said a toast was in order, and he toasted Susun, and she was smiling and then he really wanted time alone with her. No one was asking him too much about what had happened, keeping it light. He guessed they figured he'd rather forget about it. He wasn't sure about that, thinking a bit about leaving Ray back there, and Big Donny. Did they get out? He thought a few guys were coming down the tunnels behind him, but it was hard to tell. He was just focused on keeping up and getting out.

And as much as he was wondering what happened to the other guys, he was just glad to be back, listening to how Mrs. Merrill, prim and proper as ever, was mass producing baby blankets after Jordan and Ricky discovered a wool store and got everything from yarn to patterns. Jordan said Mrs. Merrill was teaching him and Tiny to knit, and Tiny said he was going to knit booties for Susun's baby. Johnny said, "It's my baby, too," and Tiny said that wasn't the baby's fault and he was still going to make the booties.

After about an hour of passing around the bottle Johnny realized he was beyond tired, he was stunned. And overjoyed. Just the smiling and the joking. He couldn't believe how amazing it felt. He said to Chumboy that he was feeling bad about the guys left behind and Chumboy said he knew Big Donny, and that the man could take care of himself. Said it was likely the guys there were glad to help out, telling him, too, that all along the way folks were willing to help. That there was a lot of hope in what they were doing. In what some folks were starting to call the northern resistance.

"Yeah?" asked Slaught. "So what are we resisting?"

"I guess what's at the other end of those railway tracks."

Chapter Eighteen

Chumboy was relieved to have Johnny back. Straight up happiness over that. So why, then, was he up half the night feeling so uneasy? It felt like things were turning, somehow, shifting maybe into something he didn't recognize, something new. But other than a feeling of unease, it was all impression and no detail. He decided he needed some serious wisdom weighing in on this one. So he was glad his Auntie had decided to stick around for a few days. She had said she wanted to see Susun, check in on how the baby was coming along. And see Johnny.

He found his Auntie in the kitchen with Tiny, drinking her morning tea.

"Just the lady I wanted to talk to," he said, pulling up a chair.

"Good morning, Chumboy. How did you sleep?"

"Funny, that's what I wanted to take to you about..."

"You got worried written all over you," she said.

"Yeah, feeling bad, Auntie, feeling bad. And I can't pin it down, it's like we're heading off into the unknown, but I don't know why I feel like that. Should feel relieved, Johnny's back and all, and instead I feel worse."

She nodded. "I feel it, too."

"She's been in here since the wee hours," Tiny said. "I couldn't sleep either. If I was weak in the mind like you, Chum, I'd say it was the full moon, or the wrong star alignment, or some of that horoscope bullshit, but I think maybe I just had a bad night."

"So, Auntie, what's your verdict—indigestion or calamity brewing?"

"Hard to say, Chumboy."

"Want to take a guess? I mean, when I try and picture what's bothering me, what's lying ahead, it's just a big empty space."

She said, "Get Susie to draw you the map."

"Like the map she's been dreaming about?"

"Yes. That one."

"You're not serious, right?" Tiny asked.

Auntie Verla shrugged. "Want to know where you're going then you need a map."

Jordan and Jeff came in, Jordan saying, "We were up all night. I mean like all night. Just awful. Feel like I've never slept. Like I may never sleep again."

Chumboy said he appreciated the dramatic delivery, but did Jordan have any crayons lying around.

"Crayons?" Jordan asked. "You kidding?"

"Nope. Got them or not?"

"Well, I think so. You wanted the kindergarten kind or maybe something a little more Grade Three?"

"When did you become such a smart ass?"

"It's from hanging around you guys. I've been corrupted." Then he added, "Mind me asking what it's for?"

"Need Susun to make me a picture."

"The map?"

Word did get around the ol' Fraser pretty quick. Guess folks were getting interested in the map. He said, "Yeah, was thinking of it."

"Then I'm going to give you some pencil crayons. I mean, we're talking a technical drawing, here."

It was him who kept the men working. It was him who was responsible for their progress every day. At the end of the first day of the Expedition he had gone to Commander Love, had said, "The man you have running your work crews, he is not the man for the job." The Commander was angry at first, but trying not to show it when he said, "Explain that to me, Ion, please, go right ahead. Explain to me how the man I selected is not doing a good job."

Bakalov had said, "Watch him yourself. He stands by the fire while the men work. He leaves them and then returns to yell and punish. When he leaves, they slow down, sometimes even stop. We could double our progress. He is Scott's man."

Commander Love had looked at him and said, "I understand. You and Scott, bit of a rivalry going on there. Not always productive, right? You can understand that sometimes competitiveness is healthy, sometimes cooperation is the better path."

"It is not about me and that man. It is about getting the job done."

"Okay, Ion, what is your plan? Telling me what one guy does badly is not productive, right? You can see that? Problems aren't helpful. Solutions are."

"These men in your army," not his army, Bakalov's army, not yet, "they don't remember how to work. I take my Twenty. They each take a crew of ten men and rotate. Show them how to work hard. Work beside them. We will make progress."

"Your Twenty?"

"Yes. I have selected twenty young men. Strong. Motivated. Willing to take risks. Be loyal."

"To whom?"

The question had surprised Bakalov, caught him off guard,

and he knew he hesitated too long, but said, "To the Commander, to you, of course."

"I see," said Love. "Well, alright. You can run the work gangs."

"You will see. We will work harder and longer now. Move faster."

"And if you don't?"

"We start shooting them."

Love laughed at first, then said, "Well, Ion, you might make some serious dents in my workforce that way. Then what?"

Bakalov said, "Do not worry, Commander. I know men. And I know work. I know what they can do, and what they don't want to do. Some men, you can inspire them to accomplish great things. My Twenty? They are that kind. The others? You have to frighten them. Either way works."

"Go to it then, Ion, but perhaps mention it to Scott, tell him to start tracking our workers. Probably useful to keep track of the mortality. Factor it into our system."

So Bakalov went back and told Jimmy to have each of the Twenty pick ten men, men with some backbone. They were going to form work gangs, work in shifts. If they refused to work, no food. If they refused to work hard, no food. He told Jimmy he had to work harder, too, to inspire the men. Set an example. Jimmy asked what if the men don't want to work on these work gangs, and Bakalov said he should know the answer by now. "Shoot them?" Jimmy asked, and Bakalov nodded.

The recruitment went smoothly, except one of the Twenty decided to try and break up the kitchen team, saying he wanted Leonard, one of Ray's friends, to work with him. He said he wanted Leonard out on the work crew first thing the next morning, give him some time to put his apron away, laughing to himself as he left.

First thing in the morning, though, they found the guy with a nice little knife sticking out of him. No one knew for sure, but most of the guys thought it was Big Donny that had done it. Bakalov had the body of his soldier dragged out into the clearing, pulled off the camo parka, and tossed the young man's body into the bush. Bakalov wondered about punishing Big Donny, sensing the lethality of the man, but decided against it. The men respected Big Donny. He ran a good kitchen, usually stayed out of trouble and kept to himself. Bakalov was always pleased to see Raymond at the door of his car with his dinner. Made Bakalov feel satisfied.

One worker standing nearby said, "Mess with the kitchen? He should have seen that coming." Bakalov turned to him and said, "Yes. You are right. It was stupid." He stared at the young man for a moment, the guy staring back, then looking away, just the right mix of defiance and deference. Bakalov passed the worker the dead man's parka, and said, "You're one of the Twenty now."

Then Bakalov went to Scott, told him he was changing the way the daily rationing was done; he wanted a two-tier system of food allowance. Plus, Love wanted him to start keeping track of worker mortality and Scott had said, "Jesus Christ, Bakalov, what are you doing out there?"

"What I need to, Mr. Scott. Perhaps you should be doing the same."

༄

Chumboy checked a few spots and eventually found Johnny and Susun sitting together in the big dining room, having a tea. "Don't you two look cute," he said.

"I'm feeling pretty cute," Slaught said. "Civilized, you know. Just sitting here with my honey having tea in a clean mug.

Doesn't get much better than that."

"That bad, was it?"

Slaught said, "Yeah, it was that bad and then some."

Chumboy wanted to know if it was true about the dogs.

Slaught was surprised. "You guys heard about the dogs? Yeah, fucking mean-ass dogs. Turned me right off the things."

"Just doing their job, Johnny, punching the clock like the rest of us," Chumboy said.

"Maybe. But I think they liked it. Vicious things. Big. And just so damn mean."

Susun said, "Probably made mean."

"Well if anyone could turn a mutt mean it would be that Bakalov guy. He was something else. The whole goddam place was nuts. Between him, the dogs and that wunderkind wacko Love, I thought I was going to lose my mind."

"The guy that runs Talos now?" Susun asked.

Slaught nodded, "Yeah. Seemed like one of those smart stupid guys. And totally fucked up over his map. Guards it like a hawk, and it's just some shit-ass gas station road map of Ontario. I'm telling you, they're all taking crazy pills down there."

Susun said, "Maybe it's because you can't get maps anymore."

Chumboy looked interested. "What do you mean?"

"No maps at all. Hector told us. Said Talos had come through and seized them all. Said Talos was burning them."

"What the Christ is that about?" Slaught asked. "Guess that's why buddy there was treating his like the Holy Grail."

"So, speaking of maps," Chumboy said, passing the pencil crayons to Susun, "want to draw me one?"

"Like, draw my map?"

"Yeah, so what is this map thing all about?" Johnny asked Susun, feeling like there was a lot for him to be catching up on, that he'd missed things. Babies, trains, maps, good Christ he might feel overwhelmed if he wasn't just so goddam happy.

Susun said, "I don't know. I've been having these dreams. Intense ones. And there's always a map, and these forms, these creatures, coming and going." She threw up her hands. "I don't know, sounds strange but there it is…"

"Auntie says women that are with child often have intense dreams."

"You dreaming our little one's future?" Johnny asked. Susun and Chumboy looked at him, and he said, "What, like I've never had a profound thought?"

Chumboy said, "Well, not since I've known you."

Slaught, just so glad to be back, said, "Yeah, well you know what they say, being on the inside changes a guy." Susun smiled and said, "My man, the ex-con." Then she added, "And yeah, maybe, I don't know. Some of the dreams, you know, they're absolutely beautiful, strange but beautiful. Other ones feel really bad."

"Bad how?" Chumboy asked.

"Dark maps. I don't know what else to say, I mean, I will be holding the map and the ink from the map will start to travel up my arm, black ink, and my arm is turning dark and I'm trying to roll up the map but I can't stop the black from spreading and it is like a fungus all up my arm…"

"Well, you know that crafty mycelium keeps everything connected, so maybe it isn't so bad after all."

"Most of them are beautiful," Susun said, "and it's usually the same one, starts out the same way but then things change, come and go. It's hard to explain."

"So could you draw it?" Chumboy asked.

"Yeah, I think so."

"I gotta say I have no idea what any of this means," said

Chumboy, "but this stupid smart guy that Johnny met, he was interested in us, in up here, and he has a map. And in your mind, you have a map. So I'm going to say that maps, somehow, are something we need to be thinking about. And if we could see your map, get an idea of what you're seeing, it might help us think about it better."

Susun said she'd try but she didn't know if she could actually draw it. It was always changing, and she wasn't much of an artist. Chumboy said they weren't looking for a Rembrandt, just wanted an idea of what it looked like.

"Could end up like one of those abstracts," she said.

"As long as it isn't a Rothko I think we'll be okay."

Johnny asked who that was and Chumboy said, "You don't want to know."

Slaught said, "Okay, we got maps and we got trains. So why the train? If they got the gumption to push back up here there must be a reason, but the train? Seems like a whole heap of effort to push a single line up, and for what?"

Chumboy said, "Probably easier than the last time they did it, blasting up through that old Precambrian Shield. Tougher than plowing snow that's for sure. And it was worth their while back then."

"Guess so," Slaught said, "but the City's such a mess, not like they don't have enough shit on their plate without stirring up more."

"Can't help themselves, gotta stir shit, that's the capitalist stew."

"And this new guy?" Susun asked. "Is this train thing his idea?"

"I think so, seems like the type. You know, big ideas guy. All that effort on these grand useless schemes and propaganda when real shit is going on. Just keeping people fed is hard enough, right? Some of the greenhouses weren't even running full bore. All kinds of problems, breakdowns. We had a shit-ton of brownouts, and then you'd get a real cold night and we'd lose a whole floor of seedlings. Craziness."

"What are people doing? There must be so many folks down there," Susun said.

"Yeah, lots, and I got no idea," Slaught said. "I know at one point they got some crazy fish farm thing going on, but the pumps keep stalling out and then, you know, their aerators fail and, well, you can picture it, right?"

And Susun was thinking yeah, she could picture it, almost suddenly felt it, the loss of air in her lungs, the smell of the fetid, thick waters, and she heard Slaught say, "You okay?" And she realized she was resting her head between her knees, trying to get her breath back and he was up, his hand on her shoulder, "Susie? You okay?"

And then she was back, breathing again and she just shook her head and said, "Yeah, I'm okay, just couldn't catch my breath there. It was weird."

"You need something?" Chumboy asked, and she said, no, she was fine, just a passing thing, that they should get going, leave her to her map.

Slaught said, "Okay, but I'm going to get Melinda to come up and check on you."

"You don't have to do that, I'm okay now."

"Well," Slaught said, "might be those seven sisters causing a ruckus in there."

"Pleiades?" Chumboy asked. "That a possible name for the baby?"

Susun smiled. "Maybe."

Chumboy said, "Well, that's some serious star power going on in there. I'm feeling better already."

It was cold. Fucking cold. Scott had a hard time believing anyone thought spring was coming. It was impossible to stay warm; he was working inside his boxcar with his parka on most of the time. And he wasn't getting his load of wood delivered until the end of the day, and there was never enough, the delivery guy saying he was always running out by the time he did the whole train, couldn't keep up. Scott complained to Bakalov, but the big man just said, "I didn't put you at the ass-end of the train."

And then the trouble with the wolves started. And that's when Bakalov really made his presence felt. Scott had to admit, at first, he was glad Bakalov had been there. They'd barely left the City and it had started, the constant howling at night. Bakalov saying it was just coyotes, nothing to worry about. Laughed at the men who were freaking out. But then the train was getting deeper into the trees and snow and dark and Bakalov said, "Now we go where the wolves go." And there was endless howling. Mostly at dusk and early in the morning, men complaining they couldn't sleep, rattled by it. The second night it sounded like the train was surrounded. The security detail said they'd seen something just after sunset, and panicking a bit they'd fired blindly into the woods that were set back about twenty feet and ran the length of the train, thick and tangled and impenetrable.

Then that night a man on the security detail just disappeared. Once daylight came they could see several sets of tracks leading away from the train. Then blood. Bakalov telling them that right there, in the snow? That was the story. A small pack took the man, dragged him to a clearing where the wolves felt safe enough to make the man into a meal. Jesus Christ.

Scott had thought the City was uncivilized. The constant violence, rioting for food. But then this. Fucking snow and wolves. It was like out of some awful children's story. What were those stories? Right, yeah, the Bothers Grimm. And Bakalov was like some character out of them, too. Showing off his huntsman skills. All the young guys in his thrall. Chrisssakes, it was a nightmare.

The security details were spooked, didn't want to make their walks around the length of the train in the dark anymore, saying it was too dangerous. Bakalov calling them cowards, said he would deal with the wolves. Went out with two of his Twenty. Came back a few hours later with a dead wolf. Thin, mangy thing. But still a wolf. Skinned it right there in the snow, sticking its head on top of a pole. The Twenty were elated. The rest of the men were more unnerved than reassured, a few guys even getting their shovels out and covering over the blood stains on the snow.

That's when things started to go really off the rails. Bakalov now taking charge, setting up safety perimeters, sending the Twenty out to secure the train. Even Love's New Army men were getting ticked off. Love telling them they were free to go bag themselves a wolf if they wanted. Until that happened, Bakalov's boys were an essential part of the expedition's success.

And with that role came privileges. More freedom, no snow detail, and decent winter clothing. The rest of the men doing the heavy shoveling had shit-assed winter gear, most of it not fitting right, or even plain worn out. The wind would kick up and it was almost unbearable, the long days—starting and finishing in the dark. Guys getting frostbite. Some of the guys envied the Twenty. Most just fucking hated them, calling them smug fucks. Bakalov's bitches.

Scott had warned Love, telling him the Twenty were getting away with shirking, weren't pulling their weight. But Love said, "You just worry about your own weight pulling, okay? Leave Ion and his boys to me."

The Twenty were going out every day, hunting, scavenging, coming back with game and loot. Taking it all to Bakalov. A few of the workers grumbling about it but Bakalov telling them to mind their business. Get back to work. That they should be thankful the Twenty were keeping them safe. Scott figured it wouldn't be long before the expedition made the Grimm fairy tales look like Mary Poppins.

Chapter Nineteen

Scott watched as Bakalov pointed to the two sets of feet sticking out from underneath a tarp. He said to one of his Twenty, a pudgy looking kid with an oversized camo parka and an AK-47 slung across his shoulder, "Get these bodies out of here."

The first set of feet belonged to a middle-aged worker. He'd been standing, cigarette in hand, not paying attention, and then slipped in the snow and got caught on the big plow mounted at the front of the train as it barreled along, was dragged for a stretch before anyone noticed the man was a mangled lump. Then, almost right away, a man went down on the shoveling crew. Maybe a heart attack. Scott was surprised there hadn't been more work-related fatalities, the men working long hours clearing the track, ten-hour shifts, half the time working in the dark. The constant clang of metal on metal, snow shovels scraping along the tracks as they would clear a section and then the train would push forward. And then they'd start over.

The pudgy guy gestured to two others to give him a hand, taking hold of the edges of the tarp and dragging the two bodies past Scott and dumping them on the tracks.

Scott said, "Don't leave them there."

The young men glanced up at Scott, but it was almost as if he was invisible. Said nothing to him. They only had eyes for Bakalov. The big man himself was now approaching with two more of his soldiers, saying, "Yes, leave them there."

Scott said, "You can't just leave the bodies here, out in the open like that."

"What do you suggest?"

"Bury them. Somehow. I don't know, isn't this your department?"

"My department? Alright, then. I say leave them."

Scott hesitated, glanced at the two young bucks soldiering up on either side of Bakalov, like some sort of pubescent honour guard. He said, "Can I speak with you privately for a minute?"

Bakalov shrugged, "Not to worry, my men are sworn to secrecy. They can be trusted."

Sworn to keep whose secrets? Scott considered making a point, asserting his authority. Doubted Bakalov would listen, though. And maybe this wasn't the time or place to test it. So he said, "Leaving the bodies here will be demoralizing. The other men might not stand for it."

"It is not up to them. It is up to me and I say we leave these lazy dogs on the tracks. It is a reminder of what happens to the weak. To men who do not pay attention. They harm everyone, including themselves. Including our great project."

Jesus Christ. Was this guy for real? Scott said, "Spare me the propaganda."

"You are going to learn, Mr. Scott, the difference between propaganda and truth. You will learn on this trip. Now leave me to run this expedition and you go back to your pencil pushing."

Fuck Bakalov. What Scott was learning on this trip was how to look out for himself. That's why he had a plan, and was putting it into play. For a while he thought things could be salvaged, that he could take Talos back. But that was clearly not in the cards. So he'd stashed a couple of snow machines while everyone had been out shoveling. He was the one who counted the snow machines, knew how many in and out in one day. So no one was going to miss the snow machines until they were missing him, too. He'd spoken to his two private security guards. He could trust them. He'd be up to Cobalt before Love even missed him. Taking the gold, turning around, and heading south. That was his plan.

Scott said to Bakalov, "The bodies, they're going to attract predators. Like those wolves that are out there at night."

"That is fine with us. Maybe we set some traps. Let those vermin come closer, my boys will teach them a lesson."

"I'm sure they will," Scott said, thinking Bakalov was getting more and more confident. Pretty soon he would be riding in Love's train car if they weren't careful. He added, "Fine, just check that neither of them has anything worth salvaging."

But Bakalov's young bloods were already on the bodies doing that.

ॐ

Auntie Verla told Tiny he was going to be a fine knitter one day, asking him how come he had so much patience with wool but so little with people.

"Wool isn't stupid."

"I suppose that's true. It can get tangled up, though."

"Not in other people's business. Wool? It does wool things."

"You dropped a stitch."

"Shit."

"Don't panic, just get it back onto your left needle on the next round." Watching him, Auntie Verla said, "That's it, there you go. Keep knitting."

"You're faster than me. I'm never going to get this finished," Tiny said, holding up the piece of knitted yellow wool.

"Yellow, it is the best colour to pick. You pick it?" Auntie Verla asked.

Tiny looked down at the tiny beginnings of the sock. "Yeah, sort of, and then Mrs. Merrill said it was neutral so it was a good colour. So I stuck with it."

"Neutral? Yellow isn't neutral."

"Yeah it is, you know, if you don't know if it's a boy or a girl."

"Susie says she knows. Says it is going to be a little girl."

"Susie says a lot of things."

Auntie Verla was quiet for a few moments, nothing but the clicking of the knitting needles against each other, then she said, "You will be able to teach the little one how to knit."

"You think so?"

"You'll be good teacher. As long as the little girl is like wool and not a person." Auntie Verla was smiling now and Tiny said, "As long as she, or he, isn't like Susie. That girl? She worries me."

"We love the ones who worry us. That is why we worry."

"What do you worry about?"

Auntie Verla said, "All of us, right now."

"What does that mean?"

"I saw Susie's map."

"Yeah? She finished it?"

"No, not yet. But she says she's close. I think she is shy about her map."

"What's it like?"

"What I saw was beautiful."

"Well, see then, nothing to worry about."

"Think that other picture is going to cause us trouble. The one Johnny talked about."

"Think you're getting worked up over nothing. This map stuff? I mean, come on Verla, a battle of the maps? Give me a break."

"You think maps are like your yellow?"

"What?"

"Neutral?"

"Well, a map is a map."

Auntie Verla shook her head slowly, and paused in her knitting. Sounded sad, she said, "No, I don't think so."

"Hey, sorry, Verla, let's stick to knitting, I don't know shit about maps." He held up his knitting needles, asking, "So you like the colour? The yellow?"

She smiled then, and said, "I like yellow. That yellow you have? It's nice and pale. It's the colour of the stars."

"I don't think stars are yellow. Think they might be red, blue? White maybe."

"They're yellow on Susie's map."

"Susie has stars on her map?"

"There's stars. What kind of a map wouldn't have stars?"

"Well, there's maps of the heavens and maps of earth. That much I do know. They're different things."

Auntie Verla started knitting again and said, "Think that if you want, Tiny. When you meet that little baby? I bet you have stars in your eyes. Probably tears, too. Hard to separate the stars from the water from you. Be all tangled up like your ball of wool is right now."

Tiny glanced down, saw the mess of wool inching up his needles. "Shit."

ক

Levi sounded like he was asking when he said, "We're leaving in the morning."

Mitch said, "Probably." Not saying too much. Frustrated. Beyond frustrated. Fucking pissed off and fucking cold.

"Think we've looked as much as we can."

Mitch said, "You think so?"

Levi glanced over at her. She looked mad. He decided to

stop talking. They'd spent the better part of the last two days searching the area around the outpost, the storage area and anywhere else they were able to spot what might be recent tracks. Nothing. They were back at the storage locker, Mitch walking around it for the third time.

"Fuck's sake."

Levi was cold. And hungry. He was tired of looking. Didn't think the gold was in the outpost, anyway. Either the Wintermen people or someone else had it. But it wasn't here. And he didn't really care about the gold. Anyway, it was useless trekking back and forth, the winds that were blowing sharp and hard yesterday would have erased any tracks they were trying to find in the snow.

He didn't know what Mitch would decide to do about her missing gold. Levi usually waited for a sign to make a decision. Something that would tell him what to do. He had no other way of making a decision. His brain didn't seem to work like other people's. But there was nothing out here to show him one path was better than another. He would have to just wait. Follow Mitch until something was clear to him.

He said, "I think maybe we should get out of the cold now. We could go back to the outpost for the night. Heat and shelter there."

She was grim looking. Mad. She said to him, "Food and shelter—that all you think about?"

"Mostly," he said, "but not all the time. Sometimes I think about home."

Chapter Twenty

Mitch was listening hard in the fading shadows, Levi looking through the field glasses. It felt warmer. The sky was overcast, powdery snow falling.

First thing in the morning, Levi had packed up their gear, thinking of the long ride home, but then at the end of it all there'd be the stand of pine, the cold, clear creek. Their small cabin, the wood pile and stable. He kept busy, Mitch not much interested in talking. Levi didn't mind that. He was content to call up pictures of home in his mind and just look at them. But then she had said, "We're taking one last look for the gold."

So he stopped the picture of home in his head and followed her out to their snow machines, following her as they headed towards a string of small buildings that edged the highway. Behind those buildings ran the rail line. She pulled up near the original storage container where she'd left the gold. And when they killed their engines they heard it. The train.

It was moving—it creaked along, loud, cold steel on steel. Sounded almost like it was dragging itself. Mitch glanced back at the locker, but then said they should go have a quick look at the train so they started out on foot, skirting around a few of the buildings until they were close enough to see.

They weren't prepared for how big it was, car after car pushing slowly by, the sound of men, lots of men, shouting and cursing as it pushed through the cleared track, men scrambling in front of it and alongside, breaking up the snow, clearing it away from the blade of the plow.

It was mesmerizing, just the sheer effort of it. The bodies of the men looking like they were one mass of beige and grey against the snow, and some of the doors on the boxcars were thrown open; inside were trucks and snow machines. But it was the first six cars that were captivating. Black and shiny, beautiful, gold scrolled along the windows, Mitch saying it reminded her of a toy train, some Victorian trinket under the Christmas tree. The rest of the cars, dozens of them, plain black, and then a few in the middle with some sort of marking on them.

Mitch asking, "What are those markings, the ones on the middle boxcars?"

Levi scanned the length of the train with the field glasses, almost sighed, and said, "It's a wolf's head, a red crest with a wolf's head on it." He was quiet, then said, "Must be Bakalov."

"Yeah? Thought he was into dogs."

"He's showing his enemy he's not afraid."

"Dickhead."

Levi just shrugged. "So what are we going to do?"

Mitch said, "I don't know."

"There are a lot of men on that train. Enough to do bad things in Cobalt."

"Not our problem, Levi. Our problem is the gold."

"Maybe we should we go help them?"

"You know what I've done for a living, right? I'm not the guy in the fire truck, I'm the guy starting the fires."

"People aren't just one thing." Levi hoped so, anyway. He said, "In that crest, on the train, it's a severed wolf's head, the red is blood."

Mitch glanced over at him, "Bakalov got you spooked, eh?"

"I can still hear his voice, coming through the tunnels, looking for us, for anyone living down there. Would set the dogs on us. Some of the kids, they were young, eight, seven, even. He'd drag them out, they'd be crying and screaming." He paused, then said, "Yeah, I guess I find him scary."

Mitch didn't say anything, thinking that was about as much as Levi had ever said at one time. He wasn't wrong, either, Bakalov was a bastard. She was having a hard time figuring out the train, the weird symbols, the elegance of it. Someone was putting a lot of thought into it. Just wasn't clear to her what the point of it all was.

They both kept watching as the train lurched forward and then came to a complete stop, men now all rushing along the sides, snow piled up that they were trying to clear. Mitch and Levi were close to the train, close enough to smell the machine of it, to see the stains from its exhaust against the whiteness of the snow, greasy and dark.

"I've never seen a train before."

Mitch looked at Levi, "Yeah, I guess you might not have."

"Subway trains. Saw those. But not like this."

The train was loud, even as it rested. Levi kept the field glasses fixed on it, moving along the row of windows and then down, going back over the set of tracks it was leaving behind, and the gaping, empty buildings. Levi thought the buildings looked sad, bereft, like the train had given them hope and was now going to leave them behind. And then he saw three snow machines, all with the Talos brand, parked along the side of a fast food building. Out of sight of the train. That was odd.

"Think someone's staying behind," he said, and passed the glasses to Mitch.

She took a quick look at the snow machines then scanned past a few of the buildings, past the stand of cedar and aspen near the very end of the train. Three men climbed down the set of steps at the very back of the train. Two of them in white camo gear, AKs slung across their backs, started towards the snow machines. The third, in a big white parka, went towards the cedar trees. He was clearly getting out of sight. She gave the third guy a closer look.

"Well, well," she said quietly, "don't you turn up in the strangest of places."

"You know him?"

"Yeah. That's Scott."

"The man who sent you for the gold?"

"The same."

"What are they doing?"

"Think the two guys are getting the snow machines and picking Scott up," she said.

Levi thought the black shiny train was beautiful. He didn't like looking at it, though, because of the wolf heads. He could see them clearly in his mind. Made him feel queasy. He wondered about the train. What it all meant. The man in the cedars linked to Mitch from before Levi knew her. Before he saw her strength and decided his future was with her. He supposed the white figure in the cedars could be a sign.

He said, "Rats getting off a sinking ship." Decided it was a sign.

ॐ

It had been easier than she'd thought to get close to the two men, coming up behind them while they were busy with their machines. By the time they noticed her it was too late. Like where the fuck did she come from? And then behind them the sound of the slide, Levi covering them with his Remington. Could tell by their "what the fuck" expressions that they didn't hear or see Levi at all, and he was only a few feet away.

She said, just walking right up to them, "Put your guns in the snow, gentlemen. Do it right now. Then you swap your camo with us and hit the road and he won't shoot you."

The first guy, his eyes a washed-out brown behind the balaclava, said, "You really don't want to be interfering in this."

"Yeah, we do. Now let's get a move on."

"You got no sleds."

"Don't worry about us. Head south and don't look back," she said. "From the looks of it you got supplies for a few days and then some, so head back to the City, no stopping, no detours. And don't worry about Scott, we'll take care of him."

The man looked surprised and said, "Jesus, are you Mitch Black?"

"Not into the chitchat, buddy, just get the coat off and beat it."

The two guys exchanged glances. Mitch said, "Tick tock, boys." And the one guy with the balaclava just nodded and said, "Okay, we're going. This whole thing is fucked right up, anyways."

The second guy, glancing over at Levi, said, "There's no way either of us is fitting into his parka."

"We could shoot you if you don't feel like trying, but I'm losing patience."

The two guys were shedding their snow gear, one of them complaining, "Jesus, this is a piece of shit coat," but still pulling it on and then getting on their snow machines, both of them glancing back, not trusting that they weren't going to get a bullet in the back.

Mitch and Levi headed carefully to where Scott was waiting. He had his back to them, watching the train. The noise of it, and the sheer draw of its bulk shuddering awake seemed to hold his attention. Not even bothering to turn around once he finally heard their boots squeaking on the snow, he said, "Took you long enough. It's fucking cold out here and I want to get a move on."

Mitch said, "Yeah, sorry about the delay, Scott, just a quick change of security detail."

He spun around, didn't even wait to focus on the two of them before he was trying to run. It wasn't clear exactly what direction he was heading off in, maybe all of them, but he moved too fast, losing his balance in the snow, face flushed as he went down in a tangle of limbs and Mitch said, "Didn't mean to scare you, just heard you'd been looking for me. Thought I'd make it easy for you."

His eyes went from her to Levi, took in the Talos security decals on the parka and said, "Where are my men?"

"Headed for home."

Scott pulled himself to his feet, dusting off the snow. "That's brilliant, just fucking brilliant. Now what? We ride piggyback back to the City?"

"No, we don't, and you better start to fucking move, because you have a train to catch." She tossed her gear bag at him and said, "Take this and get moving."

"You're kidding me, right?"

She gave him a shove. "Nope, not kidding. Now giddy-up shitbird, time to get on the ratfuck express."

॥

It was a nightly routine. It was too dangerous for the train to be moving in the dark, anything could be across the tracks: downed trees, old power lines. It wasn't too dangerous for the men to keep working, though, clearing snow away from the track, setting up camp, cutting firewood. They tried to stick as close to the train as they could, no one wanting to be the one to head into the bush to gather the kindling and firewood. That meant pushing into the darkness that lurked beyond the reach of the big searchlights mounted along the length of the train. It meant going to where they could hear scuttling on top of the snow, the howling of those fucking wolves that never shut up. So when it came time to eat, the men were relieved. They'd line up and get their container of stew or soup from Big Donny, return to their boxcars to eat, then slowly drift out to huddle around the light and warmth of the fire barrels. It was comforting, felt safe. Gave them a chance to talk a bit.

But then a red-faced guy was stumbling up the tracks, yelling, and everyone stopped talking and turned to watch him come.

"Sir, sir, Jesus, you have to come quick, it's, it's..." and then he stopped, panting, looking around at the cluster of men who were watching him, searching the faces for Bakalov's.

He was having a hard time catching his breath, looking from one face to the next, faces lit by the glow of the fire. One of the older guys said, "Hey, Cory, calm down, what is it?"

Bakalov had been watching as the guy staggered into camp, hysterical. He couldn't have that. He tossed another few pieces of wood into the fire, taking his time, walking towards the group of men, then said, "You? Did you want to speak to me?"

Leaning on the older man, trying to catch his breath, the young guy started, "It was, it was awful..."

Bakalov, interrupting, "Your name?"

"Yeah, uh, Cory. Cory, remember? You sent me..."

"Don't waste my time. What has you in such a state?"

"I couldn't do anything, there was too many of them..." he said, but he was sputtering, the guys starting to look at each other. Bakalov sensed they were getting antsy. Untrained, soft sons of whores.

Bakalov took hold of Cory's shoulders and shook him. "Pull yourself together. What is it?"

But now Cory almost seemed in shock, just staring at Bakalov as if now there was something new to fear, this man with his cold blue eyes. He managed, "It... it was awful ...I didn't know..." And then Bakalov slammed his hand into the side of Cory's head, the impact sending him off balance and onto the ground. Cory stayed down on all fours, breathing hard, maybe even crying.

The older man who had helped Cory said, "What the fuck was that?" A few guys were moving forward to help Cory up and the older guy said, "Jesus Christ, can't you see the kid's upset?" and Bakalov pulled out his pistol and asked the man if he wanted to say anything else. The older guy stared at Bakalov for a few seconds, muttering, offering a hand up to Cory and then walking away, leaving Cory wiping the blood from the corner of his mouth and staring down at the snow.

Bakalov said, "Now, stop wasting time and give me your report."

Cory, speaking slowly, said, "Sir, the bodies of the men, the men left behind on the track, well, it's wolves. Lots of wolves. I took the waste buckets to dump, went up along the railway like you told me, and, well, you know the guys who, uh, well," Cory seemed scared to use the word 'died,' and finally said, "who didn't make it today? It was them, there was wolves all over them. Like eating them. They were, they were snarling and, so many of them, I don't know," Cory ending with, "I never even seen a wolf before."

"But you are here now."

"Well, yeah, but..."

"So they did not attack you, try to kill you?"

Cory hesitated. "Well, no, but they were eating the guys..."

"And the waste buckets? What did you do with the waste buckets?"

"What?"

"The waste buckets, where are they?"

"Well I dropped them when I ran..."

"You never run from a predator. They could catch you. Easily."

"Well, yeah, I guess, but anyway, I did."

A voice from the crowd asked, "Maybe we should bury the bodies, eh? The bodies could be attracting the wolves."

Bakalov said, "It is a waste of time and energy." Bakalov could sense fear through the whole crowd. These men knew nothing of survival. Of predator and prey. But they would learn. He added, "And there will be predators out here, it is to be expected."

One of the younger guys said, "I've read that wolves don't hunt people. There's only been a few reports of them attacking people..."

"Is that what you have read, young man?" Bakalov asked. "I tell you right now, wolves will hunt anything if they are hungry enough."

There was a murmuring around the fire, and one of the guys said, "I worked in bush camps my whole life, never had any problems with wolves. Put your hand on the doorknob to go outside, they heard you. Gone. Like they'd never even been there."

"Maybe they were not hungry enough, then. There was a time, back home in the winter, the wolves got hungry, very hungry, formed into what the newspapers called these super packs." Bakalov paused, then continued, "There were reports from some villages of four hundred of them. Four hundred wolves in a pack."

"Four hundred?" the bush worker said. "That's unbelievable."

"That is the wolf. It will do what it needs to do. So will I." Then Bakalov pointed at Cory, "Go back and get the waste buckets."

"What?"

"Go get the waste buckets. We brought exactly what we needed, no more, no less. Those are the waste buckets for boxcars five and six. Go get them."

Cory just stood and stared at Bakalov, not knowing what to do. Bakalov said, "Take two others with you."

Cory looked around, no one meeting his gaze, and said, "What if no one will come?"

"They will go, pick two." But Cory didn't want to pick anyone because it seemed wrong; what, pick two guys to go get eaten by wolves?

A guy from Cory's boxcar said he'd go with him, then two brothers who were from a farm that used to have apple orchards and peaches said they'd go, too, but Bakalov said, "Decide amongst yourself, but I said three are going. So it is three."

The oldest brother said he'd go and he asked the crowd if anyone had a big flashlight to spare and someone passed his over and the three started out, Bakalov calling after them, "Any of you know how to shoot?"

The boy from the peach farm said he did. Bakalov tossed a gun to him and said, "Bring me back a few of those wolves."

"What? Are you kidding?"

Bakalov didn't answer, the younger brother saying, "We killed small things, never anything like a wolf."

"Killing is killing," Bakalov said, watching the older boy holding the gun as he stepped back a foot or so. Bakalov asked, "Are you thinking about shooting me?"

The brother looked up in a panic. "No. No. I wasn't."

Bakalov laughed, "Good, good for you to not think about trying to shoot me. Your brother will be happy you stay alive. But if it was me? I would have thought about it. I would have done it. And that is why you will carry the waste bucket and I won't. Now go get me a wolf."

Chapter Twenty-One

Larose hauled open the large metal doors of the work bay and said, "Looks like a fucking curtain of doom out there."

A thin line of turquoise along the horizon seemed to be all that was standing between them and a monster bank of ashen clouds that looked ready to fall from the sky and swallow everything right down to the ground. Still, Slaught was eager to get going. He'd slept a good twenty-four hours and was feeling rested. But also felt like it was no time to be sleeping his days away. They had trouble coming and they needed an idea of how big and bad that trouble was going to be. They had decided to head back down towards the outpost and see if they could get close to the train tracks, see if there was any activity. See if the train really was going to push up into the Territories. Or if it already had.

"That's unusually poetic for you, Harv."

"Fuck you, Chum, it's a bad looking sky."

Slaught followed their gaze upwards, thinking yeah, maybe bad, but also beautiful. Maybe that's just how things were going to be: unsettled, at odds, like the wind that felt both warm and cold, blowing in from the east. Waking up in the morning, groggy, bone tired and disoriented, he thought he was back in the jail. He sprang up, ready to get moving, but then his brain caught up with his body. Susun asked, "Everything okay?" and he smiled, glad at how familiar she felt and how different now, too. That contradiction again. And he thought maybe he was just too lucky. Was that something you could be? Too lucky?

"Hey, Johnny," Larose gave him a friendly shove, "stop day dreaming, let's get a move on." Slaught said he was just enjoying the moment, and Larose said, "See, told you, Chum, he went soft in jail. Who fucking goes soft in jail? Jesus."

Their plan was to ride south along the old highway then cut across country to the rail line that ran parallel to it, hoping if they went far enough south they'd at least know how much time they had left. They rode for almost an hour and by the time they decided to turn in towards the railway tracks, the sky was spitting down snow, stinging their faces. Chumboy slowed, stopping his machine and waiting as Johnny and Larose pulled up beside him.

"Should almost be on top of it. I'm thinking over there," he said, pointing to a huge mound of snow. "Looks like that's not any natural snowbank."

Larose was shaking his head, "They couldn't be all the way here already?"

"Only one way to find out," Slaught said, and headed towards where the railway tracks ran through the bush. As they got close, they couldn't see the tracks, huge snowbanks blocking their view. They clambered up and were now staring down a snow tunnel carved out along the tracks for the train.

Larose said, "Jesus, they're really doing it. Opening it up. That's fucked up."

"Means we passed them on the way down," Slaught said. "They're closer than I thought they'd be."

Chumboy said, "Looks like they did it by hand."

"Impossible. All the way from the City?" Larose shook his head. "It would take forever."

"It'd be some slogging, eh?" Slaught said. "What a crazy ass undertaking."

Larose, "No way, I'm telling you, it's impossible."

"Maybe," said Chumboy, "but maybe not. It's been done. An emergency rescue of a boat. Place called Robin Hood's Bay, in England. Cool name, right? Anyway, some ship was in trouble, big winter storm blowing through. Water was too choppy and they couldn't get out to the ship. So they had to haul some big ass lifeboat overland in a snowstorm. Six miles in snow, snow this deep. Maybe even deeper. Took them something like two hours."

Larose said, "How many of them?"

"Everyone and their brother and sister. Two hundred of them came out to help. Think they had horses, too, though."

"England doesn't get snow. You're giving me bullshit here."

"I'm telling you, it was a snowstorm. Late 1800s. Maybe the weather was different then, like it's different now."

Slaught was trying to picture it, first the crowd of people in England, with their caps and horses and shovels. But then thinking of the men here, on this railway. In the cold. Maybe this is where he would have been headed if he'd still been in the Facility. Been one of the guys breaking up the snow ahead of the train. Or tending to the plow mounted on the front of the train.

Slaught dropped down onto the tracks, turned and looked back the way the train had come, and saw the two bodies slumped over each other lying on the track about twenty feet back.

"Guys," Slaught said, pointing up the track, "looks like we got casualties."

They moved slowly towards the two men laid out on the track, a blue tarp shredded and lying a few feet away. Three ravens perched on top of the bodies.

"They look pretty chewed up," Slaught said, edging closer, one of the ravens hopping up a few feet away to the top of the snowbank. "Should we bring them back with us?"

"I don't know Johnny," Larose said, "not like we can do anything for them."

Slaught said, "We should at least try and figure out how they died. Who they were."

"Maybe they were making a break for it," Larose said. "Fed up with working for the railway."

"Wouldn't blame them, not in this weather," Slaught said, now pushing through the heap of snow on the tracks, the ravens disturbed and flapping away to settle on the snowbank farther down.

Chumboy watched as Slaught patted down the bodies. "Anything?"

"Nothing." Slaught just shook his head, standing then and looking down the railway track to the north. "They're from the Facility," he said.

"Yeah? How can you tell?"

"The crappy way they're dressed. Everything, the coat, the pants, their skin, everything turns grey, or whatever the fuck that colour is after you've been in there too long."

"Quite the operation, pushing all the way up here," Chumboy said, looking at the gouges along the snow wall that lined both sides of the train track. "Over there, looks like maybe they're working with some sort of plow on the front of the train, but still, must be slow going. I'm surprised they're this far."

The three stood in silence staring down the tracks. The ravens were calling, impatient, and Chumboy said, "Best leave them to it, in case they're calling their bigger buddies back."

"Wolves?"

"Yeah, there's tracks all through the underbrush back the way we came in. Ravens making quick work of it. Means they got muscle helping them."

"Feels weird just leaving these guys out here."

"Can't bring them back, got no sleds, don't even have tarps with us. But we should come back."

"Yeah, we should," Slaught said, taking a last look back at the grime and blood on the men's coats. He headed back down the tracks and then up over the snowbank and back through the snow to their snow machines.

Slaught glanced over at Chum, sitting quiet on his sled, staring up into the sky that was now completely sealed over with grey. He was watching a few of the ravens flying overhead, cawing back and forth to each other. Slaught asked, "Thoughts?"

"Weather's turning."

"Like literally, now, or like, in a bigger way?"

"Both."

"Well let's get moving then," Slaught said. "Not sure what this train is bringing but it feels bad out here."

Two more ravens came swooping in low over them, raising a ruckus and settling high up on a nearby birch. Slaught said, "They want us out of here."

"Telling us how it is," Chumboy said.

"Yeah? What are they saying?"

"That bad weather and big trouble are blowing in."

"Christ almighty," Larose said, "I'm out here with two fucking Doctor Dolittles."

൞

Love had never killed anything before. It was hard to know what to expect. What he didn't want, more than anything, was to fail. Not in front of Bakalov's crew.

He had started preparing months ago. Kept it to himself. Knew everyone would only laugh about it. The nerd trying to man-up. That was okay. He knew how change came. Hours and hours of practice. Dedication. Focus. And he had focus. So he began regular training. Down to the shooting range to work on his comfort level, his marksmanship. His instructor said he had a natural ability; Love attributed his accuracy to his video game experience. He'd had lots of that. Why not learn the real thing? Couldn't hurt to know how to shoot. Should've learned a long time ago. And the rest of them, the ones that couldn't believe it was him, Eton Love, that ended up at the top of the food chain at Talos? Well, wouldn't they be surprised.

And now he had a chance to surprise Bakalov as well. Preparing for the Expedition, Ion had reassured him, saying his Twenty were coming along, their hunting skills improving, and Love had said, "Maybe some time I'll come on one of your hunts." That in itself had surprised Bakalov. "Into the outdoors?" he had asked.

So now here they were, in the outdoors, Love's feet cold, his hands cold; he even felt the cold spreading across his back. He was bored, too. It was taking too long. Love thought about his train, of the need to look in on the cartographers, see how they were doing. Then stopped himself. It was about discipline. About trying to still his mind. Quieting all of the thoughts that were distracting. Because this was important. Time to focus his energies.

"See, see them there?' Bakalov whispered in the cold, the two men crouched down behind the blind. Bakalov pointed. "There."

And yes, Love thought he could see them, shapes against the tree trunks and snow.

Love said, "It seems far away. How far is that? Two hundred yards?"

"Yes, but you could try," Bakalov said. "Or wait, see, maybe they are coming in closer."

"Could you hit it at that range?"

"Yes, yes, of course, but you are a beginner. Better to wait and get the shot."

"Maybe," said Love, staring through the scope at the wolves. He was watching the wolves but feeling the presence of the young men some ten yards back in the second blind, watching and waiting. Judging. He needed to think only of the wolves. "Wait, they're leaving."

"Yes, they're on the move."

"I don't want to lose them, they could get into the trees. There were six, and now I can only see three."

"You want to wait, or try now?"

"I prefer to shoot now."

"Okay, it might be too far, but be ready," said Bakalov. "Be ready for the blast."

Love felt anxious, feeling the bulk of Bakalov next to him. Perhaps today was not the day. No, today had to be the day. His chance to start laying the ground work. Start wooing the Twenty. Since they had left the City he had felt the power shifting, Bakalov asserting himself more and more. Love knew he had to put an end to that. So, focusing, thinking back, hearing the voice of his instructor telling him about watching, about patience.

His eyes strained through the dim. Searched the tree line, three hundred yards away. Then looked back to the bait. Nothing there, just the winter snow now turning blue. The wind was light, he shouldn't have to worry about the wolves catching his scent. So where were they? He shifted his gaze to his right.

Slight movement.

He held his breath, tried to slow his heart, swallowed slowly. Right in front of him, not sixty yards away, a small dun wolf. Too close, maybe. Bakalov's sharp intake of breath as he clocked her as well. Love steeled himself, counting now, one thousand and one, seeing only fur up close, too close, one thousand and two, and he caught the animal in his crosshairs. Felt the slightest movement from Bakalov. Was he going to try for her? Focus. Slowly, one thousand and three, adjusting the scope, settling on a spot just behind her left shoulder as she stopped, sensing something hidden. Love released the safety, exhaling. Pulled the trigger.

And the wolf was down on the snow.

Ion said, "Oh, good shooting, good shooting. Congratulations."

Love started to breathe again, took another quick look through the scope. Yes, it was there, unmoving. "Not bad for a beginner, eh, Ion?"

And Ion said, "Very good. Very good, Commander." Love wondered about Bakalov's reaction, genuinely glad. Proud maybe? Bakalov turned to the young men, yelled, "Come on. Go get his wolf. Bring it in, we will show the trophy to everyone. Hurry."

And with that, with the sound of the men talking to each other, the howling started. First one wolf, then many, loud enough to give the group of young men pause, quieting down a bit and hurrying, weapons ready just in case. Bakalov watched until they reached the carcass, then asked, "How did it feel, your first kill, Commander?"

"Exactly like I thought it would, Bakalov."

Fucking amazing.

ॐ

"Good Christ, what is with this fucking commotion?" Tiny asked as he came into his kitchen.

It was Susun's map they were all talking about, spread out on the kitchen table, everyone staring at it. Susun had asked Johnny to meet her in the kitchen, and to bring along Chumboy. She thought she had made some progress in drawing her map. But word spread fast and it seemed like half the damned community was crowded into the kitchen.

Susun, self-conscious, had unrolled the map slowly and everyone was leaning in to get a better look. And then dead silence as they all stared at it. Then everyone started talking at once.

Tiny spoke up again, "C'mon, no offence Susie, but what's the big deal? I mean, you say it's a map? Of what? I can't even tell what it is, doesn't look like any map I've ever seen."

"Gotta agree with Tiny a bit here," Shaun said. "Can you explain what it means?"

Susun was staring at it, too, Slaught thinking she had the same expression as everyone else. Clueless. She said, "How would I know?"

"Well Susie," Tiny said, "if you don't know, who would?"

"I'm drawing what I see."

"Hey, I like it," said Jordan. "Looks like... you know... the ear guy."

Chumboy said, "Van Gogh?"

"Yeah, that guy."

Susun, not annoyed, more curious, wondering at the map, at all of them staring down at it like it could reveal some impossible truth, said, "Maybe it's not finished yet. I think there is more detail that I can't quite reach, in my head, you know, when I go to try and remember what it was like. But those are the colours. And the basic shapes . . . I think."

"Oh come on, you guys," Max sounded frustrated. "What are you going to find with this map. If it even is a map."

"Whoa up there, Max, why don't you just hitch your harshness to the post and listen to Susie for a while," Chumboy said. "Might learn something."

Max was speaking up more and more, Susun thought. Asserting himself? She said to him, "Auntie Verla thinks my dreams about the map might be important."

Max sighed, "Important. Right. Of all the problems we have."

Slaught, ignoring Max, said, "I see blue and brown. That right? Like land and water?"

She looked at him. "You guys asked me to draw what I saw."

"Just trying to understand," he said. "Do you think it's a map of here?"

"Oh, well, yeah, I think so."

"How could it be a map of here? Are you guys even looking at the same thing I'm looking at?" Max asked.

Susun, glancing up from the map to Max, said, "I can see you don't see things the same way I do, but for me, this map is important, these dreams I'm having, they give me this awful sense of urgency."

She could see he was angry about it all, but she could also see he was thinking about it, trying to piece things together. She said to Slaught, "So yeah, the blue is water. Those browns and greens, I think they're land, don't know why they're different. And this here in the middle?" she said, pointing to a blue patch, "It's the lake."

"Lake Timiskaming?"

She hesitated. "It's hard to explain. Like it's sort of Lake Timiskaming but it's also all lakes, know what I mean?"

"Not a clue, Susie," Tiny said.

She frowned, staring at it. "When it looks like this, on paper, it's different. In the dream, it's moving, layered somehow, blues and greens and things moving below the surface of the map, like it's alive." She paused, shaking her head, "Christ, I don't know guys, I don't know what it means."

Jordan said, "I think it's beautiful."

"That it is," said Slaught. "And the yellow and gold along the edges? Stars?"

Susun nodded, then shrugged, suddenly wanting to roll the map back up, protect it from the questions.

"Are those animals? On the green parts there? Looks a bit like those crazy medieval maps," Jordan said. "Oh, yeah, and I mean crazy in like the best possible way."

"It's okay, Jordan, I know it's a little out there, and I'm not the best artist, but it's a start. I'm having trouble with them, the creatures I told you about, Tiny. These strange creatures, can't quite hold them in my head long enough to see what they really look like."

Slaught said, "Well, we got to figure this business out one way or another, and this is a good start." He stared hard at it, concentrating, like he was trying to pull some meaning out of it, then he said, "Having two maps, that's what's so tangled up about this whole thing."

"These maps, could be a coincidence?" Tiny said.

"You think so? Chumboy asked.

Tiny hesitated, then asked, "How could it not be a coincidence? This guy is way down in the City. And then Susie's weird dreams. I mean come on. It doesn't make any sense."

Chumboy said, "You got to watch for the signs, Tiny."

"Susie's not that fucking Nostradamus guy now, is she? She's from Larder Lake for Chrissakes."

Susun said, "I'm not trying to predict the future, Tiny."

"Well then how does all of this work?" Tiny asked, sounding frustrated. "What difference does it make if we have our map and they have theirs?"

"A good map shows you how to get somewhere, right?" Chumboy said. "But there is always more than one way."

"But there's always one way that's better," Tiny said. "You know, the one that's faster, the one that doesn't take you through the swamp. The one that doesn't get you lost."

"Right," Chumboy said, "but maps can show you different things. Like maybe one shows you how to get from A to B by the fastest route. But another one might show you where certain plants grow, know what I mean? And other maps show who possesses what, like after the war when they carve things up. Wasn't like the land or the trees or the birds changed. Just some lines on the map."

Jordan said, "So like, what I'm wondering, you know, like, if there are these two maps, and then there's an epic map duel, how does one map win?"

"That," said Chumboy, "is an interesting question."

"Not sure we can figure anything out until it's finished. That's how I feel, anyway," Susun said.

"When's that gonna be?" Tiny asked.

"It's not like pay-per-view, Tiny. They're dreams. And I haven't had the dream in a few days."

"Well are you sleeping okay?"

"Yeah, but I think I'm trying too hard."

"Have to let it come to you?" Chumboy said.

"Yeah, something like that."

Tiny said, "For Chrissakes, if I find Susie some of that sleepy time fucking tea would all of youse get out of my kitchen?"

Chapter Twenty-Two

Larose said, "Should we be letting folks know?"

"Probably, Harv," Slaught said.

Jeff said, "And like, what do we tell people, uh, head for the hills, Talos is coming to map out the north?"

"No kidding," Larose said. "A map is a hard sell as a bogeyman."

Slaught said, "That may be, but we've got ourselves some serious trouble on the way—no doubt that iron horse chugging up the rails is loaded to the gills with men and guns."

"And mapping is a deadly serious business," Chumboy said. "This guy Love? He isn't coming up here to tell folks what's here, he's coming up to tell them what's going to be here."

"And what's that?" Larose asked.

"Guys like Love have one way of looking at things. They only see what they can take. That's what the land looks like to them. It's always the same story. We wanted our avocados and our big screens and our smartphones. And we wanted them no matter what it took. So this new guy driving his iron horse up here? He'll be like all the others, because their imagination's are stunted. Can't see anything that's really old or really new. Just trapped in the same old capitalist bullshit. So he isn't going to see rocks or rivers or trees. He can only see mines, hydro, timber."

"That's what we had here before, Chum, case you didn't notice."

Chumboy said, "Been noticing the consequences of that for the past few years, Harv."

"Right," said Larose, "but I mean, me working at the mine didn't bring on the apocalypse."

"No, our appetites did."

"You know, I've been thinking about that a lot," Slaught said, "and it was like we always wanted more. You know, I'd have a sled. Good sled. But I'd want the newest one. But then I'd get that and you know what? I'd want the next newest one. Looking back, it seems pretty fucked up to me. And now I can't remember why I always wanted another one."

"That's Capitalism 101, buddy, it can't survive without growth," Chumboy said. "Always has to eat more and more."

Larose asked, "Having a hard time following you here, Chum."

"What I'm saying, Harv, is that the train headed our way has got capitalism sticking to it like a zebra mussel."

Larose stared at Chumboy. "Yeah, made things crystal fucking clear, Chum."

Chumboy shrugged, smiling, and said, "Sorry, Harv, guess all we really need to agree on here is that we need to let folks know that the train is coming our way."

"Yeah, see, *that* I understand," Larose said, "and I can do something about that, too, right? Can't do anything about these zebra mussels or your capitalist stew or fucking Armageddon, but I can warn folks."

"See, we can find common ground, Harv," said Chumboy. "Ain't friendship a beautiful thing? Now who is going to sound the alarm for these folks?"

"Well, there aren't even that many folks to contact," Larose said, "but getting to them is going to be a pain in the ass. Trails were better when the weather was cold. Now with the melting and freezing, the wind, the trails are soggy, some just plain erased. It'll be tough-going."

"How many folks, do we know?" asked Slaught.

Jeff said, "Right, so the Donnells, the ones north of here? They're staying put. They got a few animals, couple of goats and a pig, don't want to leave them on their own. Said they're seeing wolves like never before, more coyotes, too, and didn't want to leave their animals behind. I know we missed some south of here, folk who are closer to Latchford than us. Shaun went over to get McLaren, said he'd know who was still out that way."

"I haven't seen McLaren for a while," Slaught said. "Not since I've been back."

"He moved out."

"He what?"

"Moved out. Set up camp across the lake, said it was getting too crowded in here."

"Well he ain't fucking wrong," said Tiny. "Bad enough feeding the bunch of youse but seeing the way those freeloaders tuck in around here, God almighty."

Slaught said there shouldn't be any freeloaders, everybody could contribute something, and Tiny said he'd never seen a bunch of more unskilled, lazy, unmotivated shitbirds in his entire life, didn't know where they were all coming from.

"You calling me a shitbird?" McLaren asked as he came into the kitchen, pausing to stomp the snow off his boots. "Good to have you back Johnny, heard you wanted a word with me," he said.

"Glad to be back."

"So what's this all about then? I got things to be doing out there, can't stand around yakking with you boys all day."

"Yeah, sorry about that, and thanks for coming by," Slaught said.

"Now what's this I hear about more trouble?"

"Talos kind of trouble," Slaught said. "Looks like a mittful of trouble is heading our way."

"Talos again? Thought we sent them packing."

"Guess they have a new guy at the helm. New guy, new trouble."

"Same outfit? That Black woman involved this time?"

"No, don't think so. Well not with Talos, anyway," Jeff said. "But it's always complicated with her."

McLaren snorted. "She's a bad one. Gotta watch her."

Slaught said, "Ain't that the truth. Anyway, we don't have a firm timeline on the trouble but it's soon enough. Trying to reach out to folks who might want to hunker down with us. Got the brick and cement here. Makes it easier to keep track of folks, keep 'em out of trouble. Stick together."

"Okay, I consider myself warned. Might come by, might not."

"Fair enough. Any thoughts on who might still be out there?" Jeff asked, passing him the list of names they'd come up with so far. "We only got a few days, maybe not even that."

"There's the folks down by the dam. A pair of young lads, an old guy, like me, and a couple, maybe in their fifties. Swiss, I think. Hippies, you know the type. Good folks."

"Okay, well, we got loads on our plate right now but one or two of us should head down there," Slaught said.

"Wish those Talos boys would just park their goddam sleds down in the City and stay put," said McLaren. "Seems like they can't help themselves but cause heartache for us up here."

"They're not coming on sleds."

"I'll tell you right now they can't get up that road without a sled," McLaren said.

"You're right about that. That's why they're coming on the train."

"The train? God almighty." McLaren said. "I remember back when they stopped that damn train. Goddam government. We fought like hell to get it back. And now this."

Slaught said the irony wasn't lost on him, either, but there it was. And that Chumboy figured they were coming to open up the mines, hoping maybe the weather was warming up and there might be money to be made up here again.

"Always about that almighty dollar, eh, lads? Well, alright then. If you need me, you know where to find me. But I gotta run, your good woman is waiting on me."

"Susun?"

"You got another one? If you do, you're a fool."

Slaught asked, "What are you two up to?"

"Building moose yards. Making a buffet for those skinny bastards knocking around out there in the snow. Ain't too many of them left, either. Snow's deep as sin, can't get anywhere. So Susun and me, we been hauling aspen and willow branches for them to nibble on. Cedar, too. Putting it down by the lake where they can get to it."

"Yeah?"

"Well they're going to starve otherwise, or get eaten by the coyotes or wolves—they're pretty hungry, too. Dammit, we're all hungry."

"We surely are," Slaught said. "And good luck, tell her not to overdo it out there."

"You try telling her anything. Stubborn as her cousin. Well, truth is, all the Latours, stubborn bunch."

McLaren disappeared down the hallway and was gone a few

seconds before he stuck his head back into the kitchen.
"Hemingway."
Slaught and Jeff looked at him. Jeff said, "The writer?"
"Yeah, that's right, the writer."
"What about him?"
"Well, don't know what book it is, but one of them. That's what we should do, do it now."
"Do what?"
"Well, what d'ya think? Blow up the goddam railway bridge by the dam. That'll put a stop to that train."

༙

"*For Whom the Bell Tolls*," Chumboy said. "Gotta say, little disappointed in myself for not thinking of that. Should have been the first thing that came to mind."
So they called everyone together to talk it over. Most folks came, crowding into the dining room. One or two guys banged their tables, calling out, "Bring a round here," joking around, reminding everyone that back in the day this was a favoured spot for a cold brew on a warm day. Imagine that.
"Whoa, blow up the bridge!" Jordan said. "That's a bold move, because, like, it works both ways right? Like they can't get here, but then we don't get to leave, either. Know what I mean? We're going to be trapped."
"Well, no, we wouldn't be trapped," Jeff said, "not really. We can take the actual bridge. The railway bridge is separate."
Jordan said, "You mean there's two bridges there? Man, that's weird."
Slaught commented, "Think you've ridden over both, Jordie."
Jordan said, "Whatever, man. Still, why do you need so many bridges?"

"You're over thinking it," Slaught replied.

Susun, perched on the old bar, raised her voice to get everyone's attention. People settled down as they noticed she was trying to speak. "Okay folks. We got trouble again."

Then folks really quieted down. Relieved that Johnny was back, everyone just wanted things to get back to normal. Looked like that wasn't in the cards.

"So, first, I wanted to thank everyone for helping out while Johnny was away. The support was great. You guys are great. And now we are going to have to step up again. We're about to have some more trouble with Talos."

A groan went through the crowd, a couple of folks asking if they were serious, how could that be? Didn't those people know when to stop?

"So as far as we know, they're coming at us this time with the train. And maybe the army."

That generated a round of chatter and cursing. Susun had to wait until the voices settled down, some at the back still talking about it when she said, "We have a plan, but we want to make sure everyone's good with the idea. As far as we can tell, the train right now is somewhere between the outpost and here. It's moving slow, they're clearing the track as they go, so we know we have probably a couple of days until they're on our doorstep. At the most."

"So how many are coming?" It was Shaun asking, standing at the back, holding baby Gracie.

"Don't know. We haven't seen the train itself but we think—well Johnny's pretty sure—they're running it with ex-cons from the same place Johnny was held. So they could have lots of guys on board."

"Ballpark?"

Johnny said, "There were over three hundred guys in that place. I bet at least half of them, maybe more, are on board."

"Good Lord," Mrs. Merrill said, "sending a train full of hardened criminals up here? What next, the devil himself?"

"Well, Mrs. Merrill," Slaught said, "you gotta keep in mind that most guys in the Facility weren't there for killing anybody, or even hurting or robbing anyone. They were there because they were homeless or past curfew or any number of things. Like me. I didn't even know why I was there. So just to be clear, it ain't a trainload of bloodthirsty killers coming our way, just average joes being worked to death out there."

Shaun asked, "So what's the plan?"

Susun nodded to Johnny and said, "You guys cooked it up." So he stood up, wondering how many times they'd have to go through something like this—Talos coming over and over again to get that little piece of what they had. "Well, it was actually McLaren's idea and we gotta give him credit for fast thinking. So this is the idea: blow the railway bridge at Latchford. Train can't get through, then. Simple."

"They could come across on the other bridge. What about that? I say let's blow them all," Shaun said. "If it is getting warmer—and we are all thinking it is, but no one wants to say it—then what? If they can't get up here by train then maybe in six months, well, they might just be able to drive straight up. Then what happens to us?"

"We move home?" Mrs. Merrill said, craning her neck to get a good look at Shaun.

Shaun was shaking his head, "Talos isn't going to disappear overnight. I mean, give your head a shake. It'll be martial law, they'll be rounding people up. We know how this is going to go, look what we've seen of them already. I say blow both bridges and the fucking dam."

That sent the place into an uproar, some people trying to respond to Shaun, others just muttering to their neighbours or themselves. Some looking to him or Susun to settle things down.

Susun said, "Hang on a minute, folks. Shaun might be right—we just don't know what's going to happen, with the weather, with Talos. But for now we have to deal with what is right in front of us. Think this through properly. If we do decide to try and blow up the first bridge, we can see how it goes. Decide on the rest later."

Chumboy leaned into Slaught, whispered, "Sounds like she might be going all Baader Meinhof gang on us."

"Yeah, noticing that," he said. It was interesting to see that side of her.

"I guess basically we're buying ourselves some time," Susun said. "This guy Love who's running things now, we don't know much about him. It seems as though Talos is coming up on some sort of surveying effort, maybe taking a look at the resources up here. Because maybe, like Shaun says, the weather is changing. I think this expedition of theirs is a way of laying claim to things up here. Just in case it does warm up and it's a free for all, right?"

"What if they're coming to restore order?" Mrs. Merrill said, looking around now at the folks in the room. "That's possible. If the weather is changing, and they know it, they could be coming up here to make things like they were. Open the roads. Hospitals. Schools. Why don't we stop to consider that for a moment?"

There was silence.

Slaught glanced over at Susun, wondering if she was going to say anything, but she just shrugged.

Shaun said, "C'mon, you think Talos is coming up here and

is going to be all about peace, order and good government? Suddenly the train's going to roll into town and there'll be springtime and schools?" He turned to Slaught, "So, you've seen them up close, what do you think?"

And then feeling all eyes on him. Wanting to know. Up close? Was it as scary as they feared? He took a deep breath. "I figure the weather is going to do what it's going to do. Might warm up. Might just toss us back into a deep freeze. We don't know. And Talos? They're going to do what they're going to do, too. We can't stop Talos from being what it is. It's greedy. Guess that's in its DNA. But we can do something about ourselves. Come hell or deep freeze, we gotta figure out a way of being better. Of not making the same mistakes that got us all here in the first place. So I say we handle this jackpot the best way we can. By taking care of each other and looking out for this piece of land we found ourselves lucky enough to be living on. Buying ourselves some time is just the first step. But I think we need to take it."

"So we blow the bridge?" Shaun said.

Slaught said, "That's my thinking."

"How? How are you going to blow it up? When did you all become demolition experts?" Max asked, standing off to the side, seeming pissed, maybe just feeling left out of things.

"Well, we aren't experts. A few guys have some idea," Slaught said, "worked in the mines. McLaren for one knows his way around a stick of dynamite. And that's pretty much what we got to work with. And that's how they did it in the book."

"The book?" Max asked.

Chumboy said, "*For Whom the Bell Tolls.*"

Now there was general confusion until Jordan said, "Uh, wait a minute, guys, like yeah, they blow up the bridge. But, like, doesn't everyone in the book die?"

"You've read the book?" Tiny asked.

"Grade Ten English. Had to."

Max couldn't believe it, asked, "You're basing your plan on a story?"

"Well, it's a good story," Jordan said.

"It's not true, though," Max said, "it's made up."

"That is the nature of fiction," Chumboy said. "But it isn't as though no one has ever blown up a bridge."

Susun said, "Okay, well, although questions or comments about the merits of literature are fine, we really have to decide about this bridge business before we go any further. We don't have lots of time, we'd have to get right into it, see if it's even logistically possible." She glanced around the room, asked, "So, we going to try blowing the bridge?"

Tiny said, "I think I speak for everyone when I say blow up the damn thing. Blow it to kingdom come."

Chapter Twenty-Three

Most everyone had gone to bed. The general consensus had been that they had no choice but to try their hand at some kind of demolition if they were going to have any chance of slowing or stopping the train. They managed to round up several sticks of dynamite; McLaren wasn't certain it would do the trick but Chumboy said, "We're not blowing the Golden Gate Bridge," and McLaren said he was a man who favoured overkill but that Chumboy was probably right. McLaren also told them it might be safer to store the dynamite on the outskirts of the town overnight. Old dynamite could sweat, become unstable. First thing in the morning they'd head out, survey the bridge for the best place to set their charges, and then haul the dynamite from where they'd stashed it out to the bridge and then let 'er rip.

Tiny was thinking about tomorrow, figuring it was going to be a big day and he should get some rest. Just had a bit of cleaning to finish up. Rag in hand, he headed out to the dining room to wipe down the tables. Max was sulking at one of them. Tiny said, "You still up?"

"Couldn't sleep."

The kid looked tired. Worn out. Tiny knew Max had felt bad because of what happened down at the outpost. From what Jeff had told him, Johnny might not have gone missing if Max hadn't been such a goofball that day. "You look beat, why don't you hit the sack."

Max nodded and pulled himself up. "Yeah, might as well."

"Listen, Eeyore," Tiny said, "no point beating yourself up over this thing with Johnny. It's over. Johnny's back, it's over. But now we got trouble. We're all going to have to be paying attention to what's coming down those tracks. We're going to need everyone."

"Even a fuck-up like me?" Max sounded angry.

"We're all goddam fuck-ups, Max, or else none of us would be stupid enough to have gotten ourselves into this fucking no-win situation."

Max just nodded. The room was dark and quiet, and Tiny was thinking he liked this time of day, everyone upstairs sleeping, just him and the kitchen. Peaceful. And then there was a knock on the door.

Tiny and Max both stared at the door. Max said, "It's late for someone to be passing through."

Tiny said, "Should we get someone?"

"We can handle it."

Tiny hesitated, but then approached the door, peering out through it and Max said, "You know whoever's out there can see you doing that. You look like some nosy old lady."

"I don't give a good goddam what I look like, Max, I want to know what our late-night visitor looks like."

"Well?"

"He's alone. Young guy. Maybe bit older than you."

Another knock, the guy outside shouting through the door, "Hey, I'm a traveller, just passing through, can you let me in?"

Tiny sighed, "Feel funny letting this clown in now, everyone asleep."

"I don't mind staying up," Max offered, "to keep an eye on things."

Tiny sighed, but then nodded, pushed open the door a

crack, asked, "What's your name?"

"Collins, Mark Collins."

Tiny peered past him into the darkness outside, "Where's your sled?"

"Parked it up the street some. That okay with you?"

Tiny couldn't tell if the guy was being chippy or not, but said, "No matter, just come on in, Max here might be able to help you with a hot cup of tea, maybe the makings of a sandwich."

"I'd appreciate it," Collins said, stepping inside. He was a nervous, thin-faced guy, chin ending in a point, eyes small and darting around the room. Tiny thought he looked like a weasel. Didn't like this Mark Collins.

Tiny said, "Call me if you need anything, Max, you know where to find me."

Max said he'd be fine, told Mark to have a seat, he'd bring him a cup of tea.

Once Max sat down with Collins, the guy slipped a flask from inside his grimy coat, passed it to Max and said, "Here, have a swig. Way of showing my appreciation."

When he slipped out a few hours later, leaving Max face down on the table snoring, he knew everything he needed to know about the Wintermen.

ॐ

It was warm. That was the main thing Slaught was thinking about as he watched Shaun and Jeff slide down the bank of the Montreal river to find a place to set the charges under the railway bridge.

Susun was leaning against him. "Uncanny sky this morning, eh?" she said.

They'd left town just as the dark was beginning to thin out, the rising sun bloodying up the sky behind the bronchial tips of the birch and aspen stands. Now it was giving way to rose and golds.

Slaught looked up. "Beautiful up there. Too warm and sticky down here, though. Going to be a mess if it gets cold again."

A bunch of them had come out to take a look at the bridge while Jeff and McLaren figured out how best to go about blowing the damn thing up.

Slaught saw Max, standing not far away, looking a little worse for wear as everyone around him was watching and joking. Slaught said to Chumboy, "Max looks a bit beat but everyone else seems to be getting into the spirit of the project. It's turning out to be a real community builder."

Jeff and Shaun finished exploring under the bridge, the girders all rusted and peeling paint. Climbing up, Jeff said, "This rig's seen better days."

"That's an old timey beauty," McLaren said. "Hate to give 'er a good blast with our dy-no-mite but don't see any choice."

"Hope you know what you're doing," Slaught said to McLaren.

"'Course I do," he said. "Know all about this stuff."

Chumboy said, "If you pull out your Hemingway book for instructions I'm heading home."

Slaught laughed, thinking it was good to be out here, the sky now softening, filling with pale pinks and greys. Susun had moved to the bank of the river, looking to the south with the binoculars. Keeping a watch out.

"See anything?" he called to her.

She turned and came walking back towards him, pointing behind her saying, "Just lots of wolf tracks. Could be a good sign, the population coming back up."

Chumboy said, "Maybe, or maybe they're gathering. Sometimes packs work together when they need to."

"Think they're waiting for the train, too?" Slaught asked.

Chumboy said, "Well, leaving bodies behind like that? It's like they're dragging a ripe, dripping smorgasbord through the bush. That's something that would get a wolf's attention."

"Speaking of attention," Jordan said, "when are we blowing this thing up? I think we should wait, blow it as the train comes into view. It would be so dramatic."

"Not sure we're going for the high drama, here," Slaught said. "Just want to get the thing done and over with."

"But it's going to be some of our best work, don't you think? You can't go wrong with explosions. Always a crowd pleaser."

"If you say so, Jordie. The main thing is that it gets the job done. And I'd be just as pleased if they were as far away as possible when this thing goes. Might stop them from coming closer. So the sooner they know there's a problem, the better for us. They get too close, though, they might just decide to send their shock troops up the trail anyway on sleds."

"Well, then, let's stop standing around yakking," said McLaren, "and go get ourselves that dynamite."

They were feeling almost giddy as they headed back. It was warm, the wet of the snow making the tree trunks vivid, soft big snow drifting down, the whole landscape silver and greys and white. They were packed onto the sleds being dragged by Slaught and Shaun, joking and laughing, almost forgetting what they were up against.

Until the blast.

Hard to say what was happening exactly, Shaun nearly driving into Slaught's machine as up ahead they could see snow, rock and dirt shooting high up into the air, showering down and disappearing from sight.

Slaught and Shaun stopped, killed their engines. Sat staring up ahead, but now there was just silence.

Slaught said, "Was that our dynamite?"

"Jesus Murphy," said McLaren, "if it wasn't, then I think we're driving into World War Three."

ત્ર

When they got to the crater, Tiny and Larose were already there surveying the damage. Slaught stayed sitting on his snow machine, staring with disbelief into the gaping pit that had been blasted into the snow. Tiny said, "You realize you missed the fucking bridge, right?"

"Dammit," McLaren said, "I was worried it'd be unstable. But look there, that's one hell of a hole, might have done the job down at the bridge. That's a damn shame."

Jeff was up and off the sled, walking around the pit and shaking his head. "We could have been blown to bits moving this stuff."

"Well, don't have to worry about that now, do ya? Took care of itself." McLaren sounded a bit defensive.

"Not so sure about that," Larose said.

"Meaning what, Harv?" asked Slaught.

"Meaning I think someone took a shot at our dynamite. I'd swear I heard a rifle right before the blast."

All of them were staring down into the mess of snow and rock and dirt. The gaping hole was dark, jagged around the top.

Slaught said, "Well, guess you were right, McLaren, maybe we are heading into World War Three."

Chapter Twenty-Four

Bakalov knew which piece of information would be the most valuable to Commander Love. Which one would worry him the most. The two pieces of information had come to him from Jimmy. Jimmy said a buddy of his, Markie, had been doing some side work for Scott, Scott recruiting him to try and take out the Winterman back at the Facility. But his buddy started to have doubts about the whole thing when Scott had told him go up the road ahead of the train, right into the Winterman's home town, and find out the lay of land. Scott wanted him to ask questions about the gold. Markie went but then had second thoughts on the way back, thought Scott was acting weird, jumpy. So he came to Jimmy, told him all about it. And wanted to know if he could be one of the Twenty.

Bakalov asked Jimmy what he told this Markie, and Jimmy said he told him he was out of luck, that the Twenty didn't take no snitches. Told him if a guy couldn't be loyal and keep his mouth shut, he had no place in the Twenty.

Bakalov had said that was a good answer, that Jimmy was going to do well for himself. He was a smart boy. Told Jimmy, though, to maybe string him along, to tell him that he might have a chance at joining the Twenty.

Bakalov was now walking the length of the train to Commander Love's railcar, thinking over what he had just heard, trying to decide what to tell Commander Love first. He wanted the Commander to know how useful he was. To know he could handle things. Get things done.

It was sometimes difficult to know how to handle the Commander. Build him up, yes, the Commander loved flattery. Like his shooting. Bakalov realized now the man had outplayed him. Clearly he knew how to shoot. A lesson to Bakalov to never underestimate him. But also, something else to keep an eye on, that the Commander did not seem to be doing well on the expedition. Didn't seem to be sleeping. Dark circles under his eyes, more nervous. Paranoid.

The paranoia, though, had been there from the beginning. He would be trusting, then not trusting; agreeing then questioning. Always testing. Especially that lackey Scott. The Commander did not trust him. But then neither did Bakalov. And now he had proof the man could not be trusted.

He wasn't worried about Scott, though. Bakalov could feel his own power increasing the farther they got from the City. Bakalov sensed it, at night around the fire, his Twenty there, coming together, others wanting to join them. And seeing Scott, up at his window, way at the back of the train, isolated. He knew Scott sensed it, too. Reduced to making lists, asking for accounts of things. The last time he questioned Bakalov, asking, "I've noticed you've been giving out liquor at night, around your bonfires. That's not on the register. Where is it from?" Bakalov did not bother to tell Scott that each day he sent three men to raid along the route. The train made slow progress and his Twenty got bored, so he said, go find what you can, share it with the group. He told Scott to keep his nose in his books, not in other people's business. "It's mine, that's all you need to know." Scott had said, "You don't understand, Bakalov. Out here, everything belongs to Talos." Bakalov had leaned into Scott and said, "Not me." And Scott didn't say anything. Bakalov knew then that Scott could only watch from his window.

No, Scott did not worry him. But the Commander, he had to be handled more carefully. Would take longer. But he only had so much time. The time of the Expedition. He had to go back to the City as a different man. He would not go back as the Dogman, as the rat killer. He would not do that.

So he decided to start with the bridge.

"Ion, what is on your mind today?"

The windows of the Commander's railcar were streaked with condensation. The plush chairs, the cleanliness of it. The small stove radiating heat. Too soft for Bakalov.

"Tomorrow morning we will be ready to cross the bridge. After that we have only a short distance to our beachhead."

"Yes, Ion, I am well aware of that," he said, pointing at the big map behind him, where he marked off their progress at the end of each day.

It was a ritual: Bakalov would come in, and the cartographers would already be there, going back and forth between their own railcar and the Commander's. They lived and worked in the railcar directly behind Love's. The Commander wanted them close by, protected and able to work around the clock if they had to. Bakalov would stop and visit the mapmakers, bring in field reports, then go and give the Commander the update on the day. And then the Commander would point on the map and say, "This is where we are." Bakalov wondered about that. Love rarely left his boxcar; maybe he really didn't know where they were without the map. Bakalov asked one evening, "Do you use the existing place names?" and Love had said, "There are none, Ion. You should understand that. The places don't exist until they are on my map."

Love was looking at him expectantly. Bakalov said, "Of

course you are aware, Commander, of course. But I wanted to report the successful resolution of a problem."

"A problem? Ahead of us?"

"Yes. The villagers, the ones with the Winterman. They tried to blow the bridge. Thought they could stop us."

"Blow it up?"

"Yes."

"Well, well, aren't they an unfriendly bunch. And so what have you done about it?"

"Destroyed their dynamite."

"Good. Good for you. But this is a serious business, this blowing up of bridges. There will have to be repercussions."

Yes, we will deal with them once we take their village."

"And how did you find out?"

"A source. Someone from inside the Wintermen."

"Really?" Love asked, now sounding suspicious. "And have you been cultivating sources?"

"Not me, Commander—Mr. Scott. But his man approached one of my Twenty, confided in him, said he was worried about Mr. Scott's stability."

"How complicated," Love said. He paused to think about it, then added, "And maybe best kept between ourselves at this point."

"That is what I thought."

"Good for you, Ion, good for you. Always thinking, aren't you. So, then, nothing to worry about?"

"Well, sir, I have found out something that is maybe more serious."

Commander Love positioned himself behind his desk, leaning back. "Yes, what is it, Ion?"

"The same informant, he has said there is another map."

Love sat up, leaning forward, his expression now wary.

"What do you mean, 'another map'?" he asked.

"The people here, sir, they are making their own map."

Bakalov knew Love would be angry, but it was so fast, so intense, that he thought for a moment that maybe he shouldn't have told the man. Love, face ashen, spitting his words, said, "There is. One. Map. Only. One map. I have the map. I create the map. I have a dream of the Domain. My map is *my* dream."

"I know, sir."

"Who? Who is making this map? To what end?"

"We are trying to find out now, sir, but there is a woman. And she had a dream, too."

Commander Love stared at Ion for a few seconds, thinking, then said, "That is not possible. There cannot be two maps."

Ion said nothing, waiting with his hands behind his back. Seeing what the man would say.

"Find her."

"I'm already looking."

He seemed calmer then. "What would I do without you, Ion?"

"You will never have to find out, sir."

As he left, he thought what he'd said was true: he would never abandon Love while he was still Commander. But what if the man wasn't Commander anymore? That would be different.

৵

The train had come to a stop just over the bridge and was now sitting there.

"For Chrissakes what's taking so long?" Mitch asked.

"Stop with the pacing, it's not helping," Scott said. It had been a long night, Black up every half hour and at the window, now pacing and filling the railcar with all her fucked up, nervous energy. He'd spent the evening before badgering Mitch about the gold but she'd hardly spoken a word, just telling him to shut up and settle down or she'd be tossing him out into the night. He'd gone along with her, didn't have much choice and he might be able to use her. No point pissing her off too much. And he was having his doubts now about Collins; figured the little bastard was holding out on him. He needed someone in his corner.

"It's the only way to stay fucking warm in this shithole of yours," she said.

Scott tried seeing out the window but the frost was thick on the inside. He scraped off a small section of the ice, peered out again. "Christ, all hell is breaking loose out there, tents going up, trucks and supplies being unloaded..."

Mitch said, "So get out there and find out what's going on."

"Not until you tell me where the gold is. There's no other reason for you to be on this fucking train."

"I'm here for the scenery."

"So did you stash some of it in the town?"

"Nope. Don't have it."

"Bullshit."

"I don't. And I'm figuring right now that you do. Or at least you know where it is."

Scott stared at her. "Well if you don't have it, and I don't have it, where is it?"

She just shrugged and said nothing.

Scott said, "Maybe your Wintermen are holding on to it for you?"

She shook her head, "Don't think so. But I'm having a hard time believing you didn't get your dirty little mitts on it. I figure that's what you were doing when you tried sneaking off the train near the outpost. Going to repo your stash and hightail it down south."

"I told you, I don't have it. And now it seems that you probably don't have it, either. So I have to ask you, was there even any gold to begin with? Did you find it?"

"You know, I'm not interested in having this conversation. I want to know why we're stopped."

"You're not getting off that easy."

Mitch moved in fast and hard, shoving her gun through the thin down of Scott's coat. "Get the fuck out there and find out what's going on. Levi will go with you. And no bullshit out there."

"Well, you haven't fucking changed," he said.

She pushed him backwards. "Don't forget it."

"Why not work together?" Scott said. "If you and I don't have it, let's find it together, just like we planned in the beginning. Find the gold, get the hell out of here."

"You're getting ahead of yourself. Just get out there and find out how long we're here for and what's next."

He gestured at Levi. "What's wrong with him?"

Mitch said, "What? Nothing's wrong with him. What the fuck is wrong with you?"

Scott staring at Levi. "He seems off to me. Doesn't talk or anything."

"Well you talk too fucking much," she said. "Now get your ass out there."

"Fine," he said, "I'm going, just trying to decide who to talk to."

"What about your little snitch."

"Collins? No, I had the impression he's gone over to the dark side."

"Bakalov?"

Scott nodded, "These young guys, just can't resist the lure of wolf pelts and guns."

"Yeah, what's that about?"

"Bakalov's so-called Twenty, his private pack of shitheads. You got to watch them, they're nasty little pricks. And armed."

"Well just get the fuck out there and ask someone."

Scott turned to Levi and said, "Just stay out of sight, keep your head down and follow my lead. Got it?"

Levi's expression didn't change, but Mitch said, "Don't worry about him. But if you go off script, this guy? He'll shoot you there and then. And anyone else he can. But he'll get you first."

Scott stepped out into the cold, amazed again at what an operation Love had pulled off. Already there was a row of three big military tents set up, a cook stove sending up smoke from one of them. Men were out with shovels, looking grim but doing their work, clearing paths around the train.

Scott found Jimmy Mumford minding one of the big fire barrels. "Mr. Mumford," he said, "how are you doing? Getting everything you need?" Scott sounded friendly, and felt almost boisterous. With Black in the picture there was a chance he could get this whole thing back on track. He just needed to get her on his side, and if she really didn't have the gold yet, he might have a chance. She might be unpredictable in some ways, but he could count on her being a greedy little bitch.

Jimmy shrugged, asked "Why do you want to know?"

"Just making sure you and the boys have all you need. I know it's a rough trip. Food, water . . . you getting everything you need?"

"Yeah," Jimmy said. He seemed more interested in something stuck in his teeth than in the conversation. He glanced over at Levi and asked, "That guy new?"

Scott thought that was strange; Jimmy never seemed too bright to him, never seemed to be paying attention to anything. Scott said, "Don't worry about my security detail, ok?"

Then trying to change his tone, he said, "Your job is more than enough for you to worry about, doing security out here, keeping the men safe. It's a tough job." Trying to flatter him. Make him feel like a big man. Like Bakalov did.

It seemed to work. "Yeah, we're doing okay. We're out here. Doing our job. Keeping the wolves at bay." Saying it like script.

"Anything new and exciting? I don't hear anything back there," Scott said, nodding to the rear car.

"Yeah, there was a big upset this morning. Assholes up ahead, that Wintermen bunch? Tried to blow up the bridge or something. And then something to do with the map. Anyway, Commander Love thought it was serious enough a problem to delay entry, so we're still working on clearing the track straight through to Cobalt before we take the train in. Tonight everyone is on stand down." Then he became a bit animated, "Too bad, most of us are amped right up. But Bakalov said we'll have some fun in the meantime. Don't know what he meant by that. And that's pretty much it, except they're looking for a woman."

Scott couldn't help himself, shot a look at Levi but the face was blank, somewhere else. "What woman?"

And then Jimmy was Bakalov's boy, saying, "Some bitch is stirring up trouble with a map. A map that hasn't been approved. A lie. We're going to get her and Commander Love is going to destroy the lie. And then we get to destroy the village."

Scott said, "We're delaying the invasion over a map?"

"The map, the true map, *is* the invasion. That's what Bakalov says."

"Hmm. Well, that's something." Scott, turning to go, said, "Good luck out here today."

Jimmy chewed on his lip a bit, didn't say anything for a few seconds, concentrating, like he was rearranging words in his head. Finally he said, "Don't think it will be me who'll be needing it."

"Needing what?" Scott tried to sound calm, but he was starting to get a bad feeling.

"The good luck."

Scott frowned. "What's that mean?" Wondering if the kid was trying to show off. Flex a bit of muscle.

Jimmy smiled, the grin stretching awkwardly across his face, and said, "You've been acting funny for the past day or so. Not like your usual self. I mentioned it. Bakalov said to tell you he wants to see you."

"Oh, okay," Scott said, thinking fast now. Get back to his boxcar, have Black get him the hell out of there, head north. He glanced over his shoulder for Levi but the guy was gone. When the fuck did that happen? Scott said, "I'll stop in later."

"I think you should come with me now."

"Just give me a minute. I'm going to go get my reports. Mr. Bakalov will want to see them."

"Yeah, okay. But be there in ten or I'm going to come get you."

Scott was almost to his boxcar when he heard the yelling start. He climbed up the metal stairs, threw open the door. Black was gone. And the yelling was getting louder.

Scott knew he was in trouble.

ঌ

Mitch had been wondering where the fuck the gold could be if Scott didn't have it when Levi was in the doorway of Scott's boxcar saying, "Grab the gear."

"We're going?"

"Right now."

She'd hesitated a moment, but then just nodded, grabbing

the pack and following him out of Scott's cabin, jumping down the metal stairs and then ducking around the backside of the train.

She said, "Scott coming?"

Levi just shook his head. They moved up along the far side of the train until the midway point, then Levi slipped in between two of the cars, inching forward until he was able to take a quick look, see who was around. Twenty yards away a few guys stood around a barrel, the flames barely visible. Farther down a group of men were chopping wood.

He glanced back at her and nodded, and she followed him around the corner, held her breath as they covered the few yards along the front of the train and then they were up the ramp and into the boxcar that held the snow machines. They decided to take just one machine—no point drawing too much attention to themselves.

They were loading their gear into the box on the back of the sled when a young man bounded up the ramp, not seeing them until he was right at the top, a big blonde kid, wide forehead above pale blue eyes now opened wide in surprise, the shoulders of his parka draped in a ratty piece of fur. Mitch went for her gun, but Levi was already at the side of the kid, his knife jammed hard into the side of the thick neck and then out again, blood already seeping on to the scrap of fur as Levi pocketed the knife, the kid barely gasping and then pitching forward, eyes still surprised. Levi grabbed hold of the back of the parka, struggling with the weight of the body as he dragged it away from the door.

He looked at Mitch and said, "No more Twenty. Just nineteen."

Chapter Twenty-Five

Bakalov hauled Scott down along the length of the train, the men stopping their work to watch. Scott was stumbling along, protesting as much as he could from a mouth that was bloodied and puffy.

Bakalov hadn't paid much attention to the sound of the snow machine leaving the camp. But then things had happened very quickly, and suddenly he was paying very close attention.

There was yelling. Then Jimmy came bursting into Bakalov's car, shouting, "One of us is down, he's down!" Then he stepped back through the door, "You have to come, come quick, sir!"

He'd followed Jimmy to the boxcar, the young man agitated, explaining he'd been about to go get Mr. Scott and bring him to Bakalov when one of the maintenance guys found the body. Already a group of men gathered around the ramp, a few up in the car itself. The blonde kid was on his back, his coat soaking up a lot of the blood. Bakalov told everyone to move back, asked what the soldier's name was, Jimmy said, "Beech, Cole Beech." Bakalov pulled back the hood of the kid's parka. "Stabbed." Then he thought, the snow machine, who took the snow machine? There was roll call pretty fucking quick, a couple of the Twenty dispatched to see if everyone working on the snow crew was accounted for.

Bakalov felt nothing but pleasure to discover two of Scott's security detail missing. Trying to find out where they'd gone had left Scott with the bruised and bloody mouth and an aching ribcage.

Bakalov knocked on Love's door, and after hearing the man say, "It better be important," he opened the door and found Love looking haggard, doing push-ups. Too obsessed with himself to notice the chaos outside. Bakalov pushed Scott inside and said, "This man has caused a problem."

Love straightened himself, wiped his face with a towel, then seeing a few of the so-called Twenty crammed onto the metal stairs leading up to the boxcar, he said, "Some privacy, please."

Bakalov turned to Jimmy. "Start cleaning up."

Love looked at Scott who tried to speak, a bubbling sound coming out of him. Love held up his hand, "Please, Bob, not now," and then glanced over at Bakalov. "So tell me, what is happening?"

Bakalov said, "We have one soldier dead. At least one machine stolen. Two security men missing."

"He's responsible?" Love gesturing at Scott.

Bakalov nodded.

"Well, well, Bob, you know, you surprise me."

"I can explain."

Love ignored that, studying Scott, like he was trying to size him for a new suit. Said to Bakalov, "We will need to make an example out of him."

"Yes," said Bakalov.

Bakalov was considering this, wondering what it could look like, this making an example out of someone, when Love asked, "So besides the loss of a soldier and a snow machine, what other damage have you caused?"

Scott tried to speak, his lips swollen. He mumbled, "Eton. It's a misunderstanding."

Bakalov said, "We checked further. Two more machines are missing."

Love said, "Having a little trouble with the math here. We are missing two people but three machines?"

"Mr. Scott will say nothing."

Love laughed, "I hardly think Bob here is going to hold out when the going gets really nasty, know what I mean, Ion? My feeling about this one is that he would do anything, absolutely anything, to save his own hide. Including risking the success of our expedition. Isn't that right, Bob?"

Scott, shaking his head, managed, "I don't know what happened."

Ignoring him, Bakalov said, "Scott had someone different with him just before the body was found. Not his regular security."

"Interesting. Well, I am certain that Mr. Scott will be more than happy to explain everything. Let me know as soon as anything of interest comes to light. This is all very negative. Very dark energy. I need some time to myself. I need some time to do some re-perceiving. That's what I need. New perceptions. I am feeling very stressed right now, too immersed in this experience, this drama, to make a good decision about Mr. Scott's future." He was already waving Bakalov away and turning to his map.

Bakalov left, dragging Scott back the way they had come, knowing the men were watching, talking about it. He could feel them wondering, if Scott could be treated that way, what about the rest of them? He would have to start keeping a closer eye on them. When power starts to shift, men can get ideas. Bakalov wouldn't be having any of that. It was time to start making his move.

Bakalov called Jimmy over. The group was still hovering around the boxcar, some drifting over to the barrels, "Everyone back to work. Send two men to take Beech out, away from the train somewhere."

"Like, dump him in the bush?" Jimmy asked.

"And why not? Even that is too good for him. No sign of struggle. Nothing. He failed. So yes, dump him wherever you want. And find a proper replacement. One who will not fail so easily. Then empty Mr. Scott's boxcar and lock him in it. Mr. Scott needs to get exactly what he deserves. And then I want all of you back here. We are going to have a busy morning."

"What are we going to be doing?"

"Something you will enjoy, Jimmy."

ༀ

"Think they'll be coming soon?" Susun asked. "How long does it take them to shovel that far?"

"No idea. They must be working those guys to the bone," Slaught said, "but I think we still have a day or so. We better get to it."

Almost everyone was out helping to clear the path between the hotel and the work bay. Hauling in wood from the work bay was hard enough without hauling it through a foot of heavy, wet snow.

"Maybe we should have a lookout," Jeff said. "Someone at the south end of town, keeping an eye on the rail line. Take it in shifts?"

"Probably a good idea," Slaught said. "Best to know what's coming. Larose and Shaun are taking all the weapons and ammo to the front room upstairs. Mrs. Merrill and Tiny are trying to figure out how to move the food storage somewhere safer. Somewhere that's easy to get to. Anything else we should be thinking of?"

Susun, leaning on her shovel and staring down the path, said, "They don't really even have to wait for the train. They could just come up here anytime, AKs and a dozen sleds, wouldn't take them long."

They all stared down the snow tunnel at the south end of the street, as if any minute Bakalov's hordes might come burning around the bend and into view.

Then the sound of a snow machine.

"Who the hell could that be?" Jeff looked to Slaught. "Time to run?"

Slaught took a step back but they all ended up just staring and waiting as the sound of the machine got closer and closer.

"Sounds like just one sled," Slaught said.

The sled came into view at the end of the tunnel, shiny and white. As it got closer, Slaught said, "Jesus H. Christ, if it isn't Black and her sidekick." He wasn't too surprised, thinking that it made sense she was here. She'd been part of it since the beginning, whatever this was, and Slaught had a feeling they were heading towards the end of it all. One way or another.

Mitch pulled up, killing the snow machine's engine and climbed off. The first thing Slaught noticed was that the Talos happy face logo was gone. Some weird wolf head on the side instead.

Slaught asked, "That a goodwill gift from Talos?

Levi got off the machine and said, "Took it from the train."

"You were on the train?" Susun asked.

"Since the outpost."

Slaught said, "You're lucky we didn't blow you up."

"Pisspoor job of trying," Mitch said. "Would have been better for you if you had, too. You got some serious action coming your way."

"How long we got?"

She shrugged. "Hard to say. They seemed to be setting up camp, so at least they won't be pushing in here tonight."

Seeing them all, shovels in hand, Mitch said, "Guns instead of shovels might make a bit more sense, no? Maybe just lay out a red carpet while you're at it."

"No one asked your opinion, lady," Larose said. "What the hell you doing here, anyway?"

"Good question, Harv," Slaught said, "we're all wondering that."

"I have a problem."

"Long way to come for help, Mitch," Slaught said. "Though I guess we owe you…"

"Big time, Winterman, you owe me big time."

"Granted. So, the problem?"

"Need another machine. A good one."

"That's some ask. Might as well be asking for gold."

"Funny you should say that. That's what we need the sled for, to haul our gold out of here."

"Your gold? Jesus Christ, it's still up here?"

"You tell me."

They all stared at her.

Susun said, "The gold isn't here. You must know that."

"Someone got your gold?" Chumboy asked.

She shrugged. "Isn't where we left it. And so I'm thinking it must be somewhere around here. Or with Scott. And I'm not leaving here without it, so it looks like we're stuck in the middle until your showdown with Love is over."

"Where's the map?" Levi asked.

Slaught was caught off guard. "The map? Why are you asking about that?"

"They want it."

"Who wants it?"

"The Dogman. He's getting it for Commander Love."

"Getting it for him? What do you meaning getting it?"

Levi shook his head. "Heard Scott talking to one of the Dogman's soldiers. They're coming for Susun."

৫

Jordan, seeing Mitch come through the door, her hair shaved on the sides, a bit sticking up on the top, said, "Hey, the hair, very on point, you've really nailed the apocalyptic thing. Got a little bit of that Miley Cyrus girl-gone-bad thing going on there."

She didn't even look at him, said to Slaught, "This shit-abyss secured?"

"That's a good question," Slaught said. "Think we're getting there."

"Doesn't look like it to me," she said.

Slaught told her to pull up a chair, that he had no doubt she'd think of something they'd missed. He asked Tiny if he'd mind brewing up some tea for them.

"I will, even for her, just because I'm feeling generous. But I'm not happy about it. And that Max left my kitchen in a mess last night, found him passed out in the dining room this morning. Never letting that little bastard do any entertaining after midnight again."

"Entertaining?" Slaught asked.

"Some traveller. Gone before I got up. Looks like they had themselves a little party."

"Had booze on him?"

Tiny shrugged, "From the state of Max this morning I'd say so. Boy can't hold his liquor worth shit. Says he can't remember what they talked about, but I figured from how sheepish the kid looked he probably told him everything and anything. Now I'm thinking that was probably the sonofabitch that blew our dynamite."

"Jesus Christ," said Mitch, "you people are such fucking amateurs."

"These fucking amateurs put the run on you. Twice," said Tiny.

"Fuck you," Mitch said, "I should leave you to fend for yourselves..."

"Whoa up there, everyone," Slaught said, "no need to go back over the past, right? Today is a new day with a whole heap of new shit for us to worry about. So maybe we best holster our emotions and get to it. Now then, Chum, we secure or not?"

"Getting there. We got more firewood to load in—think Shaun and Melinda are working on that. Larose is getting a few sleds loaded with fuel right up at the side doors just in case. Got to put some fencing up around the front of the hotel, block things off a bit. Can't hurt. And boarding up some of those back windows. Got a few outliers too that we gotta get to, the ones McLaren told us about. They kinda got pushed to the back burner what with the bridge and everything."

"How many?" Mitch asked.

"Three houses. An older guy on his own, two young lads, brothers maybe, and a middle-aged couple. Jeff said he'd go."

"Can't leave it to him. I'll go."

"Hey," said Jeff, "I'm insulted."

Mitch said to Slaught, "I'm going."

"We could use you here," said Slaught.

"Could be trouble, they're going to have scouts, guys out doing recon. You don't want Gentleman Jim here running into them."

Jordan said, "Yeah, exactly. No offence, Jeff, I think you should stay here with me. No point taking risks. Now this one, she's made for the job. You know, because it's like Miley said, she'd bring on her wrecking ball."

Chumboy said, "That wasn't Miley Cyrus, that was the Boss."

"Excuse me, I know my Miley," Jordan said, "and she had a wrecking ball."

Chumboy, patiently now, said, "It's Springsteen. *C'mon and take your best shot, let me see what you've got, bring on your wrecking ball.*"

"I don't know," Jordan said, "maybe he ripped off her lyrics."

"Don't even try, Jordie," Chumboy said.

Jordan persisted, "No, it's definitely Miley. Miley's badass."

Mitch, in the doorway and getting ready to head out, said, "What the fuck is wrong with you people?"

ঀ

Mitch needed to be on her own, wanted some time to think. She'd left Levi to help haul in wood and then set off to warn the folks living south of the town. The fifteen minutes or so it took to reach the houses gave her some time to clear her head. Try and decide what to do. Get the hell out, or wait around and hope she could figure out who had the gold. Scott? Didn't think so. He seemed pretty convinced she had it. She doubted Slaught and the Scooby gang had it. A random? Possible and frustrating. Then there was fucking Bakalov. He seemed an unlikely suspect—not really his thing. But best to keep an open mind. It was probably wise not to underestimate him.

But was it worth it? Getting tangled up in all of this bullshit over the gold? Maybe it made sense to just get out before that fucking train pulled into town and all hell broke out. Maybe she was tempting fate. Twice now in that fucking town she'd come too close for comfort to serious trouble. Too much gun play. And now these guys were rolling into town pumped for a fucking invasion. It was a whole other kettle of fish.

She slowed down, seeing snowmobile tracks running down a small hill. She followed the trail to a small white house and then killed her engine. Listened. Quiet. No signs of mayhem. That was something. Still, she waited. Okay. What was she missing? Sky felt empty, just grey, no clouds. The town still. Maybe that was it. There was nothing. No sign of life at all. Guessed she was too late.

She headed to the small house, reached the walkway. Imprints of boots in the snow. Man-sized. Kicked in door. Inside, a wood stove dominated the first large room, embers still glowing. Didn't happen too long ago.

Further into the cabin, a cramped kitchen area. Two young men, one bare-headed, blonde, the other wearing a dark toque, crumpled up across from each other at the table, small pool of blood meeting in the middle. The place ransacked.

She checked the map Slaught had sketched for her. A cluster of homes nearby, the two other occupied places within walking distance. She found the old man at the end of his laneway, face down in the snow. Coming out to meet his attackers, probably heard the ruckus next door. Shot point blank. Round behind his house: a tidy little grey cabin, walkway cleared, porch tended. A nice home. The door had been left open. Man in the kitchen, woman in the doorway. Didn't have a chance. And the place was a mess.

She stood for a minute. Could feel the chill settling in. Grabbed two blankets from the bedroom and covered the bodies. Closed the door behind her.

On the way back to her sled, Mitch stopped and dragged the old fellow back inside, covered him up, too. Decided to leave the brothers as they were.

Maybe she was getting soft. Wouldn't have wasted time doing that, before. Jesus Christ.

And it was no time to be getting soft. Not with that pack of bastards heading up the railway line.

Chapter Twenty-Six

They were hanging on to the wide-open doors of the boxcars, a few leaning out of windows in the passenger cars. All torches and howling as the train pushed into town, snow tumbling off either side of the tracks. Bakalov's boys riding into town as conquerors.

Love had watched as the trees rolled by. It was fucking endless. Just rock and snow and rock and snow and these endless rows of spindly trees. He had imagined something more, bigger trees, more like those European forests, great cathedrals of trees with open spaces, maybe catching sight of a stag or whatever the fuck they were. But this scrubby bush was bumming him out. What was also bumming him out were these jacked-up delinquents that were hanging off of Bakalov's every word. It seemed there was some confusion about who was in charge. He needed to set that straight.

The train lurched to a stop. Time to get on his game face. He took some time to get centred, focus. Deep breathing, imagining his entrance. Calm. Then he reached for his parka as Bakalov slid his door open.

"Show time," Love said. Then feeling his need to assert himself, he added, "No fuck-ups."

"Of course not."

So when he stepped out into the cold and there was a small platform ringed with fire barrels and men lined up along either side, he felt he was hitting the right note. Symbolic. Light in the darkness and all of that shit.

He climbed down the metal stairs from the train, felt the snow crunch under his feet, then stepped up onto the platform. He surveyed the scene and then pointed to the path that lead away from the train towards the main street of the town. "Tomorrow we will march up into the town. And it will become ours, like everything else we have passed through has become ours. And we will take this town and use it to push farther out into this wilderness. This is my promise to you: a strong and prosperous beginning, right here and right now. But for tonight, sleep and prepare yourselves for tomorrow."

They were quiet when he spoke. Quiet afterwards, too, until Bakalov brought his hands together in a slow, almost somber, clap. Then the Twenty took up the clap, then his security team, the survey crews, and then they were all echoing the rhythmic clapping. And then it happened, the creature moving fast, lunging towards Love as he was about to step down off the platform.

Nothing but fur and snarling. Love brought up his arms, but then there was Bakalov, hurling himself at the wolf, the beast's claws scraping across Love's face before the wolf and Bakalov collided, Bakalov shouting, "Get him inside!" and two of the Twenty grabbing Love and dragging him away. A tangle of man and wolf and then the wolf freed itself, bounding away into the darkness, men scattering and yelling.

When Bakalov hustled into his railcar, looking worried and bloodied, Love said, "I guess I owe you some gratitude, Ion."

"No, you owe me nothing. Just doing my duty."

"Still, impressive, tackling a wolf."

Bakalov stood saying nothing. Perhaps in shock. The man large, sweating, his adrenaline filling the railcar with an edgy, large energy, and Love felt like he was being polluted, overwhelmed. He pulled himself together and told Bakalov to go on, check in with the doctor and rest up. He would see him in the morning.

Fuck up indeed. Love carefully felt the welts on his cheek. He hoped they stayed, it would make a good story. But first he had to deal with Bakalov. Because right now, the story was Bakalov's. Bakalov the brute wrestling the wild beast and saving him? Fuck's sake. Not the optics he was after, not the right fucking optics at all. Not the strongman he needed to be. He was going to have to fix this. And he was thinking Bob Scott might be able to help out with that.

༄

"I think it fell flat."

"The grand entrance?" Jeff asked.

"Yeah. Could've done better, so much better," Jordan said. "I mean think about it. You got this awesome looking train, right? The black against the snow? Can't go wrong. A little fireworks kind of thing? Perfect. But chugging in at 10 kilometers an hour, all those guys hanging out of the boxcar with torches, I mean, whooping or howling or whatever it was they thought they were doing. Just so low rent. The way Levi described this Twenty, like some army of feral children or something, they sounded terrifying. But they weren't scary. And they weren't even attractive. Most of them look like they should go back to mom's basement, first, and second, take a hard look at their wardrobe, maybe dental? I don't know. After that, at least try, I mean just try, to get their Leni on…"

They'd watched the train roll into town, passing the night vision binoculars back and forth, taking a look from the bridge at the north end of the lake. Then they booted it back up to the hotel, dousing the lights and bolting the door. Now Slaught and a few others were watching the street, seeing if there was any movement. Nothing. Every so often Chumboy would slip out the back and take a look-see but so far, so good. None of them thought that would last.

Slaught interrupted Jordan, asking, "What's Leni?"

"Leni Riefenstahl," Jordan said, "German filmmaker."

"Yeah, one of the best if you're into fascists," said Chumboy. "They really nailed that whole pageantry shit."

Slaught said, "Christ, Jordan."

"I'm not saying I like her, I'm just saying if they're going for that look, they should've at least drawn on some classic imagery. I mean seriously, where's the drama?"

"The bloody wolves' heads stuck on the posts in the snow? Did you see those?" Slaught asked, adding, "More than enough drama for me, Jordie."

Jordan sighed, "Oh, god yes. I nearly vomited."

"That's the problem with all of that bullshit, Jordie," Chumboy said. "Up close? The bullshit just ain't got no sparkle and shine."

☫

The next morning was a weird one. Before turning in for the night Mitch had said she and Levi would spell each other off through the night keeping an eye on things. A few of them had slept on the floor of the dining room and when Slaught rolled over, feeling the floor beside him, cold and hard, he heard Mitch say, "'Bout fucking time. Your town is being overrun and you're getting your beauty sleep."

"Anything doing out there?" he asked. Sitting up, rubbing his eyes. Taking a minute, trying to get his thoughts together. This was going to be one god almighty of a day.

"They're doing better than us. Working through the night.

Levi says they're all set up and it looks like they're staying for a while. They're still clearing the rail line pushing north but also doing a lot of clearing down and around the station. Got their little bonfires all set up along the length of the train, too, regular little village down there."

"Jesus."

"Yeah, I'm here," barked Tiny from the kitchen doorway, "and I gotta tell you, this ain't going to be my finest loaves and fucking fishes moment but I got some swamp water, might pass for coffee, and some buns, too. Come and get it."

Slaught went to wash up, thinking of Susun upstairs sleeping. She'd asked him last night if he was scared, he'd said yeah, of course he was scared. And she'd just nodded, smiled, and said, "See you in the morning, Johnny." Left him unsure if it had been the right answer or not. But it was the truth. It was one hell of a mess to be in. And then before he could have his swamp water there was a loud banging at the front doors.

Shaun and Chumboy were on their feet by the time Slaught slipped up beside the doors. Mitch and Levi had positioned themselves at the far side of the room away from the doors.

Slaught said, "Couple guys with torches. No, three of them…"

"Armed?" Mitch asked.

Slaught said, "Can't really see from this angle."

Another round of banging on the door.

"I'm going to open up," Slaught said, "get ready."

Slaught popped open the door, only a bit, and one guy—soul patch trying to take hold on his chin, eyes a little too close together—said, "If we wanted in, we'd already be there."

Slaught thought the guy looked familiar, must be from the Facility. Also thought he was sounding pretty cocky, but didn't say anything. Then the guy said, "General Bakalov is seeking a temporary truce."

General? Christ almighty. Regular army out there now? Slaught said, "A truce? Didn't notice any fighting going on."

The guy said, "You will."

Slaught said, "We're not opposed to a friendly meeting."

"Come unarmed."

"Don't know if we're all that comfortable with that," Slaught said.

"Don't give a shit about what you're comfortable with or not."

It was like the kid was acting, barely making eye contact, terse. A classic interpretation of the loyal foot soldier. Slaught asked, "You for real? What's your name?"

The soul patch kid said, "Mumford. Jim Mumford. And the General wants to see your official representatives in his boxcar. We'll be back in an hour to escort you."

And then they left.

Slaught turned to Chumboy and said, "Do we have anyone official around here?"

א

It hadn't rolled out like Love had wanted. Now the task was to regain the upper hand. It was tricky. How to put Bakalov in his place when the man had performed such a showy, heroic act?

He'd asked for Bakalov to come by in the morning and now here the big oaf was, barely giving Love time to wake up. And was the man was starting to smell? Some feral odour heavy in the room. Good Christ, how unbearable.

Love said, "So you can understand, Ion, that as a man, I am deeply indebted to you. No question. But as your Commander, I have some grave concerns about your performance."

Bakalov was frowning, clearly this was not what he expected.

Bakalov said, "I hope I can reassure you, Commander, whatever your concerns."

"It's simple, Ion. Where did the wolf come from?"

Bakalov, hesitating, "... The woods?"

"Well yes, obviously, it came from the woods. But it was your duty to keep wolves out of the camp. And suddenly, on one of the few occasions I am out of my cabin, an attack? What am I to think of that?"

"It was unacceptable. I take full responsibility."

"I'm not looking for an admission of guilt. Obviously it's your fault and your responsibility. But what I want here, Ion, what I need from you right now, are solutions. Remember, Ion? I said no fuck ups. This, well, I hate to say it, this was a fuck up. And you need to fix it."

Love watched as Bakalov took his eyes from the centre point of the wall behind him and slid them over to Love. "Yes, sir. There are solutions. I have thought of these solutions and am putting them into action."

"Action? I'm seeing the opposite of action. I'm seeing men not working. I'm seeing my cartographers not mapping because the surveying crews won't go fucking outside. These wolves, Ion, you told me that is why I should bring you along. To beat back these wolves. And now I have two hundred convicts afraid to work and refusing to leave their boxcars. That means two things, Ion, do you know what two things this represents? Why this is so serious?"

Bakalov hesitated so Love said, "It means this, Ion. One, we have a wolf problem. But more importantly, we have an obedience problem. Right now, those wolves are making more of an impression on our workforce than you are. And I doubt your Twenty or whatever you call them are out there beating the bushes for your wolves, either."

"Yes, yes they are Commander. I am trying to make this right. We are establishing a perimeter, red-flagging it; it is a traditional method of control. The wolves will not cross the red line. And the surveyors are out now, four of my Twenty escorting them. And the work crews are out now, preparing the site."

"And heading up the line? Is that happening?"

"Not yet, sir. Soon."

"You know, Ion, this is absurd. Absurd. My train, my *Domain*, being stopped by some mangy, half-starved wolves? We have men, we have guns. What. Is. The. Fucking. Problem?"

"I am enlisting the aid of the locals. They will know where the wolves are, how to track them. They will be our guides. Once we wipe out the wolves we can continue to push north."

"The people here?" Love surprised. Asking the locals for help? Fuck's sake, not exactly subjugation. "I think I was pretty clear that we were going to take the town today. March all of these resistors into the streets, punish them for the bridge? You do remember that plan don't you, Ion?"

"Well, yes, Commander, but the men, I doubted we would be able to muster the men until we dealt with the wolves..."

"You didn't clear that with me. You don't have the authority to change the plans, who do you think you are?"

Bakalov was back to staring at the wall. He said, "No, no sir, I...I did not think... It seemed like the most efficient course to take. I thought you would approve."

"Well, Ion, I don't. I don't approve."

Silence. Bakalov's raspy breathing, working his mouth as he tried to find the right words. Love finding the sound unbearable, suddenly feeling tired and cold and repulsed by the large man's presence, said, "Get out of my sight and go fix this. These wolves do not exist in my dream, Ion. Make sure they don't exist in your reality. Or you're finished."

༂

At first, Susun thought maybe it should be her who went to meet with Bakalov, maybe she could get a glimpse of the other map. But Auntie Verla was shaking her head. She said, "I think we should keep those two maps away from each other for now."

Susun asked why, and Auntie Verla said, "Hard to say Susie, but that man could be dangerous to you."

"I just feel frustrated," Susun said, "sitting around and doing nothing. Like we are all just resigned to the worst. I feel useless."

When Mitch had returned with news about the killings south of the town no one had really talked much about it. What was there to say? They were all scared. Susun knew some folks were thinking that maybe this was it, that they were all going to be either killed or loaded onto the train and hauled back to the place Johnny had been, the Facility. What else were they to think after listening to those howling men last night? Seeing the fires.

"You are busy, Susie," Auntie Verla said. "Busy creating the map. And your baby. Your baby is seeing the map, too, so you need to protect the map. You should stay."

Slaught said, "The baby is seeing the map?"

Auntie Verla looked at Slaught. "The baby is seeing everything."

"Yeah?" Slaught was interested in that, how did that work? "Like literally seeing?"

Auntie Verla just looked at him and said nothing. Slaught felt his question had been a disappointment to her. He said, "Okay, well maybe I'll try and figure out this dad stuff later, but for now maybe we should figure out how we pick our official representatives?"

Tiny said, "I'm not fucking going anywhere near those bastards, so you can count me out."

No one was saying anything so Slaught glanced over at Chumboy, but he was resting his head in his hands, staring down at the floor. Auntie Verla stepped over to him and rested her hand on his shoulder. "You could get dressed, go with Johnny."

Without raising his head Chumboy said, "Yeah, I could. Okay."

Slaught said, "You up to it, Chum? Larose and I could go."

"No, I'll go. Makes sense. But this is it for me. When I come back up, I'm taking Auntie back home."

"Fair enough," Slaught said. "Okay folks, high alert. Let's lock this old joint down. Everything that can be a weapon, find it. Everything and anything. Get the food safe and accessible and don't forget about water. And firewood. Harv, can you draw up a schedule, keep things running?"

"Will do."

And then there was the pounding on the door and Jimmy was there and they were stepping out into the cold and heading up the street, men working on clearing the small hill that ran down to the old train station. Slaught could feel eyes on them as they trailed along behind Jimmy towards the train, thinking maybe he recognized some of the guys but couldn't be certain. It was hard, too, not to be distracted by the sheer energy around the train, the town full of the sounds of men shouting, chainsaws and shovels and movement. Movement everywhere, like a goddam military operation.

"Gotta say Chum, glad to have you with me," Slaught said.

"Someone's got to look out for you at the end of the world."

Chapter Twenty-Seven

It was elegant, pitch black with gold scrolls curling around the front windows. Slaught said it didn't look much like the old Northlander train, and Chumboy said it was more like Polar Express meets Texas Chainsaw Massacre. Jimmy told them to shut the fuck up.

Jimmy headed towards the centre of the train, pushing them up ahead onto the set of metal stairs. Bakalov was standing in the middle of the railcar when they climbed in through the back door, the room already looking like some whacked-out taxidermy shop: a wolf head wrapped in plastic resting on a chair, a hide draped over the man's spare, metal cot. Chumboy said, "Man, you really got your Ceauşescu going on here," taking in the man's high, thick shoulders and shaved head, some weird fur piece draped over his shoulders. "You're just how I pictured you."

Bakalov said, "You know of Ceauşescu?"

But Chumboy didn't answer, instead moving to the window that looked out over the small frozen lake, and Bakalov turned his attention to Slaught. "Ah, the Winterman, of course."

"What's on your mind, Bakalov?"

"So, right to the point, good," Bakalov said. "I have a proposition for you."

"Which is?"

"We are in your village, no?"

"Sort of obvious."

"If I am in your village, it is now my village."

"Whoa up there a minute, what about Love? We negotiating with him or you?"

A flicker of unease across Bakalov's face. "I represent Commander Love. And there is nothing to negotiate. We have taken over your village; I think any reasonable man can accept that. But we have a mutual problem and maybe we can set aside our differences for now?"

"Mutual problem?"

"The wolves."

Slaught hadn't expected that. He glanced over at Chumboy but it was hard to see what he was thinking, still looking out the window. Slaught said, "Like the bush wolves?"

"Yes, those kinds. They are attacking our men, making it impossible for them to work. Our surveyors won't go into the bush anymore. There are only so many of the vermin I can kill, and my boys, the Twenty, well, they are learning, but they are not ready. And yesterday, an attack right in camp. Our Commander."

Slaught said, "Wish I'd seen that."

"Do not make light of this, Winterman, the wolves are bold. Taking risks."

Chumboy said, "Everything's hungry."

"That's what makes them dangerous," Bakalov said. "They have killed six men in the last two days. They dragged two of our night watchmen under the train in the middle of the night and finished them there."

"What's this got to do with us?" Slaught asked.

"They will come for your people, too. They are getting bolder and bolder. If we work together, with your knowledge of the local area and our firepower, we solve the wolf problem. Then we can get back to our bigger problems."

"Wolves never bothered with us much before you guys turned up. And we never bothered much with them. Left each other alone."

"The wolf, it is imperative that he kills. He does not kill because he is hungry. He kills because that is his nature."

"Don't think you're describing wolf," said Chumboy. "Think you're describing yourself. And Talos."

"I promise you, they will come in the daytime. Come to where you gather your wood. Make things impossible for you. Take the weak ones first. I will not protect you. So you should cooperate now, while you have a chance. This does not mean you surrender. It is not giving in to me—other enemies have cooperated before. In the Great War, Russians and Germans were enemies, but they worked together for a common cause. It is just expedient. A shared enemy."

"The Kovno truce?" Chumboy asked.

Bakalov turned to Chumboy, looking pleased, "Ah, you know your history."

"Not *my* history buddy, I'm Algonquin, got nothing to do with me. Doubtful it's anyone's history, though. More like bullshit."

Bakalov smiled, "I explain to you. Wolf has always been problem in Russia. And that winter, in 1916, it was the world war, fighting was brutal. Wolves could not resist the weakened and tired soldiers. Opportunists. Scavengers. That's what they are. The soldiers helped each other, stopped their fighting to hunt the wolves, so, like us, they could get back to their bigger problems."

Slaught said, "You telling me you think those guys stopped battling it out in the trenches, got together, killed a bunch of wolves and then got back to killing each other?"

"That is the Kovno truce. We need such a truce."

Slaught sighed. "Okay, Bakalov, we're out of here. That is the stupidest fucking thing I've ever heard."

He turned to go, but Chumboy wasn't moving from the window. Slaught followed his gaze across the lake. A few deer were on the far side of the lake. Maybe browsing on the cedar branches that Susun and McLaren left there. Pale brown, white undersides. Small and delicate, too. They were beautiful. It was something to see.

He looked over his shoulder when he heard the racking of the rifle. "What are you doing?"

"Hunting," Bakalov said, laughing. "It will be a nice change for dinner."

"You hardly see deer anymore," Slaught said. "Especially out in the open."

Bakalov didn't say anything, carefully sliding the window down.

"You're shooting them from in here?" Slaught was surprised, and mad, too, wanting to be out of there, out of the train car with its stuffy heat and this man, too big in the cramped space. Like an ogre.

"Why trouble myself," Bakalov asked, "if they present themselves like that to me? Make themselves such an easy target?"

"I think you should wait," Chumboy said, seeing the second deer stop, head come up out of the branches.

"You can cry for Bambi if you want. But it is natural for me to kill and eat this animal. So I will."

"But the deer has company."

And they watched as the first wolf appeared, about twenty yards to the left of the deer. A big dun-coloured creature. Two more followed, but the deer kept grazing. The smallest deer glanced over, but only to watch as four more wolves came from directly behind, then a pair of big blacks emerged from the woods, joining up with the rest of the pack.

Chumboy could hear Bakalov's breathing change as he watched. Slaught said to Chumboy, "Never seen anything like this before. Deer must be hungry to take a chance playing chicken. Think you should let this thing play out, Bakalov. These guys out there have it rough. Maybe they need that deer more than you do."

"Survival of the strongest, that is what makes sense out here, Winterman. I'm surprised at you. I am predator. Wolf is predator. We compete for scarce resources. That is nature."

Chumboy kept watching out the window and said, "Hawking a western mash-up of Darwin and some worn out capitalist creed, are you? Why would any Russian worth their salt go for Darwin when you got Kropotkin? You know, those ideas about mutual aid and cooperation. Might be more useful to you."

"I don't know of this Kropotkin. But I know the wolf."

"No, you only know yourself. Don't think you know much about the wolf at all."

And then the smallest of the deer jumped a bit, then the three of them bounded away, the wolves barely seeming to notice, spreading out along the far side of the lake. Then the big dun walked towards the line strung along the far side of the lake, red flags hanging from it, rough-hewn pennants. The wolf walked under the line and sat down. Staring at the train.

The sight of the wolf seemed to transfix them all as they stood together at the window. Chumboy said, "Maybe the wolf knows you, though."

Bakalov still had his rifle resting on the windowsill. "I am going to kill these wolves."

Slaught said, "We're going." Saying it but not moving, eyes on the wolf.

Bakalov said, "If you do not come willingly to help hunt these demons, I will force you. Bad things can happen, Winterman, you know that. I think you have women and children up there with you, no?"

"You're something else, you know that?" Slaught said. "We're up here minding our own business and you charge in here, creating problems, then demand that we solve those problems. Or else what? You're going to pick on people you think might not be able to defend themselves? What's wrong with you?"

Bakalov was staring out at the wolf. It was big, must've weighed well over a hundred pounds. And as strange as it seemed, Slaught was convinced the wolf was staring back at Bakalov.

"Fucking cur," Bakalov muttered, and Slaught felt him move slightly to reposition his rifle, centring the scope on the animal sitting in the snow.

Chumboy said, "Don't do it."

Bakalov, not hearing him, slowed his breathing and focused on the target. Slaught, sensing that Bakalov had his shot lined up, standing so close he could hear the man exhale, thought he'd had enough of this shit and slammed his elbow up into the big man's arm. He knocked Bakalov sideways, the rifle crashing against the top of the window and slipping out of Bakalov's grip, clattering back onto the floor of the boxcar. Slaught scooped up the rifle, taking hold of the barrel and swinging it up and cracking it across the back of Bakalov's head. The big man staggered, but caught himself on the edge of the open window, bellowing. Then the door flew open and the place was swarming with the Twenty, who immediately went for Slaught. Chumboy backed up against the window.

Jimmy, trying to take control of the situation, yelled at Slaught, "Stay still, motherfucker."

"You made a mistake, Winterman," Bakalov managed. He said to Jimmy, "Put them in a boxcar with the workers, keep him there there until I am ready." Then to Chumboy he said, "You will be coming with me soon enough. Or we'll go up the hill and drag your people out of there one by one. Understand? We will go out at dusk. We're going to track that wolf and kill it."

Chumboy asked, "You think he's coming for you?"

Bakalov was quiet. Slaught, as he was being pushed out through the door, asked, "Is that a thing? Wolves singling a guy out like that?"

"Ask him," Chumboy said, "he's the one who believes in fairy tales."

༄

"So your little red flags weren't as spooky as you thought? Jesus Christ, what a shocker."

Love, hands flat to his desk, looking down, shook his head.

"This is unprecedented, Commander Love."

"Really? That waving red pieces of cloth doesn't scare the wolves? That is ridiculous, Ion. Just ridiculous. I am not a great hunter, not like you, oh no, but I think to myself, what is the one thing that could stop a wolf? A bullet. There's a radical idea, eh? Use a fucking bullet. Not some rag flapping in the breeze."

"It is not just rags, it is the fladry. It has worked for generations, centuries even. It is proven. This wolf was different."

"Different, Ion? Different how?"

Bakalov hesitated. Tell the man the wolf was a demon? No. "It was very bold. There was something about it. Something different."

"I see. Well, we have a problem. Because the men are once

again refusing to leave the immediate vicinity of the train. *Again.* Nothing is getting done. And no obedience. We cannot be out here, hundreds of miles from civilization, and have no obedience. Staging an invasion becomes unconvincing if your soldiers are hiding in their boxcars, no? You know, Scott warned me about this very thing, that our soldiers could turn on us. Perhaps, Ion, I should have listened to him, not you."

"The soldiers are not turning, Commander, they are scared, yes, but we will get the wolf, and all the other wolves."

"So you have your guides, or sherpas, or whatever you call them?"

"Yes, I have two men. One of them is the Winterman, the other is an Algonquin. He will know the hunting."

"Algonquin?" Love thought about that for a minute. "Bring him to me, I want to chat with this Algonquin."

Bakalov said, "Of course. Anything else, sir?"

"Yes, there is, Ion. My presence will be felt in this shithole today, felt by everyone, understand me? This is the first day of our occupation, and I am not fucking around. I want a bigger platform outside my car, I want torches, lots of fire, can you see it? Picture it? I want your Twenty to be lighting their torches from a big central fire, and I want bonfires, big fucking bonfires, blocking the trails at either end of the town. With guards posted there, no one is getting out of this shit-ass town. No one. So tonight, stage set, I am going to give a short speech. Get things ready. And make sure there are no fucking wolves dive-bombing my fucking stage, can you do that? And once my speech is over, I want you to bring out Scott."

"Scott? What are you going to do with him?"

Love said, "That would be none of your concern, Ion, just have him there."

"Yes, of course."

"Oh, and perhaps you could find the woman with the map. Could you at least do that for me?"

ॐ

"I hope you realize the gravity of your situation."

Chumboy didn't see any reason to answer Love. He'd been waiting in Bakalov's boxcar, wondering if maybe they had just forgotten about him in the uproar over Johnny, but then a heavy-set guy around thirty showed up, a thin strip of wolf pelt fixed to the shoulder of his parka. He came in gun-first and said, "Get up, you're going to see the Commander." Chumboy asked him if he wasn't a little old to be playing Lord of the Flies with these clowns. The guy said he was a late recruit but there were lots of perks, and he was on board as long as he got better meals.

And so now Chumboy was with Love, the soldier waiting outside the door for him to finish up.

"So, you're an Algonquin."

Chumboy just watched the man, taking in the white linens, the orderliness of the boxcar. But the man himself a mess—hair greasy and standing up, unshaven, dark circles under his eyes.

"I'm talking to you," Love said.

Chumboy stayed quiet, the man now pacing, shoulders bunched up and tense.

"You know I could kill you right now. I can do anything I want. To anyone. So I suggest you play nice with me."

"Not real clear on the game we're playing here, that's all."

"Well, you're an Algonquin, right? I thought maybe, you know, your take on things, spiritual things, warrior stuff, could be useful to me. Know what I mean?"

"No idea."

"Okay, let me lay it out for you. You know how I see myself? Sort of as a mentor. Or maybe a gatekeeper. That's it. A gatekeeper of the new ways of being. I can show others. Create a new way of being human, of living."

"Nothing new about you, buddy."

"You're wrong there, Mr. Algonquin. What's new about me? I'm not just selling ideas. I'm not selling a new political ideology. I'm selling a new energy."

"Maybe. But that energy is hanging around you like bad juju, Loveman."

Love frowned. Glanced over his shoulder as if the energy might actually be visible there. "Can you see it?"

Chumboy wondered if the guy was serious. He said, "Can smell it. Just like those wolves out there."

"I'm not spooked by your Aboriginal voodoo."

Chumboy didn't know what to say to that, the nervous energy pouring off the guy was straight up weird.

Love said, "You think you're some sort of shaman or something. Whatever. Right now, with this train and my map, my map coming to life, to fruition, I feel powerful, like an ancient Druid."

Chumboy couldn't help himself, he laughed. "You best go back to that spiritual buffet you've been picking over and get yourself something a little more useful. God almighty, a Druid?"

Chapter Twenty-Eight

Slaught and Chumboy were trying to see through cracks in the door of their boxcar.

Once Love had finished with Chumboy, he'd told the soldier to take him to one of two boxcars they were using to lock up the men who were refusing to work. He was shoved into a crowded boxcar that already had Slaught and Big Donny and about forty other guys packed into it. Bakalov, Big Donny told Chumboy, had said he'd kill them if they didn't get out and start working, and then hauled out three guys and shot them right in front of the boxcar. Still, the rest of them figured being shot was better than being gnawed upon by a pack of wolves. They were taking a chance that Bakalov wouldn't want to waste too much ammo. Rumours were they were running out of everything, including bullets.

So they'd spent the day trying to find a way out of the boxcar, a few guys taking turns watching out through the slats on the boxcar, letting everyone know what was going on outside. Seemed busy even though there weren't many guys out there. Hard to know exactly what was going on but by the time twilight was setting in and the guys were getting hungry, a bunch of guys were building a big bonfire out front.

Slaught, eye pressed to the thin opening, said to Chumboy, "Something weird going on out there."

The rest of the workers, the ones who had gone out to work for the day with the promise of protection and food, had formed a big circle behind the Twenty. Bakalov was now dragging Scott through the snow towards the centre of the circle. Scott was protesting, yelling at Love to stop behaving like a crazy man.

Chumboy glanced over at Slaught. "Man, Johnny, you look like shit."

"Yeah, it's three times now they've beaten the shit out of me. Three times."

Chumboy thought about seeing Johnny hauled off the boxcar, thrown into the snow, the young men kicking at him, insulting him. The wolf in the distance, still sitting and watching for a while then joining his pack, disappearing into the trees. Chumboy asked Slaught, "Was it worth it?"

"Each time? Don't know. Not even clear why I got the first two beatings, except being in that fucking shitbox. But this last time? Yeah. It was."

Chumboy nodded. "Did the wolf speak to you?"

"What? Like did I hear something?"

Big Donny was crouched not too far away, his back to the wall of the boxcar. He said, "He asked you if the wolf spoke to you. That's a simple question."

Slaught said, "Simple? Not to me it isn't. But no, I don't think so."

"So, why, then?"

Slaught sighed. "Guess it reminded me of football, you know?"

Chumboy smiled. "You and me—we have very different points of reference. So nope, no idea what you mean."

"It was like, to me, right then, they were choosing teams."

Chumboy was now looking right at Slaught, asked, "And?"

"Well, they were both asking me, you know, they were trying to pick me for their team."

Chumboy said, "That happened to you often?"

"What? Both teams wanting me, like growing up, you mean?"

"Yeah."

"Well, Chum, I can play ball."

Big Donny said, "Don't guys like you usually play for the winners?"

"Guys like me?" Slaught bristled a bit, still watching through the slats, now leaning even closer to see what was happening outside. Bakalov and Scott came into view, but Slaught lost sight of them as Bakolov shoved Scott into the circle of men.

"Yeah, guys like you," Big Donny said, "you know, the kind of guy that gets the prom queen. Maybe you were even prom king. I don't know about that shit, though."

Slaught moved along the boxcar, trying to get a better view, wondered if he was that kind of guy. Didn't think so. Susun didn't seem like a prom queen, anyway. He said, "Yeah, don't know about that, either. But I like an underdog."

Chumboy tried peering through a lower crack that ran along the door, "Just seeing snow and feet. Wait, hang on... Love's talking..." Everyone in the boxcar was quiet now, listening to the scene outside. Chumboy said, "Okay, Love's saying something to Scott, Scott's shouting." And then they were all up and trying to listen. They heard Scott yelling, "This is insane," and Love addressing the crowd gathered around him, saying, "See this man here, this man we trusted and made part of our project, of our Expedition. This man has betrayed us. He has betrayed the Domain. The word is 'treason,' gentlemen."

"He's some big fucking drama queen," Big Donny said.

Love went on a bit longer, sending a ripple of murmuring through the crowd. Slaught asked, "Did he just say gold?" He listened hard as Love said, "This man was trying to steal from the City, to take the gold for himself. To deprive Talos of the resources it needed to rebuild the City."

Scott, almost pleading now, saying, "I don't have the gold. I don't have it."

"I know, Mr. Scott," Love was saying, "I know you don't have it because you're looking at that gold right now. That gold made this, the Domain, possible."

Scott, sounding disbelieving, maybe outraged, said, "You spent the gold on this fucking train?"

Slaught had never thought of that but it made perfect sense. How else to finance his expedition? Love had not only taken the gold, he'd spent it all. Mitch Black was going to be some pissed.

༈

Love knew he was in a tricky situation. Scott was down, weakened in the eyes of the crowd, but he wasn't exactly going quietly. And could the man just not shut the fuck up and let Love think? His begging wasn't helping, and it was making it hard for Love to concentrate. And his feet were cold. This fucking place and this fucking cold. It was playing havoc with his inner alignments.

So many problems, not just this cowering weasel in front of him, but Bakalov, too. Even now, all of the men in the crowd seemed to be watching Bakalov. Trying to determine what their leader thought. The big man of action. They weren't waiting to see what their Commander would do, weren't hanging on his words—the man who had created all of this, the man who had brought Scott to his knees—but were watching Bakalov, looming over Scott, fists clenched, massive. Strong. Oh, the loyalty.

Bakalov's boys were hunching up, moving in closer, the circle around Scott becoming tighter. Love realized he had to do something, right now. He'd seen guys like this before; it didn't matter if it was the schoolyard or the boardroom. If they smelled blood, you had to give them something.

Love said, "The gold was meant for our great project. When it was needed, the hidden was revealed to us, confirming the rightness of this project. Our destiny."

Scott, turning now, said, "This is bullshit, you all know it's bullshit ..." But then Bakalov stepped forward, and there was the crack of his fist. Scott tumbled down onto the snow, weakness almost a physical presence around him. The circle moved closer.

"You pick yourself up, Mr. Scott," Love said, trying for what he thought of as an elegant violence, restrained but authentic, "and start walking. You walk the length of this train and then keep walking, out towards the woods. I'm sending you to the wolves, Mr. Scott, as a sacrifice, because you are like them, you deserve them. Sneaky and greedy. Now start walking."

Scott, panicked, searching the faces around him, but then Bakalov hauled him to his feet, saying, "You heard the Commander, start walking."

"No, this is crazy, I'm not going out there, I'll get torn to pieces."

And then it was as if the group imagined it, some of them picturing Scott stumbling through the snow, sounds of howling and hunger. But others saw themselves in Scott and they shifted uncomfortably, eyes now down on the snow, not wanting to see the fear in his eyes. Feeling the shifting moods, Love barked at Bakalov, "What are you waiting for? Are you going soft on us?"

Bakalov hesitated, confused by what Love had said, what he wanted, and the pack seemed to lean forward as one. They, too, did not know what was expected, but they sensed a challenge.

And Love knew there and then what he would have to do to stop this gang of young bloods from tearing him apart. He could do it. After all, Ion had shown him how.

He stepped down from the platform, walked to Bakalov and held out his hand. "Give me your weapon."

Bakalov drew his pistol out slowly, saying, "If there is something you wish me to do Commander..." But Love barked again, "Ion, the gun!" And then it was in Love's hand and he took a deep breath. The crowd shifted uncomfortably, but, Love noticed, did not speak or try and stop him. They were waiting to see who would come out on top.

Love pushed past Bakalov and stood in front of Scott, who frowned, saying, "Look, Eton..." But Love said, "I told you to walk," and feeling strong and scared he pulled the trigger. Scott lurched backwards and the crowd was silent. Love could almost taste obedience in the air. He turned and as he passed Bakalov, dropped the gun onto the snow and said, "Now get me the woman with the map. And launch my invasion."

Yeah, he'd watched fucking Planet Earth. He knew how things died.

঎

"Shit. They're inside."

Susun listening at the top of the stairs. Hearing the voices, and what sounded like the chairs being kicked over. She whispered to Jordan, "Get everyone to the front of the building. Quiet, you understand? And send Shaun over here."

And Jordan went, feeling sick, ready to cry, and walking as soft as he could. Mrs. Merrill was halfway down the hallway with an armful of bedding. Jeff, Shaun, and Larose had been gathering furniture and carrying it towards the top of the stairs, just in case they needed it to block off the stairs later on. No one thought later on would be now.

Jordan whispered to Jeff, "They're here. Inside the building. Susun says to go to the front end." He saw Shaun and whispered, "Top of the stairs."

Shaun, inching towards the top of the stairs, said, "I can hear them, in the kitchen."

"Wasn't locked?" Jeff asked.

Jordan said, "Left it open for Johnny and Chum."

"Yeah, so where the fuck are they?" Larose said. "Christ almighty, of all the times… hope nothing has happened."

They had waited for what seemed like hours for Slaught and Chumboy to make it back from the train. Finally, after a constant parade of people going to look out the front windows and then saying, "No sign of them," Mitch had said, "For Chrissakes, I'll go look for them, okay? You guys are fucking driving me nuts. Get your shit together while I'm gone."

That was all of fifteen minutes ago. And now someone was down there trashing the place, breaking glass and slamming doors. Then it was quiet, and they heard a voice from the bottom of the stairs. "Hello? Everyone up there hiding?"

Larose jerked his head at Shaun, get those kids out of sight. Then they waited, holding their breath.

"We just want the woman who drew the map. Send her on down and we'll leave you in peace. Deal?"

Susun, standing in the doorway at the end of the hall, everyone looking at her, took a step towards the stairs. Then she felt Mrs. Merrill come out of the room behind her, calling down in her high-pitched, reedy voice, "Okay, I'm coming down but you have to keep your word." Then she took Susun's hand, whispering, "Get out of here, somewhere safe. You and the baby."

And then she was going down the stairs, almost rushing. Before she changed her mind.

॥

It was a mistake. Bakalov realized it now. To think the gold was unimportant. And to think he could outsmart the Commander. The Commander knew of the gold all along. Had everyone guessing and chasing each other while he created his vision. And Bakalov also realized that the Commander no longer trusted him. Had disrespected him in front of the Twenty.

He had a choice. Fix things to please the Commander. Or kill him. For now, he would try pleasing him. He sensed that things were not ready for him to assume command. To move into the Commander's boxcar with the desk and the map. Soon. But not yet.

Earlier, he had sent Jimmy and a couple of his soldiers up to the hotel. Infiltrate. Bring back the woman. Wait further instructions. Now he saw one of them heading towards him, leading an older woman. This could be it. Could help restore trust with the Commander.

He asked, "Is this her?"

"She won't stop talking…"

Mrs. Merrill sniffed a bit and said, "You don't have to be rude, young man. I came along nice like you asked. Now can I please see the man in charge." Then, as if just noticing Bakalov, she asked, "Are you the man in charge?"

Bakalov turned to the soldier without answering her and said, "Gather the rest of the men, and check the train perimeter. Make sure everyone is accounted for. Then get ready to head up to the hotel. Wait for me."

"I was speaking to you," Mrs. Merrill said. "Are you in charge? You act as if you are in charge."

But Bakalov just took her by the arm and started towards Love's boxcar, not thinking about the old woman next to him, but about the things he had failed to do: failed to handle Scott, failed to get the guides to cooperate, failed to stop the wolves from killing. That was the problem, it started with the wolves. Demons. That's what they were.

"I'm speaking to you," Mrs. Merrill repeated. "Where are you taking me?"

But Bakalov just said, "I'm not speaking to you," and pulled her up the metal steps and knocked on Love's door.

"Yes, come."

Bakalov pushed Mrs. Merrill through the door.

Love was agitated, and Bakalov wondered if the adrenaline was still pumping through him. Killing a man could do that to you. He said, "This is the woman who had the map."

"Are you in charge?" Mrs. Merrill asked, straightening the lapels of her grey wool coat. "I am only interested in speaking to the man in charge." But Love's hand was out, saying, "The map. Give me the map."

Mrs. Merrill flushed. "What is your name?"

He was close to her then. Close enough that she could smell his breath, he said, "Give me the fucking map."

She looked past his shoulder to the map on the wall. "Well, it looks just like that one. All maps look the same to me."

Love stepped back. His gaze shifted to Bakalov. Back to her. "You have no map."

She said nothing, smiling awkwardly but starting to panic, afraid now.

Love hissed at Bakalov, "There is nothing fucking special about this woman. Get her out."

Bakalov took hold of her arm, pulled her towards him and shook her. "Show him your map!"

Mrs. Merrill was on the verge of tears. She sputtered, then stopped and raised her chin. "This is all foolishness, you know. This map business. Foolish."

Love turned towards his map, as if trying to calm himself. Silence for several seconds while Mrs. Merrill looked back and forth between the two men. Love turned back to face Bakalov, "Give me your map. The one from your father, or your fucking grandfather, or whoever it was. Now."

Bakalov let go of Mrs. Merrill. "Commander... you don't need it..."

"Give me the map."

Bakalov felt sick, but it was an order. And he was not prepared to end this man now. He had been focused on the wrong things. Obsessed with his own failures, caught off guard. And the Commander was getting more and more powerful.

He tried once more as he reached into his pocket for the map. "But it is of no use to you."

"You're wrong, Ion." Love took the map and flipped it onto the desk behind him, letting Bakalov know he did not respect the map, did not respect Bakalov anymore, either.

"The usefulness of the map, Ion, is to motivate you. You bring me the real woman and you get this back for the family scrapbook. Otherwise? It goes into one of those big fire barrels of yours. Now get her out of here and don't come back until you have the right woman and the right fucking map."

"Myself, and my Twenty, we will go now, go now to find the woman."

"Burn them out if you have to, Ion, but bring me the map."

Bakalov left, hauling Mrs. Merrill along with him by her arm. Once out in the cold air, he tried to move his mind to solving his problem, did not want to be bothered with the woman who had started nagging him about what he was going to do with her and could she go back to the hotel. He pushed her towards the soldier outside Love's boxcar and said, "Take her back to the hotel." And the soldier said, "Sorry, sir, I'm only to take orders directly from the Commander."

Bakalov barely waited to hear the soldier out, dragging Mrs. Merrill towards the boxcar where all the workers were being held. Slaught and Chumboy, too. Mrs. Merrill said, "You're not putting me in there?" But he pushed her up the ramp, unlocking the door and sliding it open enough to shove her inside. Slammed the door shut again. Threw the bolt. Took a deep breath.

So now he knew where he stood. At the edge.

Chapter Twenty-Nine

The man was leaning against a railcar near the front of the train. He was smoking. She walked up to him, but it was almost as if he couldn't see her.

Susun said, "Hello?"

He squinted at her, looking genuinely perplexed at her appearing there in front of him, as if he couldn't process it.

"Hello?" she repeated. When he didn't answer, she said, "Are you alright?"

His gun came up, fast. He said, "Who the fuck are you?"

"I have what everyone is looking for. I thought I would make it easy for you."

As soon as Mrs. Merrill had descended the stairs out of sight, Susun had made her way to the back of the building and down into the basement. Once in the basement, though, it felt wrong to be hiding. If the man wanted the map, was willing to hurt people to get it, why not just give it to him? It was just a piece of paper. The map would still be in her dreams.

She liked how it swirled around in her head, liked waking each morning to new colours and forms, the map shifting and changing in her dreams. But this morning when she had woken up there were very vivid images in her mind. She added them to the map. Looked at it. Sat with it. And knew it was finished. So maybe it was a good time to hand the map over. Give him the paper, but keep the images in her mind.

She took a quick look around the basement, found some winter gear, the parka too big but it would do. She grabbed matches and extra mitts, already had her little knife with her so tucked it into her parka pocket. She slipped out the set of basement doors that took her to street level and then headed for the train. There was a large gathering of men farther down, past the end of the train where there was a clearing in the snow. Loud voices and shouting came from there, but she saw the man smoking and approached him.

He now asked, "You have the map?"

"Yes," Susun said. "What's your name?"

"Matt Hughes," he said, then added, "I thought you'd look different."

"How?"

"I don't know. Just different. Older maybe?"

"Today I feel old."

"You're pregnant?"

"Yes. I think it is a little girl."

He did not know what to say so he gestured with the gun. "Get moving. See the dark grey railcar, there? We're going there."

And so they walked, blood under their feet all the way, Susun wondering, wolf blood? Maybe men that were shot. Hard to say. She slowly placed one foot in front of the other and he said, "Squeamish, are you? Better get used to it."

She said, "I'm not afraid of blood."

He pushed her along until they came to the car. "Up here," he said, pulling her up the metal steps. He knocked on the train door, slid it open and said, "Go in, get in there."

A big man, bald and barrel-chested, stood behind a large black table. "You found her?"

The man holding her hesitated, wanting to take credit but

afraid of being caught in a lie. Susun said, "Yes, he found me. I was trying to get past the train," but Bakalov was suddenly right in front of her, the back of his hand felt like a slab of cement as it cracked against her jaw, sending her to the ground.

"I was not talking to you, bitch."

Susun felt warm blood running into her mouth, the strange metallic taste. She wiped at it with her hand, her mouth stinging as she said, "But you will."

When she saw his foot drawing back to kick her body she rolled away from him, yelling, "I'm pregnant."

Bakalov said to Hughes, "Get her up."

Hughes reached down, helping her up now. He avoided meeting her gaze. She moved away from Bakalov and placed a chair between them. "Don't come near me again."

Bakalov laughed, "Or else?"

"Do you want to know where the map is or not?"

"Yes. I want the map."

"If I give you the map, will you leave?"

"Give it to me."

"Will you go away? You don't need anything else here."

"You don't tell me what I need. Just tell me where the map is."

She hesitated, and he said, "Give me the map and I will let you go. If not, you can join the wolves. In the snow."

Susun felt Hughes look over at Bakalov but he said nothing. She doubted Bakalov would let her just leave. She had been trying to follow her instincts, but this now felt wrong. How could that be? She said, "I have it with me."

"Show me."

She reached inside her parka, felt it there, worn now, passed from hand to hand in the community, opened and folded and shared. She brought it out and passed it to the big man, his thick fist grabbing at it and then moving to the small side table to open it up.

He stared down at it for a few seconds, then turned to her and said, "You think it wise to risk everything on a stunt?"

"That's the map."

"This is a child's drawing."

"It's the map. I saw it in my dreams. I can't help how it looks to you."

"You little bitch," and he crumpled the map and tossed it on the floor. He looked to Hughes and said, "Get Jimmy."

Susun felt the small knife in her coat pocket. Bakalov's eyes were still on Hughes, so she moved, dropping down and scrambling fast towards him. He turned to swipe at her but she stayed focused, moved fast and strong and plunged the knife into his leg just above his knee. He roared, swore, reaching for her again, but he was off balance. She grabbed the map, and while Hughes watched her, ran from the boxcar.

৯

Bakalov was wearing the knife in his leg as he hobbled down the stairs of his boxcar. On the way out he swore at Hughes, bellowing, "Dumb fuck, go find her."

He leaned on his rifle to get off the last step, sharp pain shooting up the length of his leg. He slung the rifle over his shoulder. Better. The cold air felt good. He'd been too warm, maybe that was why he was feeling dizzy. Or maybe it was his leg, but it was only a small knife. Could not have done much damage.

It was fairly quiet outside. Some of the Twenty were down towards the back end of the train, a few men loading wood into a boxcar. Light from the windows at the front end of the train drew his attention. The cartographers still working. The Commander's light on, too.

What to do now? Tell Love he lost the map? And the woman? Was she even the map woman, and could that really be the map? He didn't know anymore.

He found himself headed towards the Commander's railcar but knew he did not want to tell him. It was not possible. But Love would be asking soon, would want to know why it was taking so long to find the woman and her map. Bakalov could not believe the mess he found himself in. There was no end to the fucking up.

And his map. He needed that back. He could go after her but he did not think that time would be on his side. By the time he found her, Love may have already destroyed his map.

He hesitated. The throbbing in his leg was making it hard for him to concentrate, to think. His head had started to ache. He wiped his brow with his glove. He was warm again. Sick, maybe? A soldier positioned outside of Love's boxcar approached him and said, "Are you okay?" Then he noticed the knife. "You should get that out. There is a doctor here. Maybe you should get it looked at, get stitches or something."

Bakalov said, "What's your name?"

"Manning."

"I don't know you."

"No sir, I'm part of the Commander's security detail." He added, "You don't look so good, sir, I could escort you to your quarters."

Bakalov nodded. Took note of the man's hand resting on his rifle; he was ready to protect the Commander. There was another man, also dressed in the black uniform, stationed just outside the Commander's train car.

Bakalov said, "I am good, Manning."

Bakalov started to head towards the main road, trying to put some distance between himself and Manning. He could feel the soldier still watching him. He got to the bottom of the small hill that ran up to the main street of the town and he heard Manning call out, "Mr. Bakalov. Wait, please. The Commander wants to see you."

Bakalov stopped. This was not how he wanted it to go. Not yet. But how to make it the way he wanted it?

Do what he should have done before.

Long before the Commander killed the wolf. That had changed the Commander. And changed the way the men saw him. And he should have done it long before the Commander took his map.

Bakalov turned and made his way back towards the train, limping and stumbling a bit, slipping his gun into his hand, and then taking hold of his leg and acting as if it was almost useless He dragged his leg up the steps into the Commander's boxcar, keeping Manning's focus on his injury. Not the gun. If he could get inside, he could then decide the fate of the Commander.

Stepping through the door, he was reassured by the feel of metal in his hand. But then Love said, "Really, Ion, you give me no credit at all."

Love, leaning against his desk, appeared relaxed, arms crossed. Two men waited inside on either side of the door. Manning appearing in the doorway behind him. Trapping him.

"You, Ion, are not the man you once were. You've become, I don't know, what's the word? Diminished. And, sadly for you, I am having the opposite experience. I'm growing. Personal growth, Ion, that's what it all about. And you..." Then he noticed the knife jutting out of Bakalov's leg. "What do have we here?"

Bakalov did not speak. Tried to draw himself up, but the pain was too sharp.

Love looked to the men in his railcar, "Anyone? What is happening here?"

One guy shrugged, then Manning said, "We heard some yelling earlier, maybe ten, fifteen minutes ago. Then saw someone running into the woods." He glanced at Bakalov's leg, adding, "Guess it wasn't him who was running."

Bakalov said, "I saw the map. It is not a real map. Scribbles. It was not important."

"The map? Where is it?"

"The woman left with it."

"And where did she go?"

"Into the woods."

"And did she do that to you?"

Bakalov said nothing.

"You know, Ion, we could have done great things. But you got greedy. I'm exceptionally disappointed."

Bakalov, swallowing hard, said, "I understand."

Love was quiet for a few seconds, then said, "Do you? I don't think you do. I mean, I think you were coming through that door to kill me. So should I kill you? I'd be well within my rights, wouldn't I?"

"Yes."

"But you see, Ion, that will not help me realize my goals, understand? There are things you can do for me besides die that will help me. So what you are going to do is go get that woman. And if you're right and it is just meaningless scribbles, or whatever you said, fine, we expose it as meaningless. But I can't have that map, or a rumour of another map, or any other dream bullshit of this woman, out there. Can't have it. You're going to bring me the map. These men are going to take you until you pick up her trail, then you are going to find her. If you don't go, then I am going to have you tied to a tree out there and left for those wolves of yours. Understand that, Ion? With that bloody leg it won't take them long to find you."

Then Love made a face and said to the man behind Bakalov, "And is that normal? Such a small knife and so much blood?"

"Maybe he's one of those bleeders, know what I mean?"

Bakalov interrupted, said, "It is dark."

"It is always fucking dark here, Ion, this is the darkest, shittiest fucking place I've ever been. And that's why I am going to finish up and get the fuck back down to the City. Stop wasting my time and get out there."

"It will be hard to find her."

Love shrugged and said to Manning, "Get your men, get the fuck up that hill and clear that hotel. Apparently Bakalov's minions have secured it. You can kill everyone, I really don't care, just get it done. But first take this man out and find those tracks." Then he turned back to Bakalov, "You're the great hunter, get out there and hunt."

ᛉ

Mitch had no luck finding Slaught. Tried the work bay. Nothing. If he wasn't hiding out, he might be locked up in one of the boxcars. From where she was, she could see the train, some of the boxcars open, ramps down, but most shut up tight. And there weren't nearly as many men around as she estimated there should be. Who knew how many were inside? But there was no way she was going down there to find out. The snow had turned hard with the cold weather, a thin layer of ice on its surface, every step sounding like an explosion. No sneaking around on a night like this.

Her best bet was to head back to the hotel, just in case

Slaught had turned up. She made her way up the small trail that snaked up to the main road. A big bonfire burning farther up the road was blocking the main street at the north end. Couple guys tending it. She could hear their voices, the sounds carrying in the clear, cold night. Too busy bullshitting each other to be paying attention to her moving along the far side of the street, crossing to the hotel, then down along the side to the door.

Lights were all out. Mitch slipped into the entranceway, and immediately heard voices from the kitchen. Might be friendlies but she doubted it, the voices unfamiliar. She had no idea what was going on, for all she knew the place could be crawling with Bakalov's crew. She went farther along the narrow hallway until she was just outside the kitchen door. Took a quick look. Again, guys not paying attention, leaning against the big table with their backs to her, looking into the dining room.

A stocky guy was holding a flashlight, another one had a bottle of booze.

The guy with the flashlight said, "It was fucking awesome, Jimmy, fucking awesome."

Jimmy said, "Which house did you do?"

"Some old guy with his chick. And he got mouthy right away, told me to get the fuck out of his house."

Passing the liquor bottle, Jimmy said, "What'd you do, teach him a lesson?"

"It was over so fast man, so fast. Couldn't believe how fucking fast it was. Like we walked in, and the guy in the kitchen said, who the hell are you, and I told him to shut the fuck up and he told me to get out," taking a swig, "and so I just shot him, and his old lady started screaming, and I just shot her, too."

Jimmy said, "Wish I'd been there."

"No fucking doubt you wish."

Mitch slipped into the kitchen, as the two guys kept talking.

"Yeah, cuz you know what I woulda done? I'd have taken his face and, bam, right into the fucking wall."

"Yeah?"

"Fuck ya. I mean I wouldn't take any shit from him," Jimmy said, gesturing for the other guy to pass him back the bottle. "Let him get away with that? No fucking way. You know what else I would've done?"

Jimmy reached to take the bottle, but stopped as he struggled to process what he was seeing, Mitch with her knife in his buddy who went down fast, the bottle smashing to the floor and then everything stinking of rye. Jimmy scrambled to retrieve his gun from the table but Mitch sent a toaster into his face a few times, not giving him a chance to say what he would've done, and leaving him on the floor.

She kept going, into the next hallway, the rest of the building quiet. She started up the stairs but saw Levi coming down. "They're in the building," she told him.

"Think three came in," Levi said.

"Two were in the kitchen. Won't be bothering anyone for a while though."

"The third one left with the old woman."

"Old woman?"

"The Merrill woman. She went instead of Susun when they came for the map. She told Susun to hide."

"Did she?"

"Hide? Don't know."

"Slaught turn up?"

"No, not yet."

"There's a couple of boxcars under lock and key down there, he's probably in one of them. Anyone here hurt?"

Larose, coming down the stairs said, "Nice of you to show up."

"That's what I thought, asshole."

Jordan was coming down fast behind Larose, saying, "Could we not be bickering? Seriously. We have, like, some major, major, epic..."

Mitch said, "Spit it out."

Jordan said, "They're coming."

"The Twenty?"

Jordan said, "Don't know, they're coming from all sides. And it looks more like the four hundred to me."

Chapter Thirty

"Shit's sake, we got next to nothing here," Tiny said, sorting through boxes of ammo. "We're low on everything."

"I thought all of this was supposed to be over, that we'd dealt with Talos and it was finished," Larose said, sounding scared, trying to make sense of things.

"What, thought it was going to be happy ever after for you?" Mitch asked.

"I wasn't talking to you, lady," Larose said.

Tiny said, "That's right, though," looking over at Auntie Verla, sitting in the corner knitting. "In fact it was you that said it was over. That it was going to end in the snow. Those were your words. And now all of this map crap. What's going on?"

"I'm knitting you a toque, Tiny," she said.

The wool was blue and yellow. "Well, thanks, Verla, but right now I'd like to know if you got any insight into this map business? Why didn't he just ride up on his train and make the fucking maps? What's with all the guns and the howling and killing? Doesn't make any sense."

"Nope. No sense," Auntie Verla said.

"And what's with Susie? What's that about?"

"You're asking me questions," Auntie Verla said, concentrating on her stiches, "I don't have the answers for."

"But these dreams of hers," Tiny persisted, "you think she's actually dreaming this shit? You've talked to her."

"Mothers-to-be sometimes have strong dreams, Tiny. And Susie is a strong woman. I saw that when I first met her. Under those cedar trees."

"And that's when you said it was all going to end? Remember that? You told Johnny it would end in the snow, right? That was your prophecy or whatever. And he went out there, him and Chum, *in the snow*, and finished it with this Talos outfit, sent that one over there," pointing to Mitch, "packing. So I just don't know why we're right back in it."

Auntie Verla put down her knitting, the ball of blue wool slipping off her lap and rolling out along the floor, all of them watching it until it came to a rest, and Auntie Verla said, "I never said it was Johnny that would end it."

"What? What does that mean?" Tiny asked. Then, sounding panicked, he turned to Larose, "Where's Susie?"

They all looked at each other, Shaun saying, "She went to hide, right? When they came for Mrs. Merrill."

"Jesus Christ," Tiny said, "I should have gone with her. Where the fuck could she have gone to hide?"

"I don't know, but I hope it's a good spot," said Jeff, "because they're coming. And there's more than we thought."

Mitch said, "What are you seeing?"

Jeff focused the night vision binoculars on the far end of the street. He could see a group of men heading up the street, mismatched uniforms, must be the Twenty. Behind them, though, looking a little more solid, about six guys in dark gear, and then maybe another half dozen in regular camo. "Spooky as shit looking out there. There's two groups, no wait, there's more guys coming up behind, hard to tell. But there's the Twenty, and then some kind of security guys? Looks like they got AK-47s."

Mitch said, "Give me those," grabbing the binoculars. "Shit, those are Galil ACEs. Fucking overkill. Jesus Christ I can't believe this."

Larose and Tiny were at the window, Tiny asking if someone should go downstairs, cover the front doors and secure the kitchen.

Everyone was sounding panicked, grabbing for the weapons while Auntie Verla sat with her knitting. Jeff picked up a pump action and said, "Not much good with this." Then he asked Mitch, "So what's our plan? Should I go cover downstairs?"

"What am I, the fucking den mother?"

But everyone was quiet, just waiting for orders. She said, "Fuck's sake. Okay, half of you, downstairs and secure the doors. And check around for Susun, we'll need everyone. Best shots, stay up here." Then she looked around the room. "Can any of you actually shoot?"

Larose said him and Shaun could shoot just fine but Chumboy was the best shot. Mitch said, "Well he isn't fucking here, is he?" Then she told them to get the two end windows opened up, get in position there.

"And somebody get downstairs and block those doors, use anything you can get your hands on." Mitch looked around, scared faces staring at her. Jesus Christ, what fucking slim pickings. "Okay you," pointing to an ashen-faced Max, "you go with this old geezer here and keep those dickheads away from those front doors. Someone gets through, just shoot them. Understand? No chit chat, no questions. Just fucking shoot. Can you do that?"

"Damn straight we can," McLaren said, "don't you worry about us."

Mitch told everyone to get a fucking move on. She figured they could hold them off for a while but those guys out there could make mincemeat of the place with a little bit of time. They were going to need more. More firepower. More bodies. More time. "Okay, we're going to let them get closer. If we start now, they're just going to scatter. Let them get close, maybe we can at least take out a few. And aim for the guys in black. They're going to do the most damage."

Mitch checked her own weapon, feeling them all watching her, hanging on every word, nodding. Serious like. As if this bunch of fucking misfits could actually pull this off. Christ almighty.

Auntie Verla put down her knitting and said to Mitch, "I think you could use a green toque, but that little man of yours, still not sure about him." She paused for a moment, looking intently at Levi. He just looked back at her, eyes flat, grey. Auntie Verla said, "Why don't you take him and get on down to that train station. Free some of those boys down there to come and help us out." Auntie Verla patted her large wicker knitting basket. "Not to worry about us, I've got the makings for some nice Molotov cocktails in here. We'll be alright for a while."

ॐ

Big Donny said, "So what the fuck? Didn't break you out of that shithole jail so you could sit around on your ass."

He was looking over at Slaught slumped down on the bench. Slaught was trying to open his eye, the left one crusted and feeling puffy. After Mrs. Merrill had been tossed into the boxcar, she had tried clearing away some of the dried blood with her hankie, but it hurt like hell. Slaught had asked about Susun, and Mrs. Merrill said she was safe, hiding, and after that Slaught relaxed a bit. Felt like maybe he had dozed off. He woke to the sound of more howling. Sounded like a fucking chorus out there.

"How long I been sleeping?"

"All fucking afternoon, and through that racket out there, Jesus," Big Donny said, but Mrs. Merrill said it was more like a minute. "Doesn't matter how long," said Big Donny, "I broke this guy out of the Facility. Now he thinks he's fucking Sleeping Beauty."

But what the fuck to do? They were locked in the metal boxcar and no matter how many times he searched it from corner to corner, he couldn't see any way out.

"So why did you break me out?"

"Owed you. For looking out for Raymond, here. And cause of the spooky kid. Owed him, too."

"Levi?"

"Don't know his name. Didn't know he even had one. But yeah, him and Raymond were pretty tight for a while, living down there in the tunnels. The kid saved Raymond's ass more than once. Raymond," Big Donny said, "has a way of getting himself in trouble. Don't you, Raymond?"

Raymond shrugged. "Maybe."

"Well, Ray," Slaught said, "we're right back in it now."

And then they all jumped. A gunshot, close by, made the men scramble back from the door. Then the sound of metal on metal, the bolt sliding and then the door was pulled open.

"Well," said Slaught, "speak of the devil."

༄

Jumping down from the train, Slaught landed beside the body of a soldier lying face down in the snow. He asked Levi, "Did you do this?"

Levi shrugged. "Yeah. Most of them are heading up towards the hotel, but I ran into this guy down here. Think there's a few more at the other end of the train."

"Where'd you come from?"

"Came up from behind, across the lake. Mitch went for the front end of the train."

Guys started jumping down out of the boxcar, tentative at first, but when it was clear no one was shooting at them they got a little more comfortable, milling about, talking about what they should do next. Levi had weapons for Slaught and Chumboy, Slaught passing his over to Raymond and saying, "You hold onto this, I'm not good with a gun." Then, hearing the steady howling from across the lake, he asked Levi, "Did you see the wolves out back? They've been howling their heads off for the past few hours."

Levi said, "Saw them. Must be over a dozen."

Slaught, curious, said, "They not interested in you?"

"Not really."

"How does a city kid like you get so comfortable in the bush? Don't make sense to me."

"There's animals in the City."

Slaught was skeptical. "I suppose."

"In the tunnels, I learned a lot from the rats. When to run. How to hide. They're smart."

Slaught said he figured that might be true. Then Levi pointed to a guard sitting alone in the open door of one the boxcars. The guy just sat and watched them as they came his way.

They got closer and he asked, "You letting everyone out?" Sounding surprised.

Slaught stopped, trying to see if the guy was armed. "Yeah," he answered.

"Packed in there like hogs, eh?"

"Yeah, I was one of those hogs."

"What are you going to do now? Can't exactly run away. We're all stuck. Guess we just have to sit around and wait for orders. No one knows what the fuck is going on."

Chumboy and Big Donny came up from behind, Raymond, some of the guys from the boxcar and Mrs. Merrill with them.

Big Donny said, "Thinking of heading up towards the hotel. Should get Mrs. Merrill somewhere safe."

"Doesn't sound too safe up there," Slaught said. "Sounds like those young punks are gathering up there, howling and all. Blocking the main entrance, I'd guess."

"The side door is open," Mrs. Merrill said, "that's how the boys got in before. We could try there. I don't care to be out here much longer."

"Mrs. Merrill," Big Donny explained, "finds that the criminal element agitates her."

"Oh," Mrs. Merrill said, colouring a bit, patting Big Donny's arm, "not Donald here, he's turned out to be a real gentleman."

"Hard to tell who's a criminal out here, anyway," Chumboy said, then asking the guard, "Shouldn't there be more bodies around? Where is everybody?"

The man shrugged. "Few guys went into the bush, a bunch went up the hill to sack the hotel. Some hiding in the boxcars, scared of the wolves."

Slaught said, "And who are you?"

"Hughes, one of the security crew."

"And what are you doing if everyone else is so busy?"

Hughes shrugged, "I was left to guard the woman. But she's gone."

Slaught felt a stab of both hope and dread. "What woman?"

"The one that got away," Hughes said, pointing over his shoulder. "She went across the lake."

Slaught, thinking of the wolves, thinking of Susun, asked, "Long brown hair, tall?"

"Yeah, sounds like her."

Slaught asked, "What way? What way did she go?"

"Into the woods. Bakalov went in to find her."

Slaught was having trouble breathing. Levi said, "Go find her. We'll go up to the hotel."

"But fucking Bakalov," Slaught said. He asked the guy in the doorway, "How long ago? When did Bakalov leave?"

"An hour ago, maybe longer. But he'll be moving slow. She got a knife into him. He took off with it still in his leg."

"Jesus," was all Slaught could manage.

Big Donny, smiling, shaking his head, said, "Take it easy, Winterman. If that bastard has a knife in his leg he isn't going to get too far."

"Susie," Slaught said, "she just had this little knife she carried, for cutting twigs and stuff. Not going to slow Bakalov down."

"I tell you right now, it's going to slow him down for sure. He's going to be losing blood like a stuck pig."

"Why's that?" Chumboy asked.

"Been putting a side of rat poison with his supper every night. Motherfucker didn't have a clue."

"What's that do?" Slaught asked.

"Going to turn that big fucking Dogman's blood to water, that's what it's going to do."

Levi said, "If he's bleeding, the wolves will be on him."

"He's going to take them right to Susie," Slaught said.

"Let's go," said Chumboy, "no point standing around thinking about it."

Slaught said, "No, you should head up to the hotel. We got lots of folks trapped up there, Love is still in the mix, and we have no idea which way the majority of these guys are going to go if things get out of hand. We need all hands on deck up there. Plus we need a few of you to check the train, don't want any troublemakers hanging back. I'll go after Susun. It'll be just me and Bakalov. Compared to the hotel, those aren't bad odds."

"But you got those wolves out there, that changes things," Raymond said.

"Don't worry," Chumboy said, "Johnny's playing for team wolf, he should be fine."

Slaught sighed, glancing down the length of the train to the darkness of the bush. "Let's just hope they know it."

※

"Why isn't it up to date, Harris?"

The head cartographer stammered, "The wolves... no one has been going out, there haven't been any updates to process into the maps. Uh... we have been working off some field notes but... uh, there just isn't very much ..." Harris' voice trailed off.

Love surveyed the room. Large sheets of paper tacked to the wall, piles of scribbled notes and six fucking stupid faces.

"Why do you think you are here? Hmmm? Why?"

Nobody said anything.

"I'm waiting."

Harris said, "We're making a preliminary survey. Inventory of infrastructure. Sketching maps." The man sounded tentative.

Love sighed. Decided to take a few seconds, breathe slowly, try to calm himself. "I don't see any proper maps here," he said, grabbing the sheets on the wall and ripping them down. "This is crap. Nothing but crap." He tried to steady his breathing, refocus. He could hear sporadic gunfire; at least things were happening up at the hotel.

"Sorry, yes," Harris said, "they are not of the best quality. But we can't just conjure..."

"Yes, you fucking can. That's exactly what you are going to do. You are going to fucking conjure me a map. A map with roads and rivers and dams and mine sites and a fucking future. You understand? And you have twenty-four hours to do it."

"Well, we need to sleep..."

"I don't fucking sleep," Love yelled, "so you don't fucking sleep!"

And with that, Love left, slamming the door of their railcar.

Chapter Thirty-One

Snow in slow motion, straight down and sparse. Big flakes. Looking up, she could watch it emerge from the dark blue sky and drift down around her. To the west, the horizon was a pale green, lying low behind the jagged tops of the jack pines. Above that the night was pushing down, the glowing greens giving way to navy. She could hear sounds, but couldn't identify them. Skittering sounds. Shuffling in the underbrush. Scratching on the crust of the snow. The night woods waking up as the twilight started to give way to darkness.

Beautiful, but strange. Unsettling.

She kept moving, making her way carefully in between the houses that sat above the lake, then up along the snow machine trail towards the woods. Her footsteps were loud, breaking through the skin of ice that came with the cold turn of weather. She stopped. A split in the trail. The snow machine trail heading down to her right. To her left, a narrow footpath.

Which way to go to put the most distance between her and Bakalov? Maybe even get away. She might be able to outlast him, have more stamina. He was bleeding. Perhaps she should go deeper into the woods. Or maybe everyone was out looking for her and she should sit tight and wait to be found. Or maybe no one was looking. She wasn't sure what had happened to Johnny or Chumboy, and when she'd left the train station the men gathering there seemed loud, riled up. They were probably up at the hotel, now. She did not want to imagine the worst.

Perhaps she should try to circle back to the hotel to help. It hadn't felt good to leave everyone behind. It had been a gamble. If it was really the map that Talos wanted, it might have worked. But they wanted what the map represented. Wanted to stop the story of her map. She understood that now.

She rested her hand on her stomach, glad for the company. "Should I let the stars guide us?"

The stars were faint overhead, waiting on the growing darkness to reveal them. The green light now just a ribbon along the western horizon. She took the footpath, looking up into the treetops, branches spread like pale veins against the sky. She wondered about Johnny. Wished he was with her, the two of them walking with the stars.

Howling. Real wolves, she thought, not one of those boys. She stopped. She knew the wolves were out there; she had seen their tracks, and every now and again she had come across one of their kills.

Then a shot, cracking the night. She hunched down instinctively. Impossible to tell in the cold empty landscape where the shot had come from. The sound seemed to be all around her in that moment. She could feel her heart pounding. Was the baby's heart pounding, too?

The howling started up, then more voices joined in, the sound prolonged and pained. Susun decided to head back. She hoped Bakalov had stuck to the main trail; she did not want to run into him on the narrow footpath. If she could get to the ridge above the lake, she could circle around and try and get close to the hotel from behind.

The howling grew upon itself as she backtracked. She was trying to rush, but then she slipped off the trail, going down into the snow along the edge. It was jarring—hurt her back.

Best to slow down. Slow down her breathing, too.

She caught the faint bob of a light through the trees. Flashlight. She stopped so she could hear. The sound of footsteps, the crunch of the snow. Where had the flashlight gone? The trees in front of her were dark and she was unable to see the light now, but she had seen it in the woods. And if she could hear his footsteps, he could hear hers. He must be somewhere nearby.

Then startling her, way too close, Bakalov calling, "Map lady? Where are you?"

She started back down the trail but could not move very fast, slipping down again, her leg plunging though the sharp ice into the soft snow below. Stuck. Seeing the glint of the flashlight through the trees again, the voice calling, "I just need the map. Then I take you back. Before the wolves get you."

He yelled at her through the darkness for a while as she freed her leg and set off again. They were both moving, and she could hear the thick sound of his heavy boots punching through the snow behind her, sounding closer now, his voice crystal clear. She saw the flashlight reaching towards her against the snow, the ice on top glistening then returning to darkness. He was maybe fifty yards behind her. She could hear his wheezing, maybe he was slowing down. Then to her right, a slight cracking sound of the icy crust on top of the snow. Moving too fast, too steady for a man. Too light. Wolves, maybe.

She kept her eyes on the trail, but it was hard to see now. All the snow had turned blue in the darkness. She listened hard and then she was certain: it was wolves, the sound of their paws breaking through the snow, sometimes sliding a bit, claws scrambling on the ice. They were moving parallel to her, stalking her. Two or three, maybe more.

She decided she needed to lose at least one of her pursuers. She felt, but could not be sure, that Bakalov was gaining on her.

To her right was a clearing that sloped down into the deepening shadows of the tag alder and dogwood scrub. If she could reach it, she would be hard to spot. But how to get across there without his hearing her leave the trail? And the snow might be too deep; she could get bogged down.

She got down on all fours and began moving across the thin, icy surface of the snow. It crackled under her mitts as she made progress away from the man. He began yelling again, swearing. Swearing, too, at the wolves.

The wind was picking up as she reached the line of small trees. She could see that on the other side was a short open area and then what looked like dense bush. It was colder, now. She sat back on her haunches thinking, curling her hand up in her mitts. Too cold. And Bakalov was too close. And the wolves? She was pretty sure they were even closer than the man. Shadows, impressions. But they were there.

She pushed through the dogwood and found herself maybe twenty yards from the bush. She stayed crawling and began to move towards the trees, thinking her best bet would be to find a sheltered spot. Try and hunker down for the night before she found herself too far away from the town or out in the open, the wind now sending snow, sharp and tiny, spitting at her face.

"You fucking little bitch." His voice raspy.

She held her breath. Afraid to move now, knowing he heard her and was close. She slowly turned her head, how had she not heard him? Paying too much attention to the noise she was making herself. Still, he must be at least twenty yards away. Make a run for it? Stay put? He must be on the other side of the scrub, which meant he'd probably heard her but he couldn't see her, the thin beam of the flashlight searching now through the darkness.

She heard the man curse, fire his gun into the darkness.

Susun knew then that the wolves had caught up to them, were spooking Bakalov. She decided to make a run for the trees, taking a few steps but plunging through into the snow, the snow up to her hip, hauling her leg out and getting her balance on the trail again. The man was yelling some more, couldn't tell if it was at her or the wolves because she could only hear the crunching of the snow under her feet, close to the trees now. Bakalov firing again, at her? At them? Seemed like the bullet was close.

She was moving as fast as she could, her bulky clothes slowing her down. And then something moving through the trees on her left: a wolf, not huge, but big enough, just a few yards behind her. She could smell it, feel its presence, and she thought of yelling at it but didn't want to draw Bakalov's attention.

Then she hit a patch of ice. Sheer ice. And a slope, too, her feet going out from under her, and she was skidding, then sliding, sideswiping the wolf that had been picking up steam behind her. Tangled up together, they slid sidewise down the steep incline, then hit the edge. Susun sensed the drop coming and scrambled to grab hold of something, hearing the wolf also clawing at the snow, clipping her chin. Then both of them went over the drop and hit the snow below. Breath gone, Susun flailed her arms outward to fend off the wolf. She looked into the dark space under the outcropping of rock she had just fallen over. Bakalov, somewhere above her, was yelling and then muttering and yelling again, *you little bitch*. She rolled in under the outcrop, and then in the darkness the man's ragged breath. He was right above her, at the edge.

Holding her breath. Listening as Bakalov paused, the beams of his flashlight sweeping overhead. Then he moved on. Then more howling and the sound of Bakalov's yelling farther away, cursing her, cursing the wolves. She didn't know where the wolf was, sensing it close, smelling it, too, the wet of its fur. She pressed herself against the rock wall behind her and closed her eyes, trying to shut out the yips and howls and the man's now frantic shouts.

ℵ

Mitch could hear someone in the next car. Figured it must be Love.

There was so much noise and confusion, howling and shooting from up at the hotel, it hadn't been all that hard to get close to the train. She told Levi to go check if Slaught was in the boxcars at the far end, to try and sort out who was who in the bunch of guys down there. She'd take the front end.

She was careful, going around to the far side of the train, slipping along and up into the first car. It was empty. Fancy but chaotic, the bed messed and strewn with papers and folders, several drinking glasses half full of thick green liquid were on the floor, the bedside table, the chairs. Dirty plates, too, food barely eaten. Mitch figured it was Love's railcar. And from the looks of things he wasn't living his best life. Fucking weirdo. Then she could hear some hollering coming from the next railcar. Someone sounding pissed, ranting. She guessed it was Love and it sounded as though he was finishing up. Figured it wouldn't be long before he was back. She decided to stay put.

Get it over with.

As he whipped open the door to his compartment, he came up short, saying, "Who the fuck are you?" Then wary, slowing down his momentum into the room, he asked, "Are you the map woman?"

"Where's the Dogman?"

Frowning now, "Who are you?"

"I'm asking the questions, buddy," she waved her Beretta she'd been holding down at her side. "So, again, where's Baldie?"

He didn't seem nervous enough, and Mitch figured he'd just remembered he was armed. Now he'd be thinking of how to reach underneath his fleece vest to get at the gun and fire it before she took his face off with hers.

He asked, "Do you know Ion Bakalov?"

"Done business with him."

"You must be Mitch Black." Love was impatient, "What are you doing in here?"

"Looking for Bakalov and you."

"Well now you've found me, aren't you lucky. You know, I've heard all about you. I had a chance to discuss you a bit with Bob Scott. You knew Bob Scott, old friend of yours, right?"

Love had now moved his hand to his vest pocket, resting it casually there. Still had miles to go unless he was fucking Wyatt Earp. She said, "I know Scott."

"Uh, wrong tense, Black, you *knew* him. So my condolences to you. See, I shot him. Right out there in the snow." Waiting for a response, but getting none, he said, "I shot him because he lied to me about the gold. He told me he hadn't tried to steal it. Or, I mean, let's be honest, better to say he didn't try and have you steal it for him. And you've been looking for the gold all over the place. Is that what brought you to the Winterman?"

Mitch said, "You talk a lot."

"You've taken up with the Winterman? Bad decision if you have—right now all my men are up there cleaning house. This is going to be my new outpost, you know. We're pushing into the hinterland. Restoring civilization."

Mitch glanced around the compartment, checking that there was nothing else she had to worry about other than whatever was under Love's vest.

"If you're looking for your gold," Love said, "well, congratulations, you've found it."

"It's here?"

"You're standing in it."

"You used the gold for this fucking train?" Un-fucking-believable.

Love said, "Yes, on the Domain, for the grand vision. To do a reset on the planet. A hyper-upgrade. That's what I'm doing with your gold. Money well spent wouldn't you agree?"

Talking fast, maybe to distract her. He started to cross over towards the map that hung on the wall behind his desk, using that opportunity to try and casually slide down the zipper on his vest. Christ, he was slow getting to that gun.

She asked, "That some gas station road map?"

"Much more than that, it's the past. You know what I'm doing here? Do you understand? See, this map, it's the world that existed before. Now, on *this* map," he turned his back to her as he focused on the big map sprawled across his desk, "I'm drawing the world anew. Like a god. Creating it, you understand? Drawing the riches underneath the ground, harnessing, taking. The map, it's just the beginning. I'm going to draw the whole known world next. Will put my mark on it."

Mitch said, "Still with the talking."

He turned around, smirking, gun out, and so Mitch shot him. Blood splattering across the map.

She tore the map off the wall and grabbed the bloody one off the desk, left the boxcar, crumpling up the maps and tossing them into the burn barrel.

"So much fucking trouble over some bullshit maps," she said to no one.

ဢ

It was hard to tell who was who. That was the problem. Some had clearly headed up the hill with the Twenty, falling in, seeing if, after prison and the work gangs, there might be some excitement to be had. But most of the guys in the boxcar had simply stayed put, hanging around the fire barrels. Why get involved? Wasn't their fight, anyway.

There were several guys still close by, though, wearing the black uniforms, looking like Love's men. Probably tasked with watching the train. A few others were positioned at the bottom of the hill. She'd already stuck her head into the cartographers' car, told them they were free to take their naps. But what to do about the rest of the men hanging around the town. Who knew which way things could go?

She yelled from the platform of Love's railcar, "Hey, Love's dead. Consider yourselves unemployed."

A bunch of the men turned her way, and a few started to head over. One of them yelled, "Bullshit. Who the fuck are you?"

"The one who killed him."

One of the security guys said, "You better fucking account for yourself right now. Where the fuck did you come from?"

Mitch put a bullet into the guy's leg, and he let out a scream and fell onto the snow. She said, "Don't have time for bullshit. You got a hundred unhappy and hungry workers, you got the worst bunch of fucking idiots up the road trying to torch a civilian target, and you got no bosses. You guys need a Plan B."

The other guys were uncertain now.

"General Bakalov..."

Hughes said, "Gone. And injured. Saw him heading off into the woods myself. One of the Wintermen guys went after him. Bunch of them went up to the hotel, too." He bent down, saying, "I'm taking this guy to the doctor. Someone help me? It's the fourth car down there." Another guy joined him, pulling up the bleeding man who then looked at Mitch and said, "Fuck you, bitch."

Some of the workers were now drifting over, attracted by the shooting. A few of the soldiers followed Manning, Love's senior security guard, as he drew his weapon and pushed his way into the ring of men, Mark Collins right behind him. He asked one of the guys in black, "Who's the chick?"

One of them said, "I think it's Mitch Black."

Manning, peering up at her, now bringing up his gun, said, "I thought she was dead."

"No, on the run. She was hiding out down south from what I heard," the first security guy said, now also levelling his gun at her.

Mark Collins said, "She has a price on her head."

Manning was starting to say maybe they should lock her up when Raymond shouted, "Hey, wait a minute, buddy, do I know you?"

Everyone turned to look over at Raymond, including Mark Collins. Raymond got a good look at him and said, "You fucking weasel-faced bastard."

Collins panicked, recognizing Raymond from the night he'd closed the door on Raymond and Slaught, leaving them to the dogs. Collins said, "Hey man, I didn't..." but then just started to run, pushing a few guys out of the way. Raymond plunged after him, leaping on his back and bringing the guy down onto the snow. Men scattered every which way; a few guys, including Manning, grabbed at Raymond, hauling him off as Collins tried to scramble to his feet. Raymond was still yelling as Manning swung his AK around and shouted for everyone to get the fuck out of the way while he dealt with this clusterfuck. Then Levi was right there beside Manning, no one even noticing him until he'd shot Manning, then Collins.

Levi just stood there while Raymond looked around, fishing in his pocket for the gun Slaught had given him. He waved it around, then said to the group of men now looking in confusion from the dead soldiers to Levi, to Raymond, "No more bullshit. You got a problem with what we are doing, go back to your boxcars and stay the fuck out of our way."

Mitch jumped down off the train steps, came over and said to Levi, "Where's everyone else?"

"The hotel. 'Cept Slaught, he went to look for Susun."

Mitch could hear the howling and whooping from up by the hotel. "Okay gentlemen, you know your choices. Stay out of the way or help out. Now, who wants to come along and put those pups up there in the kennel?"

A few guys moved over to Raymond and two guys headed back to the train, one of them muttering, "Fuck this shit." The last of the security men nodded at Love's body on the steps and asked Mitch, "What do we do with him?"

"Feed him to the wolves for all I care."

Chapter Thirty-Two

He'd been out walking for a couple of hours when he came across Bakalov.

He'd already searched through the houses across the lake, thinking it would make sense for her to hide in one of them. Nothing. He headed out then along the series of bush trails that ran from the edge of the town out to their traplines and fishing holes. The tracks were confusing, the snow trampled up a fair bit.

Then he saw the dark bulk against the whiteness of a birch tree about ten yards off the trail. He stopped. Must be Bakalov. He waited, listening in the dark. A faint squeaking of the snow, like something shifting its position. Not the body, but something past it. Then a low growl. He shone his flashlight. The neon dots of several eyes looked back at him. Wolves. Maybe six or seven. Sitting deeper into the forest. Waiting.

Slaught turned his attention to Bakalov. Maybe he was still alive? He called out the man's name. No response. He could see that the man was sitting in the snow, leaning against a tree trunk. Slaught figured he'd decided to make a stand here against the wolves. Maybe gotten too weak to keep going. Slaught put his flashlight on the body. Thin coating of snow up the man's right side where the wind would have caught him the hardest. Around Bakalov's knee the snowsuit was soaked red, the knife out of his leg and in his right hand lying limp at his side. Rifle across his lap.

Slaught called to him again. Moved up behind the tree, trying to keep an eye on the wolves, too. They were growling a bit more, worried he might be messing with their kill. A couple of them began inching closer. He reached around the tree, checking for a pulse. His flesh had that feeling—cold and hard. Inanimate. Eyes were closed.

Slaught took the rifle, checked the chamber. Empty. He kept moving. The wolves stayed put. Keeping an eye on their prize.

So he was moving, but wasn't making much progress, and he didn't know which way to go next. He thought of heading back, getting Chumboy to come with him. Kept telling himself, okay, another ten minutes, and if he didn't find anything, he'd go back. But he didn't seem able to stop, he wanted to find her so badly.

He had stopped calling her. It wore him out and he hated the silence that followed. So he wandered, staring down at the snow for any sign of her. He thought it felt warmer, maybe it was going to be a nice day. Would that be possible? No, not if he didn't find her. So he kept looking.

∾

Just as Mitch, Levi, and several men from the train were making their way towards the Fraser Hotel, Jimmy woke up. His first thought was that he didn't feel very good. It was like he was caught in sludge, could barely move. Everything just seemed so hard. He tried lifting his head off the ground but there was a sharp, splitting pain. He lay still for another moment or two, trying to open his eyes, get his bearings.

Slowly, he shifted his body to get his arm under himself. He propped himself up. He found if he moved very slowly, his head didn't feel as much like it was being attacked by a hammer from the inside. He brought his free hand up to his face but if felt pulpy and a bit crusty. He pulled his hand away fast. Gross.

What the fuck?

He sat up.

In the dim light he could see a body across from him. And the room stank of rye. Noise from outside the room was seeping in as his mind cleared. Shouting. Explosions?

It occurred to him he could be in some real serious trouble.

He felt around on the floor, looking for his gun. Couldn't see it. Crawled very carefully around the table to the other body. Jesus, he was dead.

Taking hold of the edge of the table, he got himself to his knees. Fuck, everything fucking hurt. He tried pulling himself the rest of the way up but had to stop. He rested for a minute or so, then tried pulling up one knee and steadying himself. Then he slowly pushed himself into a standing position. Rested by leaning on the table. He saw his gun lying on the table. That was something at least.

Son of a bitch. From the sounds of it, fighting was going on outside. And it sounded pretty fierce and close by. Jimmy had never been in a situation like this before. He thought finding Bakalov made the most sense. What he didn't want to be was stuck inside the hotel. Behind enemy lines.

Then he thought, hang on, maybe that was the best place to be. Could hear himself saying to his buddies, *can you say maximum havoc*?

"They're all gone," Auntie Verla said, looking in her knitting basket. "It's too bad. I thought I had one more."

The first one hadn't gone off, the glass bottle landing in the snow as if caught in a cushion. That caused some panic in the upstairs room because two of the soldiers in the front of the group looked up, saw the open window, started sending up some cover fire as a few of the Twenty made for the front doors. "Jesus Christ," Larose had yelled, "Jeff, fire that fucking gun of yours." But Jeff was just staring at the gun in his hands in disbelief. "Christ, Harv, I don't know what to do. I don't know, I've never shot anyone. Maybe this is wrong? I mean, killing someone? I don't know if I can do this..." Larose told him not to fucking worry because it wasn't like he was going to be able to hit anyone, so just fire the fucking gun. Jeff just leaned his gun out the window and fired it, the impact sending him falling back into the room, swearing, and Tiny tossed another Molotov straight down at the doors below and then the soldiers were scrambling back as flames coated the entrance to the hotel.

Larose had just tossed another one down and sent two men scrambling away from the door, one guy busy dousing the flames spreading across the other guy's back. Larose yelled "That's what I'm fucking talking about, keep 'em coming, Verla!" A couple more went sailing down. Then she told him she was out.

"Jesus Christ, the luck we have," Larose said.

"No, hey wait, over there on the far side," Jeff said, "someone's coming."

"Let it be Johnny, for fuck's sake, we need some reinforcements."

Tiny stuck his head up to peer over the windowsill, "No, doesn't look like Johnny. Oh wait, Jesus, it looks like some guys, Mrs. Merrill, maybe Chumboy? Looks like they might be trying the side entrance."

Larose said, "Shaun, get the hell down there, make sure that fucking door's open, don't want them getting trapped out there and spotted."

Shaun came down the stairs two at a time, yelling over to Max that he was checking the side door. Max was leaning against the stack of tables and chairs that he and McLaren had piled high against the glass doors. Cold air was blasting through the holes where the glass had been shattered by the Twenty, who were taking turns running forward and hurling things at the door, every now and again taking potshots at the building as well. Their rock throwing, it seemed, was doing more damage than their shooting, but either way the barrier wasn't going to hold. Shaun glanced at it and said, "Jesus Christ, I'll be right back to help with that."

He was thinking of what they could use to fortify the front barricade as he barreled into the kitchen, too preoccupied to see Jimmy leaning against the counter. He sailed right past him in the dark towards the door when he heard the click of Jimmy's gun.

"What's the rush?" Jimmy asked.

Shaun stopped dead. Waited, not saying a word, and Jimmy said, "Got guests?"

"No, just coming down to lock it," Shaun said.

Jimmy didn't know if the door was locked or not. Wasn't locked when he'd come up from the train. Had they locked it behind them?

Shaun said, "What happened to your face?"

"Fuck you," Jimmy said, moving carefully around the table towards the door, getting into position behind it, getting his gun up and ready. He said to Shaun, "Open it."

"No one's out there."

"Great. Then once the door's open, you and I can step outside, and I can kill you out there. Make less of a mess."

Shaun said, "I'm not opening the door."

Jimmy considered this for a minute. If he shot this guy right here, whoever was outside, or upstairs, might hear. If he opened the door himself, he wouldn't be able to keep an eye on the guy. And he didn't feel like he had time to tie the guy up. "Open the door or I'm going to go straight through to the front to put a bullet in the guys out there. And tear down that lame ass barricade you have."

"If it's so easy why haven't you already done that?"

Jimmy wasn't about to tell this shithead it was because he was having trouble seeing out of one of his eyes, that his head hurt, and he was waiting until the tide seemed to be turning to make his big move.

Then the door flew open. Jimmy thought, Geez, it wasn't locked after all, and Mrs. Merrill came stumbling into the kitchen, obviously in a hurry. The door bumped Jimmy, knocking his gun up and back and then a couple of other guys pushed the door open again and piled in as Shaun said, "Chum, careful..." and then the last man in, Big Donny, pulling the door to close it and there was Jimmy, suddenly looking small and confused. Big Donny said, "Tsk tsk, shouldn't play with guns," and his big fist wrapped around the muzzle and yanked it from Jimmy's hand. Then he said, "My, my, imagine running into you in a kitchen. Guess it's time I paid that debt I owe you."

ॐ

As it turned out, after all his searching, she found him. Slaught heard her before he saw her, could hear her chattering, her voice light, happy sounding, talking out loud. By now the morning sky was humming with violet and wispy dove-coloured clouds were sailing behind the bare branches of the poplars. He scanned the woods—where was she? And then there, emerging slowly along a narrow path, he saw her. Walking towards him.

She saw him and smiled, gave him a little wave and he thought for a minute he might cry. Wasn't sure why, maybe because she looked so happy as she stepped carefully along the trail, still talking, looking down so she didn't slip off. He didn't seem to be able to move, spellbound by her, her footsteps leaving tracks in the fresh snow that became one with the wolf tracks that were crisscrossing the land like sutures.

She was close now and still he couldn't move, and she said, "I dreamt of you all night."

His mouth dry. "I looked for you all night."

She smiled. "You were beside me. But you were a wolf. It was so vivid it might have been real."

"Maybe," he said. "You okay?"

Susun nodded. "I'm cold. But fine."

"I'm cold, too," Slaught said, "but it's a damn beautiful morning isn't it?"

Chapter Thirty-Three

Tiny said it was like a goddam meet and greet. There'd been a steady stream of men into the hotel that morning, all of them wanting to see the map and the woman who had slept with the wolf. Susun had said she wasn't sure what had happened during the night, between the cold and exhaustion, it was all a confusion. But the story had gotten around, grown as it went, and now it had a life of its own.

Hughes was now saying he helped her get away, and most of the workers and soldiers that had been so abruptly decommissioned by Mitch were now more than willing to fraternize with the enemy.

Jimmy, along with the other surviving members of the Twenty and one of Love's security detail, had been rounded up and herded into the boxcars. Big Donny said he'd take them back to the City with him but wanted to see some improvement in their attitude, otherwise he was leaving them at the outpost. He also announced that he was going to try his hand at being a train engineer. Had always wanted to be a railroad man.

Big Donny was enjoying a certain degree of celebrity status for having the foresight to slowly poison Bakalov, and most of the men wanted to head back to the City with him and Raymond. It was going to be all aboard, Big Donny had said, laughing. The rich folk down in the City were going to be in for a surprise when the train came chugging back into town loaded with ex-cons. Big Donny and Raymond were thinking of a few versions of their future but all of them started with parking the train in a nice spot and building out from there, making some kind of village. Maybe down in the Valley. If the weather changed, maybe they'd start up a train service. Never knew.

Slaught and Chumboy had spent a couple of hours helping load up the train, Larose and Shaun cutting and hauling some wood for the train's trip back. Larose said to Big Donny, "Think it's enough to get you most of the way, fewer of youse now anyways," and Big Donny said, "Yeah, and that's a good thing, there's a better quality of crowd now."

Mitch and Levi were along for the ride until the train hit the City, then they were heading back down to their place in the state park. Slaught was surprised, thought Mitch might go try and fill that vacuum at Talos, what with all their big shots being down for the count. She said a promise was a promise, they were going home. And that she was sick and fucking tired of big shots, anyway.

As for Levi, he was eager to get going. He'd hauled most of the gear down to the train and was just putting the last of their belongings into his knapsack when Susun said, "Before you go, I'd like to show you the map." Mitch, waiting in the doorway, said, "So sick of fucking maps," but Levi said, "I'd like to see it."

Slaught said he wouldn't mind having another look, too, so Susun unrolled it, saying to Slaught, "Hold your side, okay?"

Johnny smoothed the edges, staring down at it as a few others crowded around.

At first, he just saw the colours, the parchment of the map and against it, lines and shapes, blue-green arteries running and flowing across the surface, mesmerizing, and then the ochre and evergreen of the land. He thought maybe it was one of those optical illusion type things, almost looked like it was moving, dazzling. But then there were shapes, filling in the edges and marching across the parchment that was their land. How had he missed them? Elaborate, but not quite right, all claws and streaming hair and scales. The monster that was raven, the monster that was wolf, the monster that was spruce tree and the monster that was human, all on the map together.

"I'm not sure what I'm seeing," he said.

"That's good," Auntie Verla said, leaning in beside Tiny, "keeping an open mind."

Slaught said, "It's a strange one."

Larose and Tiny glanced at each other. Larose started shaking his head, and Tiny said, "Susie, seriously, what the fuck is this map about?"

Levi was edging his way around the table, cautious. His eyes travelled the map. By now it was wrinkled and stained, but he was seeing the golden stars tumbling along the rivers and creeks, stardust and children and rats sitting high up on the cedars, showing him traces of this place where his life had turned and become something different.

"You just have to really look," he said. "Look closely. It shows the way back from the end of the world."

Acknowledgements

Work on The Wintermen story began in 2010. Ten years is a long time to spend with characters so I would first like to thank them. They were good company. I wish them all the luck.

Heather Campbell, my publisher, the brave soul that she is has been a delight and honour to work with. Latitude 46's commitment to northern literature, to stories that are from a particular place, is admirable. And Morgan Grady-Smith was a perfect editor – thoughtful, nuanced and meticulous. What more could a writer ask for.

There are many folks who have helped me along the way. Laurence Steven of Scrivener Press was the first to publish The Wintermen. Chaz Bufe of SeeSharp Press took some time to read and comment on the first manuscript. It helped. And to Tony Burgess, Hal Niedzviecki, Louis Palu, Dave Bidini, Jason Collett, Mary Lawson, and Karen McBride, thanks for being so generous with your time and support. And to Dan Bloom, Mr. Cli-fi, for his attention to the role fiction can play in addressing climate change.

Great appreciation for Natasha Greenblat's passion for storytelling, Alex Bird for his creative wizardry, and Leah Lalande for a great cover concept. I would be remiss not to thank the folks at Chat Noir Books for their commitment to northern writers. And all the good folks I work with at Timiskaming First Nation, for the generous lessons about what really matters.

For sharing a terrain of imagination with me for a very long time, thanks to Anthony. And of course, to Charlie, my best friend, and to my stellar daughters, Mariah, Siobhan and Lola, stars indeed with their insights, patience and just sheer marvelousness, a bunch of thanks. For all the creatures who live inside my home, as well as the darlings in the fields and woods nearby – eternal gratitude. And hopes for your forbearance.